SPLIT IMAGES

SPLIT IMAGES

A Novel by

Elmore Leonard

QUILL
WILLIAM MORROW
New York

It is the policy of William Morrow and Company, Inc., and its imprints and
affiliates, recognizing the importance of preserving what has been written, to
print the books we publish on acid-free paper, and we exert our best efforts
to that end.

Library of Congress Cataloging-in-Publication Data

Leonard, Elmore, 1925–
    Split images: a novel / by Elmore Leonard.
        p.   cm.
    ISBN 0-688-16971-6 (alk. paper)
    I. Title.
    PS35 62.E55S75   1999
    813'.54—dc21   99-23233
                                              CIP

Printed in the United States of America

First Quill Edition 1999

1 2 3 4 5 6 7 8 9 10

www.williammorrow.com

For Bill Leonard

SPLIT IMAGES

ONE

IN THE WINTER of 1981 a multimillionaire by the name of Robinson Daniels shot a Haitian refugee who had broken into his home in Palm Beach. The Haitian had walked to the ocean from Belle Glade, fifty miles, to find work or a place to rob, to steal something he could sell. The Haitian's name was Louverture Damien.

The bullet fired from Robbie Daniels's Colt Python did not kill Louverture immediately. He was taken in shock to Good Samaritan where he lay in intensive care three days, a lung destroyed, plastic tubes coming out of his nose, his arms, his chest and his penis.

Louverture said he had an argument with the people who lived in the same room with him in Belle Glade. He paid forty dollars a week for the room and twenty dollars deposit for a key to the bathroom. But they had stopped up the toilet and it couldn't be used. They cleaned fish, he said, and threw the heads in the toilet. Speaking in a mixture of languages and sounds, Creole and Bahamian British English, he said, "I came here to search for my life."

The Palm Beach Police detective questioning Louverture that evening in the hospital looked at him with no expression and said, "You find it?"

Lying in the white sheets Louverture Damien was a stick figure made of Cordovan leather: he was forty-one years old and weighed one hundred seventeen pounds the morning he visited the home on South Ocean Boulevard and was shot.

Robbie Daniels was also forty-one. He had changed clothes before the police arrived and at six o'clock in the morning wore a lightweight navy blue cashmere sweater over bare skin, the sleeves pushed up to his elbows, colorless cotton trousers that clung to his hips but were not tight around the waist. Standing outside the house talking to the squad-car officer, the wind coming off the ocean out of a misty dawn, he would slip a hand beneath the sweater and move it over his skin, idly, remembering, pointing with the other hand toward the swimming pool and patio where there were yellow flowers and tables with yellow umbrellas.

"He came out. He crossed the yard toward the guest house. Then, once he was in the trees over there I didn't see him for, well, for a couple minutes. I started across. Got about right here. Yeah, just about here. And he was coming at me with the machete."

They could hear the high-low wail of the emergency van streaking west on Southern Boulevard, a far-off sound, fading.

As Mr. Daniels rubbed his bare skin the squad-car officer would catch a glimpse of the man's navel centered on his flat belly, tan and trim, the cotton trousers riding low, slim cut down to bare feet that were slender and brown. The squad-car officer, twenty-seven years old and in pretty good shape, felt heavy in his brown and beige uniform, his gunbelt cinched tight to support about ten pounds of police gear. He was from West Palm and had never been in a millionaire's home before.

"Sir, you chased him out of the house?"

"No, I thought he was gone. I got the gun, came out to have a look around. . . . I see *him* coming out, I couldn't believe it. He was still in the house when we got home."

The wind had been blowing for several days, the sky overcast, an endless surf pounding in. Mr. Daniels said he hadn't heard the man, it was more like he sensed him coming across the yard, turned and there he was.

The squad-car officer wondered at first if Mr. Daniels was a movie star. He had the features and that kind of sandy brown curly hair some movie stars had and never seemed to comb. The few lines in his face disappeared when he opened his eyes that were pale blue and seemed amazed in the telling of how he had actually shot a man. Twice in the chest.

"Sir, how many rounds you fire?"

"I'm sorry—what?"

"How many times you fire your gun?"

"Twice."

"What was he about, twenty feet away?"

"Closer. Ten feet maybe."

"Swinging the machete."

"What? Yes, raising it."

"But he didn't get a swipe at you."

"No."

Mr. Daniels seemed surprised, or else he seemed dazed or preoccupied, thinking about it and the squad-car officer's question would bring him back to now. Otherwise Mr. Daniels was polite and seemed anxious to be of help.

People were always seeing movie stars around Palm Beach and Mr. Daniels mentioned George Hamilton twice. He

11

mentioned Shelley Berman and he mentioned Burt Reynolds. Mr. Daniels and some friends had gone up to Jupiter to the Burt Reynolds Dinner Theatre, saw "God's Favorite" and came back, had a few drinks at Charley's Crab, then stopped by a friend's house to visit. He said he got home at approximately four-thirty, quarter to five.

Out visiting that time of the morning. The young squad-car officer nodded. He had seen a young woman down at the far end of the living room that was like a hotel lobby. Younger than Mr. Daniels. Light brown hair parted on the side, not too long; black turtleneck. Eating an apple.

"Sir, your wife was with you?"

"She's in Aspen."

That stopped the young squad-car officer. "Aspen?"

"Colorado. She's skiing. A houseguest was with me."

"Could I have that person's name?"

"Angela Nolan. Put down journalist. She's been interviewing me for a magazine, some kind of story."

"So she came in with you?"

"Yeah, but when I realized someone had broken in, the way the place was tossed, I told Miss Nolan, stay in the foyer and don't move."

The squad-car officer paused. One of Mr. Daniels's words surprised him, bothered him a little.

"Sir, you know what if anything was taken?"

"No, you'll have to search the guy. I didn't touch him."

"How 'bout the help? Where were they?"

"The servants? They came out after."

"Must've heard the shots."

"I suppose so."

The young squad-car officer had a few more questions, but a detective arrived with the crime-scene people and the squad-car officer was sent out to South Ocean Boulevard to wave traffic past the police vehicles lining the road. Shit, what traffic? He was curious about a few things. He wondered if the houseguest, Angela Nolan, had seen any of the action. He wondered if Angela Nolan was staying in the main house or out in the guest house.

The young squad-car officer's name was Gary Hammond.

On the third day a woman who worked in a shirt factory in Hialeah and said she was Louverture Damien's wife came to Good Samaritan to sit at the man's bedside while he died.

Officer Gary Hammond was stationed outside the Haitian's hospital door now—in case the poor son of a bitch ripped out his tubes, somehow crawled out of bed and made a run for it. Gary would talk to the woman from time to time.

How come if she was married to Louverture she was living in Hialeah? To work, the woman said. Well, how come her husband didn't work there? The woman said because her husband believed to work every day was a bad thing. "If work was a good thing the rich would have it all and not let you do it." Grinning then, showing her ugly teeth.

Jesus, the old broad was putting him on.

The woman was as skinny as the man in the bed. An old leather stick with a turban and nine strands of colored beads. She told Gary her husband had found nothing in his life worthwhile. She told him her husband was sometimes a thief, but not a dangerous one. He was too weak or cowardly to hurt anyone.

Gary said if he was harmless then what was he carrying the machete for, to get some coconuts?

The woman told him her husband had no *mashe*. She said her husband run. The man say to him to stop. Her husband stop. The man say to him to come back with his hands in the air. Her husband does this. The man shoots him and *li tomber boum*, her husband falls with a great crash.

Gary said, "You believe that?"

The Haitian woman said, "If he lie he could tell a good lie, he can tell grand stories. But I don't know." She said, "I go home tonight and fetch a white chicken and kill it."

Gary said, "Yeah? Why you gonna do that?"

The woman said, "Because I'm hungry. I don't eat nothing today coming here."

Gary said, "Oh."

He told the detective investigating the case the man had died. The detective said, well, there were plenty more where he came from. They stood between two squad cars parked near the gate entrance to the estate.

Eyes half-closed in cigarette smoke the detective said, "What do you think this place would sell for?"

Gary said he supposed about a million.

The detective said, "Try three and a half. You know how many rooms are in that house? How many just bedrooms?"

The young cop had a hard time figuring the house out. It was classic sand-colored Spanish with a red-tile roof, common enough in Florida, except it was big as a monastery with wings and covered walks going out in different directions. Hard to make out because of all the vegetation: the shrubs and sea grape, royal palms, a hedge of hibiscus full of scarlet flowers hiding the wall that ran about three hundred feet along South Ocean Boulevard.

The detective said, "Six bedrooms up, four more in the guest house not counting the servants' wing. The place will sleep thirty without putting anybody on the couch."

How'd he know that?

"Authentic iron hardware on all the doors, you can pick any lock in the place with a screwdriver. It's got a sauna will hold about twenty naked bodies of either or both sexes."

The detective had been a Detroit cop before coming to Palm Beach. Middle-aged stocky guy with short arms that hung away from his body. That shitty-looking thin hair greased back in a shark-fin pompadour the young cop bet would hold for days without recombing. The guy sounded a little bit like Lawrence Welk the way he talked, not so much with an accent, but seemed to say each word distinctly without running words together. He seemed dumb, squinting with the cigarette in his mouth to get a half-assed shrewd look. But the guy did know things.

The young cop was still wondering about the houseguest. Was she staying in the main house or the other one? He asked the detective if he'd talked to her. Angela Nolan.

Yeah, he had talked to her.

She corroborate what Mr. Daniels said?

The detective, with nineteen years Detroit Police experience, began to look at the young squad-car officer from West Palm a little closer, dumb-shrewd eyes narrowing.

Why?

Gary Hammond said he was curious, that's all. Was there something going on there? You know, hip-looking broad here, the guy's wife off skiing?

The detective said, "You mean you want to know do I think he's fucking her? Yeah, I think he's fucking her. I think he'd be out of his fucking mind if he wasn't. Robbie Daniels doesn't strike me as being double-gaited or having any abnormal ideas what his dick is for," the detective said. "I mean outside the popular abnormal ideas that're getting more normal all the time."

Gary said he was just wondering.

The detective was not on the muscle. Sounding a little

sour was his everyday tone when he wasn't intentionally kissing ass for information or some other purpose. At those times he sounded appreciative, sometimes humble.

He said, "Did I ask him, you want to know, if he's dicking her? No, I didn't. Did I ask if they're tooting cocaine, maybe blowing a little weed? No, I didn't ask him that either. The man comes home to his residence, finds this Haitian in there in the dark. The Haitian comes at him with a bolo or some fucking thing and Daniels shoots him. Now, you want me to try and find some holes in that? You want to implicate the broad, the houseguest, like maybe she's in with the Haitian, left the door open? Or how about we take a look, see if Daniels has got any priors? That what you want?"

"Well, for one thing," the young cop said, "the Haitian told it different."

"I bet he did," the detective said. "I bet he said he was fucking assaulted. You been out to Belle Glade lately?"

"Sure."

"You see how they jungle-up out there, how they live, you want to call it that? There's all kinds of work out there. Every day five, six in the morning the buses are waiting. No—this guy comes all the way from Belle Glade, stops by four-thirty in the morning see if they got any odd jobs, cut the grass or some fucking thing. Comes strolling up to the guy with a machete and the guy shoots him, you think something funny's going on."

Gary Hammond was patient. He was going to say what was bothering him.

"He said something to me, Mr. Daniels. He said he come in—he realized somebody was there from the way the place was tossed."

"Yeah? . . ."

"He used the word *tossed*."

"So?"

"I don't know, it seemed weird. Like he used the word all the time, Mr. Daniels."

The detective said, "He say it was going down when he got home? How about, he looked at the guy but couldn't make him? TV—all that kind of shit come out of TV. They get to be household words. *Tossed,* for Christ sake."

"What about the Colt Python?"

"Cost him four and a half. I told him I could have got him a deal in Detroit."

"I mean is it registered?"

"Jesus Christ, get out of here, will you."

"Okay, but can I ask one more thing?"

"What?"

"Robbie Daniels—he isn't a movie star, is he?"

The detective said, "Jesus Christ, the man owns companies. He's got a big plant in Detroit supplies the auto industry with something or other. Has a development company owns land in seven states and down in the Caribbean islands. Resort hotels, condos, all that development shit. He's worth like in the neighborhood of a hundred million bucks—you want to know he's a fucking movie star."

The detective, wearing a light blue wash-and-wear suit over a dark blue sport shirt and a cream-colored tie, the open suit coat tight around his arms and shoulders, waited for the young squad-car officer to drive off before he buzzed for somebody to open the gate.

Mr. Daniels wanted to talk.

The detective had not been told this. He knew it the way he would know from a woman's glance in a bar there it was if he wanted any. The only difference here, he didn't know what Mr. Daniels had in mind. The detective had already gone down the list.

He isn't gonna ask you you want to play tennis or fucking polo, anything like that. Ask you you want to join the Seminole Club.

He isn't gonna ask you who your stockbroker is.

He isn't gonna waste his time, chitchat about this and that. Though it would start that way.

What can you do he can't—outside of pressing two hundred ninety-five pounds straight up over your head? He thought about this following the drive that was lined with royal palms, but couldn't think of a good reason why the man would want to talk to him.

The detective's name was Walter Kouza.

"What's going to happen, not much at all," Walter Kouza said. "They'll run it past a grand jury, Palm Beach County Criminal Court. They have to do that in the case of a homicide. The jury will practically be instructed to call it justifiable and that's it."

"I have to appear, though," Robbie Daniels said.

"Yes, you have to appear, tell what happened. You're the only one knows, right? I take the stand, describe what the crime-scene people found—evidence of forcible entry, your gold cigarette lighter in the guy's pocket, Exhibit A, the machete—you'll be out in about twenty minutes."

There would be a silence and Mr. Daniels would nod to himself, getting it straight in his mind. The detective was surprised Mr. Daniels didn't act bored or like he was better than anybody else. He seemed like a nice down-to-earth fellow. Sat with a leg hooked over his chair. White cashmere today against his tan; faded jeans, gray and white Nike tennis shoes with the strings untied. The detective bet the guy never picked up his room when he was little or combed his hair. He still didn't.

He did kind of look like a movie star.

Or a cheerleader.

That was it. And the detective was the football coach. Big Ten. The two of them sitting around shooting the shit after the game. Only the coach called the cheerleader mister and maintained a pleasant expression.

Silence didn't bother the detective. He liked silence, waiting for the other fellow to speak. He liked the afternoon sunlight, the way it filtered through palm trees and filled the living-room-window wall twenty feet high. Sunlight made a silence seem longer because there was no way to hurry sunlight. You couldn't turn it off. He liked the cheerleader-coach idea too and thought of Woody Hayes. Woody Hayes had probably never spoken to a cheerleader in his life outside of get the fuck out of the way. But this coach would talk to this cheerleader, yes *sir*, and wait until spoken to.

What he didn't like was not seeing an ashtray around anywhere; he was dying for a cigarette.

"Will there be any problem with the gun?"

"The one you used? No, I don't see a problem. I assume, Mr. Daniels, the gun's registered."

The cheerleader nodded again, thoughtful. "Yeah, that one is."

That one. The guy still nodding as the detective waited, in no hurry.

"Hey, listen, why don't we have a drink?"

"Fine," the detective said, "if you're going to have one."

He thought a servant would appear and they'd have to wait around for the servant to appear again with his silver tray. But the cheerleader jumped up—let's go—and led the detective through a back hall, up a narrow spiral stairway to an oval-shaped castle door Mr. Daniels had to unlock. Not the wrought-iron crap, Walter noticed, but Kwikset deadbolt double locks. The door creaked. Walter saw shafts of light in narrow casement windows, an oriental carpet, bigger than any he'd seen off a church altar, books from floor to ceiling, inlaid cabinets. Spooky, except for the oak bar and art posters that didn't make sense.

Walter said, "You must read a lot."

Robbie Daniels said, "When I'm not busy."

They drank Russian vodka on the rocks, Walter perched on a stool with arms, Daniels behind the bar—long-legged guy—one tennis shoe up on the stainless-steel sink. Hardly any sunlight now: track lighting, a soft beam directly above them and the rest of the room dim. Walter wanted a cigarette more than ever. There was a silver dish on the bar, but he didn't know if it was an ashtray.

He said, "Detroit, I had a bar down in the rec room, all knotty pine, had these ashtrays from different hotels, you know, different places."

"That's right," Robbie said. "I forgot, you're from Detroit."

"As a matter of fact born and raised in Hamtramck," Walter said. "Twenty-three sixteen Geimer. Went to St. Florian's, Kowalski Sausages right down the street if you know that area, or you happen to like kielbasa. Yeah, my old man worked at Dodge Main thirty-two years. You know they're tearing it down. GM's putting up a Cadillac assembly plant, buying all that land around there from the city. The city tells the residents, a lot of them these old people, what they're gonna give them for their houses, that's it, take a hike. Ralph Nader, you say GM to him he gets a hard-on, he's mixed up in it now . . . Yeah, technically I was born in Hamtramck, been a Polack all my life." Walter Kouza paused. His eyes, deep beneath his brows, showed a glimmer of anticipation.

"You know who lived not too far away? John Wojtylo."

He waited. "The pope's cousin. Yeah, you know. John Paul the Second?"

"Is that right?" The cheerleader gave him an interested little grin.

"Yeah, the cousin use to work over to Chrysler Lynch Road. He was a sandblaster. Only the pope spells it different. Wojtyla. With a *a* on the end 'stead of a *o*. He's a Polack too. Hey, and how about that other Polack, Lech Walesa? He something? Doesn't take any shit from the communists."

Walter's blunt fingers brought a pack of Camels and a green Bic lighter from his shirt pocket. "And you live, your residence is in Grosse Pointe, if I'm not mistaken." He looked again at the silver dish on the bar; it was within reach.

The cheerleader was nodding, very agreeable. "Right, Grosse Pointe Farms."

"I could never keep those different Grosse Pointes straight. You live anywhere near Hank the Deuce?"

"Not far."

"There Fords all around there, uh?"

"A few. Henry, Bill, young Edsel now."

"They got, in the barber college right there on Campau near Holbrook? Heart of Hamtramck, they got a chair Henry Ford sat in once, got his haircut. I don't mean at the barber college, when the chair was someplace else."

"That's interesting," Robbie said. He took a drink and said, "You mentioned the other day you were with the Detroit Police."

"Nineteen years," Walter said. "Started out in the Eleventh Precinct. Yeah, then I moved downtown, worked Vice, Sex Crimes, Robbery . . . " Walter lighted his Camel and pulled the silver dish over in front of him. Fuck it. "It was never boring, I'll say that."

"You ever shoot anybody?"

"As a matter of fact I have," Walter said.

"How many?"

"I shot nine people," Walter said. "Eight colored guys, one Caucasian. I never shot a woman."

"How many you kill?"

"I shot nine, I killed nine." Walter let himself grin when he saw the cheerleader begin to smile, eating it up.

"They were all DOA except this one guy, a jig, hung on three hundred sixty-seven days, if you can believe it. So technically his death wasn't scored as a hit. I mean he didn't die of gunshot, he died of like kidney failure or some fucking thing. But it was a nine-millimeter hollow nose, couple of them, put him in the hospital, so . . . you be the judge."

"How about down here?" Robbie said.

"The guy was a quadriplegic, I mean when he died."

"Have you shot anyone down here?"

"In Palm Beach? I don't know if I tried to draw my piece it would even come out. No, I haven't, but the way things are going, all these fucking Cubans and Haitians coming in here . . ." Walter stopped. "I got to watch my language."

Robbie gave him a lazy shrug, relaxed.

Walter said, "Anyway, with the refugees coming in, lot of them jerked out of prison down there in Cuba . . . I know a gun shop in Miami I mentioned to you, guy's got three outlets, he's selling five hundred thousand bucks worth of handguns a *month*. Guy's making a fortune. He's got a range, he's teaching all these housewives come in how to fire three-fifty-sevens, forty-fives . . . Can you see it? Broad's making cookies, she's got this big fucking Mag stuck in her apron. But that's what it's coming to. It didn't surprise me at all a man of your position would have that Python. It's a very beautiful weapon."

The cheerleader was pouring them a couple more. "What do you carry?"

"Now? A Browning nine-millimeter." Walter laid his cigarette on the silver dish, raised his hip from the stool as he went in under his suit coat, pulled the weapon from the clip-on holster that rode above his right cheek and placed it on the bar, nickel plate and pearl grip sparkling in the cone of overhead light.

"Nice," the cheerleader said.

"Detroit I packed a forty-four Mag and a thirty-eight Smith Airweight with a two-inch barrel. But that's when I was working STRESS. As a matter of fact, eight of the guys I took out it was when I was with STRESS."

"I sorta remember that," Robbie said.

"Stop the Robberies, Enjoy Safe Streets."

"I'm not sure I ever knew what it meant."

"Yeah, Stop the Robberies . . . and so on. That was . . . let me see, I was on it back in '72, '73. We'd go in teams in a hot street-crime area, inner city. Dress like you live around there. One guy's the decoy, the target. Stroll down the street maybe act like you're drunk or you're a john looking for some quiff. The other guys lay back, see if you attract anything. See, we used teams of four. That would be your decoy, your backup, he'd be like another bum or civilian of some kind, then you'd have two more guys in the car, they covered you. We cut street crime way down, confiscated something like over four hundred guns. We had to shoot some people to do it but, well, it's up to them."

The cheerleader seemed to smile as he frowned, liking the idea but with reservations. "Isn't that entrapment?"

Walter said, "Hey, they named the game. All we did, we played it with 'em."

Robbie said, "May I?"

Walter said, "Sure." If the guy owned a Python he could handle a Browning. He watched Daniels heft the nickel-plated automatic, extending it now to take a practice sight. But then looked up, lowering the gun.

A woman's voice said, "Don't shoot. I'll leave quietly."

Walter made a quarter turn on his stool.

The houseguest, Angela Nolan, stood in the oval doorway. She was wearing a long navy blue coat with her jeans, over what looked like a workshirt and a red neckerchief. She said, "I'm on my way."

Robbie raised his eyebrows. "You're finished with me?"

"No, but . . . " the girl paused. "Could I talk to you for a minute?"

Robbie said, "Maybe some other time."

"I've got a plane. I just want to ask you something."

"Yeah . . . Go ahead."

"Could you come downstairs?"

"Not right now," Robbie said.

It was the girl's turn. Walter Kouza waited, feeling something now, a tension that surprised him: the two of them trying to sound polite, but with an edge, Mr. Daniels's edge just a hint sharper than the girl's.

She said, "Thanks, Robbie, I'll see you."

He said, "Angie? Don't go away mad."

The doorway was empty. Walter swiveled back to the bar as Robbie added, "As long as you go," and shook his head, patient but weary.

Walter said, "Gee, she walks out—I thought you extended her every courtesy. She's a writer, uh?"

Robbie was fixing up their drinks.

"Suppose to be doing a piece for *Esquire,* part of a book. At least that's what she told me. Like, 'The Quaint Customs of the Rich' or some goddamn thing. She tells me go ahead, do whatever I do, she'll *observe,* take some pictures and we can talk later. Fine. I'm on the phone most of the time I'm down here."

"I can imagine," Walter said.

"But then I sit down with her, she turns on her tape recorder—you know what she asks me?"

Walter shook his head. "What?"

"What's it like to be rich? Am I happy? She goes from

that to, What do I think about abortion? What do I think about busing . . . I couldn't believe it. Or, If you can have anything you want, what turns you on more than anything? Another one, related to that. If you have all the money you could possibly spend in a lifetime, why do you keep making more? I try to explain that the money itself is only a way of keeping score, but she doesn't understand that."

Walter didn't either.

"But then if I don't have time to sit down and talk, she gets pouty. I couldn't believe it. Really, like I'm taking up *her* time. She seems intelligent, you know, has some good credits, but when a broad comes on like it's the Inquisition and then gives you that pouty shit . . . I said wait a minute. I agreed to be interviewed, yes, but you could get fucking washed out to sea tomorrow and I doubt anybody'd miss you."

"You told her that?"

"Why not? She came to me."

"Jesus, that's pretty nice stuff. I thought maybe she was like, you know, a girl friend."

Robbie said, "A girl friend? You look at her close? She's okay, but she's got to be thirty years old, at least. No, what she does, she gets you relaxed, talking off the cuff like she's your buddy, but what she's doing is setting you up. She's a ball buster," Robbie said. "I told her that. I said you don't care what I think. You interview somebody with a name, you just want to cut off his balls, make him look like a wimp. You know what she said? She said, 'I don't have to cut 'em, they come off in my hand.' I said well, not this pair, love. Go fondle somebody else."

Walter Kouza said, "Jesus." He never again thought of Mr. Daniels as a cheerleader.

He considered himself an ace at sizing people up:

A guy shoots and kills an intruder. The guy seems not exactly shaken but awed by it. A bright eager good-looking guy. Sort of a millionaire Jack Armstrong but very impressionable.

Yeah?

Walter Kouza would run through those first impressions again, then piece together step by step the revelations of that afternoon in Mr. Daniels's study.

He remembered Mr. Daniels, Robbie, opening the second bottle of vodka and going downstairs for more ice . . .

Yeah, and he opened another pack of Camels while Daniels was gone. Tore off the cellophane, dropped it in the silver dish full of cigarette butts, mashed Camel stubs. He remembered seeing words engraved around the rim of the dish he hadn't noticed before. *Seminole Invitational 1980* and the club crest covered with butts and black smudges. Shit. He got off the stool to look for a regular ashtray and almost fell on his ass. There weren't any ashtrays. He was standing there looking at the inlaid cabinets—beautiful workmanship—when Daniels came back in, closing the door this time, turning the lock, and said, "While you're up, let me show you something might interest you." Took out a key and unlocked one of the cabinets.

There must have been two dozen handguns in there, a showcase display against dark velvet.

"Jesus," Walter said.

There were Smith and Wesson thirty-eights and three-fifty-sevens, in Chief Special and Combat Masterpeice models, two- and four-inch barrels, He had a Walther P thirty-eight, a Baretta nine-millimeter Parabellum. He had Llama automatics, several, including a thirty-two and a forty-five. A Llama Commanche three-fifty-seven, an Iver Johnson X300 Pony, a Colt forty-five Combat Commander, a Colt Diamondback and a Detective Special. He had a big goddamn Mark VI Enfield, a Jap Nambu that looked like a Luger. Christ, he had a ten-shot Mauser Broomhandle, nickel-plated, a Colt single-action Frontier model, a couple of little Sterling automatics. Walter's gaze came to rest on a High Standard Field King model, an ordinary twenty-two target pistol except for the barrel. The original five-and-a-half-inch barrel had been replaced by a factory-made suppressor, or silencer, that was at least ten inches long, fabricated in two sections joined together.

Walter pointed. "Can I see that one?"

Robbie handed him the twenty-two target gun.

"You turning pro?" Walter said and chuckled. He looked at the suppressor closely. "Jesus, Parker-Hale. You mind, Rob, I ask where you got it?"

"I'll tell you this much. The guy who sold it to me," Robbie said, "has a metallic gold-flocked sawed-off shotgun that matches his Cadillac."

Walter remembered saying, "Well, this little number right here," hefting the twenty-two, "this is the one the pros use, not to mention the CIA."

Robbie said, "Wait." He unlocked the cabinet beneath the handgun cabinet and said, "I've got some pieces here might surprise you, to say the least. The thing is, I'm not supposed to have them."

Even at this point he would seem naive and trusting, looking at Walter with his earnest nice-guy expression.

Walter said, "Rob, this is my day off. I don't run anybody in when I don't have to and I haven't been surprised at anything since I found out girls don't have weenies."

Robbie said, "I trust you, Walter," and brought out a forty-five U.S. Army submachine gun with a wire stock. He said, "M-three."

Walter said, "Jesus Christ."

Robbie was bringing out more submachine guns. "Sten, very old. Uzi, the Israeli number, needs some work but usable. German machine pistol . . . Ah, but here's my favorite . . . " It was MAC-ten with a thirty-two-round clip, all cammied-up for field duty. The compact little submachine gun was painted with

27

free-form shapes in rose and dark blue on a light blue background, like a wallpaper design.

Walter stared. He took the weapon in his hands, caressed the pipelike attachment screwed onto the barrel stub.

"Silencer's bigger'n the gun, isn't it? Jesus. How much you pay for this?"

"Fifteen hundred," Robbie said, "in Miami."

"With the silencer?"

"No, the suppressor was five hundred extra."

"I could've got you the piece in Detroit for a K," Walter said. "The suppressor—yeah, that's about five anywhere you shop." Walter started to grin. "What're you doing, Rob, going to war?"

Robbie said, "Nothing that big."

Walter was sitting at the bar again when he explained about the trial coming up next month in Detroit: this family bringing suit against the police department and Walter Kouza for something like five million bucks. "Remember I said I shot a guy but he didn't die right away? . . . Rob?"

"I'm listening."

"Well, this was only a couple years ago, not when I was in STRESS. The guy I shot's got a brother was in Jackson, was in Marquette, and learned a few things there talking to the jailhouse lawyers. Comes out, he files this suit in his mother's name. Like by shooting her son I denied the family all the millions he would have made at the car wash, plus another few million pain and suffering, even though the guy's fucking paralyzed from the neck down, can't feel a thing. Me and the department, we denied the mother all the benefits she would have gotten if the asshole had not been shot. Yeah, they come all the way down here, give me a subpoena."

He remembered saying, "Hey, come on, Rob, bullshit. We're about as much alike . . . listen, I'll tell you something. I was six-two and had curly hair and I had a name like Mark Harmon, Scott Hunter . . . Robbie *Daniels*, shit, and I had *money?* I'd be fucking dead by now. I'd have burned myself out by the time I was thirty. No. I'm Walter Chester Kouza and there isn't a fucking thing I can do about it."

He said, "Can I drive a limousine? Rob, you drive a car you can drive a limo. I'll tell you what, though, I would never wear any chauffeur's uniform, fucking hat with the peak . . . Bodyguard, that's something else. Sure, I'd drive you though. Like around Detroit? Sure."

He remembered Robbie saying, "You sound like someone—yeah, you sound just like him. What's his name, you know . . ."

"Is this fellow, he's got an orchestra, he goes a-one and a-two and? . . . "

"Karl Malden. That's who you sound like."

Walter said, "Karl *Malden?*"

He could see Robbie over by a wall of books. Slim guy, standing hip cocked. One hand, he's like rubbing his stomach underneath the white sweater, stroking himself. The other hand, he's pointing to different books, taking some of them partway out and shoving them back in.

Robbie saying, "A guy is hired to kill somebody, a woman, and falls in love with his intended victim. A man with no money, no known enemies, is murdered. Who did it?"

"Guy's wife," Walter said.

"Lot of who-done-its," Robbie said, "But I'm not talking about that. Here's one. A famous hunter risks his life simply to put his sights on Adolf Hitler. Great book. Here, another one. The hired assassin is out to kill de Gaulle. This one, Winston Churchill. Here, the president's daughter is shot."

"His daughter?"

"Ah, but were they aiming at the president? Presidents are always good."

"Like Abraham Lincoln," Walter said. "Guy pulled that one didn't know what the fuck he was doing."

"Here, the victim's J. Edgar Hoover. This one, Martin Bormann."

Walter had never heard of Martin Bormann.

"An African dictator . . . A right wing newspaper columnist. Here, a guy *running* for president . . . Another African dictator. Dictators are fun. Murder in Moscow, a triple with the victims' faces removed. Beauty."

"Who's behind all this?" Walter said. "I mean in the books."

"Who's paying for it? Big money, big oil, the CIA. Self-appointed world savers . . ."

He remembered Robbie sitting next to him at the bar, in the cone of soft light.

Robbie saying, "I didn't say who do you think deserves to be killed. It's not a moral question I'm asking. I said who would you *like* to kill, anybody in the world, assuming you have the resources, whatever you need. You can go anywhere, hire anyone you feel can be trusted, like that."

"I already got one," Walter said, "the Ayatollah. What's his name, Asshollah Khomeini, take that sucker out."

"Not bad," Robbie said, "but I think we should be a little more realistic. I mean you land at Tehran, but where are you? I think it's got to be someone who's relatively accessible."

Walter thought some more, smoking, drinking his vodka. He wished he had a beer to go with it.

He said, "This is fun, you know it?"

Robbie grinned. "I thought you'd like it."

"Jesus—Fidel Castro!"

"You want a challenge, uh?"

"Slip into Cuba by boat," Walter said, "wait for the sucker to drive by someplace."

"I think you're into a storybook situation there," Robbie said. "You're right, there're some good ones. Yasir Arafat, the PLO guy. Qaddafi in Libya. I don't know what you might think of Ahmed Yamani." Robbie paused. "No, I guess Yamani's all right."

Good. Because Walter had never thought one way or the other about Ahmed Yamani in his life.

Robbie said, "But those are the kinds of names that are done in books and the situations are about as real as the heroes. You know what I mean? The hero's a superstar. Former Green Beret, CIA, KGB double agent, colonel in Army Counter-Intelligence. Can speak about seven languages including Urdu and Tamil. Expert with any kind of weapon ever invented and has a black belt in Tae Kwon Do. His hands are lethal weapons, ah, but manicured. You know the kind of guy I mean?"

"Sure, very cool. Has all these broads around—"

"But grim," Robbie said. "The serious type."

Walter was nodding. "Yeah, dedicated. Never looks around—wait a minute, the fuck am I doing here? Like any normal person."

"That's what I mean," Robbie said. "Looking at it realistically . . . and we put our minds to it, decide to take somebody out . . . who would it be?"

"Somebody who's a real asshole," Walter said, thinking hard. "In fact this fellow—tell me if I'm wrong, Rob—he's not only a rotten son of a bitch should be put away, he's fucking evil. Hey, and he can be dangerous. You don't just walk in and do him."

Robbie was nodding. "That's the guy."

Walter thought some more; he looked up.

"You got one?"

"Well . . . I might."

"Who is it?" Walter waited.

Robbie smiled. "Not yet."

"Come on, Rob, you can tell me."

Robbie said, "I'm not even sure you want to make the move. You've been a cop a long time."

Walter said, "You kidding? I'll quit today."

"What about your wife?"

"She can stay in Florida, get a job wrestling alligators. No—Irene'll be fine. Don't worry about it."

Robbie nodded. For a moment there was silence.

Walter said, "Come on, who is it?"

Robbie said, "Walter, I'm gonna have to insist on a couple of things. First, no more Rob, or Robbie. From now on I'm Mr. Daniels. Is that understood?"

Walter managed to smile. "No problem, Mr. Daniels. How's that?"

"The other thing," Robbie said, "the day you come to work for me you're gonna have to quit smoking."

TWO

BRYAN HURD WATCHED Walter talking with his hands to his lawyer. They were in the hall outside the courtroom, tenth floor, Detroit City-County Building.

You could be wrong about him, Bryan thought.

Or maybe he's changed.

When Walter saw him he tucked his chin in like a fighter but grinned as he said, "There he is. Bryan, how the hell are you? Lieutenant Hurd now, uh? Homicide, getting up in the world. I was just saying to Eddie—Bryan, shake hands with Eddie Jasinski. Eddie's representing me in this deal. I was just saying to Eddie, you believe it? Secret Service're standing there, the guy squeezes off six rounds, empties the piece, then, *then* they're all over him. They all got a hand in there, all want to touch him, tell everybody how they grabbed the guy—what's his name, Hickle?—he's in there somewhere under this pileup, you can't even fucking *see* him."

No, he hasn't changed, Bryan thought.

"Then this other thing, Jesus Christ, the motive, thing with the broad? What's her name, Jodie Foster? Gain her respect and love—I never even heard of her. You can understand the guy wanting to make it with say, you know, Raquel Welch, one of those. I could even understand—no, I'll tell you the broad I'd kill for, Jesus, Norma Zimmer. But doing it for some teenage broad? Guy's got to be out of his fucking mind."

He hasn't changed a bit, Bryan thought. He was going to ask him who Norma Zimmer was, but Walter's lawyer was taking him aside, getting ready for the hearing.

Angela Nolan sat in the second row of the nearly empty courtroom, sunlight on pale varnished wood all around her. She began to write in her notebook, underlining key words or when she felt like it.

Wayne Circuit Court.

Pretrial evidentiary hearing. A motion by Kouza's lawyer to exclude Kouza's record as STRESS cop. Plaintiff's lawyer wants it in.

Judge. Robert J. Solner, 50s. Familiar with everyone. Goofs around with lawyers and witness (?). Tells story, lawyers laugh on cue, witness only smiles.

Defendant. Walter Kouza. Eats Certs like candy.

Def. Lawyer. Edward Jasinski, 50s. Expression of perpetual disbelief. Or fear.

Plaintiff. Ms. Jeanette Moore, 40s. Buddha in black dress and turban, white purse. Doesn't move or speak.

Plaintiff's son. Curtis Moore, 20s. Stud. Good moves, stage presence. Brother of *Darius Moore,* deceased—what it's all about.

Plaintiff's Lawyer. Kenneth Randall, 50s. Bill Russell in $500 gray suit, pearl tie. Cultured black cool.

Witness. Might be a cop. Or another lawyer. Nifty.

Angela looked up, glanced around. She wondered if Robbie would make an appearance, give his new bodyguard moral support. It wouldn't surprise her; strange things were happening.

Mr. Randall said, "Your Honor, we gonna be somewhat relaxed today, are we not?"

Judge Solner said, "What's the matter, you have a hard night?"

Mr. Randall said, "I hit my knee playing racquetball, Your Honor. Hit it with my own racquet, like a fool."

Walter Kouza and Edward Jasinski, sitting at the defense table, seemed lost, their heads turning in unison from the judge to Kenneth Randall, and back again, back and forth; spectators.

Judge Solner said, "Sounds like a good time to get you out on the court."

Mr. Randall said, "I'll stand up, Your Honor, you want me to. The pain isn't quite unbearable."

Judge Solner said, "It's all right, stay where you are . . . Mr. Jasinski, this is your motion, I believe."

"Yes, Your Honor"—rising briskly—"Your Honor, since the Detroit Police STRESS operation ended some eight years ago I see no reason to refer to my client's record as a STRESS officer, as exemplary as it may be, in any way, shape or form during trial proceedings."

Mr. Randall said, "What Mr. Jasinski means, the city's already paid out five, six million in STRESS-related damages. STRESS is a bad word and he doesn't want it mentioned front of a jury."

Mr. Jasinski said, "Your Honor, this case has got nothing to *do* with STRESS!"

Mr. Randall said, "Same instability on the part of the

police officer is involved. The point I want to make, Your Honor, is that Mr. Walter Kouza, based on his record with STRESS, should never have been allowed on the street. And if he hadn't, my client's baby boy would still be alive."

Veins stood out in Mr. Jasinski's neck. "The kid was nineteen years old! If he wasn't on probation he was in DeHoCo!"

Judge Solner said, "Mr. Jasinski, I didn't want you to have a heart attack in my courtroom. Calm down. Mr. Randall, save your act for the jury and tell the court how you want to proceed."

Mr. Randall said, "I'd like to call a witness, Your Honor, who was on STRESS back at the same time as Mr. Kouza and was also present—in fact it was his investigation—at the time the defendant shot Darius Moore. I'd like to call Lieutenant Bryan Hurd, Detroit Police Homicide, Squad Five."

Judge Solner did not say anything for several moments, his gaze not moving from Mr. Randall. He said then, "You represent the plaintiff and you're going to ask a police officer to describe the actions of a fellow police officer in a suit against the police department?"

Mr. Randall said, "Like expert testimony, Your Honor." And seemed to smile.

"Lieutenant, what was the purpose of the STRESS operation?"

"To interdict street crime in high-incident areas."

"Sounds like you're reading it," Mr. Randall said. "So you mingle with the civilians, pretend to be one of us?"

"That's right," Bryan said.

"Which suggests to me," Mr. Randall said, "an omnipresent, omniscient police force indistinguishable from the citizenry, ready to stop crime in progress or prevent its occurrence. Was that the lofty aim?"

36

Bryan said, "Or hold crime to acceptable limits."

"Now you sound like General Haig. That what the book says?"

"There is no book," Bryan said.

"Give you a gun, send you out to do the best you can, huh? . . . What kind of gun you carry on STRESS?"

"I carried a Smith and Wesson nine-millimeter."

"What else?"

"That's all."

"Didn't have another one down in your sock?"

"No."

"I thought STRESS cops carried two, three guns," Mr. Randall said. "Well, let's see." He looked at his file, open on the table, and said, "Lieutenant, I've got one, two, three . . . *four* incidents here in which Mr. Walter Kouza fired at fleeing robbery suspects after identifying himself as a police officer, killing all four of them. Tell me something. Why didn't he fire a warning shot?"

Bryan said, "Because a warning shot can kill someone blocks away, somebody looking out a window."

Mr. Randall said, "All right. What if you fire straight up in the air?"

Bryan said, "When the point man fires there's no way for his backup to tell a warning shot from any other kind. They could reach the scene and fire on a suspect who's already surrendered."

"Sounds very military," Mr. Randall said. "War in the streets. That how you feel about it?"

"No," Bryan said.

"I believe you quit STRESS after three months. Why was that?"

"I didn't like it."

"You're in Homicide now—you telling the court you don't like killing?"

"I thought it created more problems than it solved."

"Not to mention lawsuits," Mr. Randall said. "What did you think of Walter Kouza as a STRESS officer?"

Angela Nolan waited. She had underscored *black cool* in her Kenneth Randall notes and added: *Showboat, but fun to watch.*

Under *Witness* she had crossed out the line of notes and written in *Lt. Bryan Hurd*, as he spelled it for the court reporter. Now she underscored it and added *NIFTY* again in capital letters. She liked the way he sat straight but relaxed in his slim-cut dark navy suit and did not become indignant. She liked his hair and his bandit mustache, his hair long but not too long, not styled, and the way his mustache curved down and made him seem a little sad. She liked the way he looked directly at Walter Kouza as he answered Randall's question.

"I think he had a tendency to overreact."

Mr. Randall said, "Yeah, but isn't that the type volunteered for STRESS? All the gunslingers?"

Mr. Jasinski said, "Your Honor, I object to that." Sounding quite angry about it.

Judge Solner said, "So does the court. Mr. Randall, stand up to examine the witness. Maybe we'll get through this sometime today."

Pushing himself up with deliberation, his hands flat on the table, Mr. Randall said, "Yes, Your Honor . . . Lieutenant . . . let me see. How many officers did you have in STRESS?"

"I'm not sure," Bryan said. "Less than a hundred."

"Out of about five thousand. All volunteers, were they?"

"That's right."

"And how many people you boys kill?"

"Objection!"

"Let me rephrase that," Mr. Randall said. "How many suspects, directly related to the STRESS operation, suffered mortal wounds? . . . How's that?"

"I believe twenty-two," Bryan said.

"How many Walter Kouza kill?"

"I don't know exactly."

"We'll allow you to guess."

"Eight."

"Eight it is," Mr. Randall said, "but I'm sorry you don't win nothing. Your Honor, twenty-two suspects were killed and Mr. Kouza, alone, accounted for more than a third of them. I believe the court should consider the significance of that proportion and let a jury hear about it." Mr. Randall paused, referred to his notes and looked at Bryan Hurd again. "How many people—strike that. In the death of how many suspects were you directly responsible, lieutenant?"

"While on STRESS? None."

"Well, have you killed anybody lately?"

Yes, Angela Nolan thought. She could see him firing a gun as she might see it in a dream or a movie. She saw it again in slow motion, looked at it closely and saw his expression the same as it was now. He fit the role of homicide lieutenant in a filmic way, look and manner adaptable to motion pictures. And yet his manner was natural, almost boyish.

She was surprised then at Bryan Hurd's answer.

"No, I haven't killed anyone lately."

"Homicide detective, you haven't had to use your gun?"

"The shooting's over by the time we get there."

"How about when you make an arrest—you have your gun out."

"Sometimes."

"What I'm getting at," Mr. Randall said, "you use your gun if you have to. Whereas another police officer might use his gun because he *likes* to. Is that a fair statement?"

"It sounds fair," Bryan said.

"So now," Mr. Randall said, "tell us what you saw . . . No, first tell the court how you came to be at the Moore residence that afternoon."

"A *capias* had been issued on a suspect in a felony homicide," Bryan said. "He skipped bond . . ."

"Not Darius Moore or any member of the Moore family."

"No."

"The suspect, did he live at that address?" Mr. Randall consulted his file. "Seven-twenty-one Glynn Court?"

"No. The address came from a tip. Someone called it in."

"Give you his name?"

"No, it was an anonymous call."

"So you all mount up and ride out to . . . 721 Glynn Court to arrest this murder suspect. Tell me something," Mr. Randall said. "Mr. Walter Kouza was not with Homicide, was he?"

"No. He was with MCMU at the time," Bryan said. "Major Crime Mobile Unit. We called them for backup."

"So how many people you have to make this arrest?"

"Three from Homicide, four MCMU officers."

"Feel you had enough troops for the job?"

Bryan didn't answer. He stared at Mr. Randall, waiting, and Mr. Randall said, "All right, now you're there. Tell us how Mr. Walter Kouza came to shoot Darius Moore, subsequently ending his life."

"Objection!"

Judge Solner said to Mr. Jasinski, "Counselor, try to keep it down." He said to the court reporter, a young woman poised over her machine, gazing off, "Helen, strike *subsequently ending his life.*"

Now Jeanette Moore, the mother of the victim, raised her voice without moving and said, "He died, didn't he? He wasn't cripple by the man he wouldn't have died. I know that much."

Her son, Curtis Moore, grinned and poked his mom on the sly with his elbow.

Mr. Randall leaned over to say something to the woman, putting his hand on her shoulder, while the son, Curtis Moore, stared up at the lawyer and began to shift in his seat as though he wanted to say something. Curtis Moore's hair was in tight cornrows; he wore a white T-shirt beneath a black leather jacket trimmed with bright metal studs and the words *Black Demons* lettered on the back in red.

Mr. Randall said, "I'm sorry, Your Honor . . . "

Curtis Moore said, "They kick in the door." Now Mr. Randall had to hobble a few steps to get his hands on Curtis's shoulders.

Bryan Hurd said, "We knocked several times. We could hear movement inside, voices . . ."

"Look like some gang out on the porch," Curtis Moore said, Mr. Randall squeezing his shoulder blades. "They come dress like some gang, they ought'n to make house calls."

Beautiful. Angela was smiling as the judge told Mr. Randall he'd be held in contempt, bad knee or no bad knee, if he wasn't able to control his clients.

She saw Bryan Hurd smiling, not giving it much, not enough to show his teeth, but smiling all the same. She saw him looking at her now, as though he were using the smile to bring them together. But as she smiled back she knew this was between the two of them and had nothing to do with anyone else or anything that was said. They continued to look at each other until Mr. Randall asked a question.

Bryan Hurd, said, "I went over to one of the front windows. That was when Walter, Mr. Kouza, kicked in the door."

"Yeah, then what happened?"

"Well, we went in."

"How many of you?"

"Sergeant Malik, Mr. Kouza and myself."

"Where were the others, the other four?"

"On the sides and around in back."

Mr. Randall said, "It wouldn't seem anyone could slip out, make an escape then."

Bryan said, "It wouldn't seem anyone could escape from jail, but they do."

"Got to watch myself with you," Mr. Randall said. "Go on, tell the court what happened then. Who was present in the house? You busted the people's door down, now you're in there."

Bryan nodded toward the plaintiff table. "Mrs. Moore was coming down the stairs at the time. Curtis was in the living room. Darius was in the dining room, directly behind the living room."

"What was he doing?"

"He started—it looked like he was going into the kitchen when Mr. Kouza yelled at him to stop."

"What did it *appear* he was doing when you arrived?" Mr. Randall asked. "In fact, the whole family. What were they doing?"

"I think they were getting ready to have something to eat. There was a pie and a bottle of Pepsi-Cola on the dining-room table. One of those big plastic bottles."

"So Mr. Kouza, he yelled at Darius, uh? What did he say to him?"

"He called for him to remain where he was."

"Yeah, but what did he say exactly?"

"He said, 'Freeze, motherfucker. Don't move.' "

"Like that?"

"Somewhat louder."

"Then what happened?"

"Darius turned and started back."

"Toward the living room?"

"That's right. But he was still in the dining room when Mr. Kouza fired."

"I thought Darius was shot in the spine," Mr. Randall said.

"He was," Bryan said. "From the front."

"Must have been a powerful weapon Mr. Kouza used."

Bryan didn't say anything.

"Was a *Magnum*," Curtis Moore said. He was standing now, Randall trying to get to him. "Was a big forty-four *Magnum*. Ask *me* what the motherfucker use. He want to shoot everybody, except this one"—pointing to Bryan Hurd on the witness stand—"stop him."

Mr. Randall had his hands on Curtis now, easing him down, saying, "Your Honor, please take into account this young man's emotional state, seeing his brother—" And stopped there.

Judge Solner said, "I've seen enought of Mr. Moore today. He can leave on his own or the court officer will throw him out. Right now."

Angela watched Curtis Moore stroll out of the courtroom in his black leather jacket and tight maroon trousers. All he needed was the Bee Gees playing behind him, his drag-step pace right on the beat. She wondered if any magazine would go for an interview with Curtis. Outside of *Easy Rider*.

Bryan Hurd was looking at her. He wasn't smiling now

but almost. She looked at him with the same expression. She couldn't be cool with him. She didn't want to be. She wanted to make a face and see him smile, knowing he would. But the face would have to relate to something he would recognize. She knew him but she didn't know him.

Mr. Randall said, "I've only one more area to cover, Your Honor," and turned to Lieutenant Hurd again. "Was Darius, at the time he was shot, was he holding anything in his hand?"

"He was holding a knife," Bryan answered.

"What kind? Big butcher knife?"

"He was holding a silverware knife."

"Just a plain, ordinary silverware knife?"

"That's right," Bryan said. "With banana cream pie on it."

Twenty minutes later it was over. Angela watched Walter Kouza coming out, glancing back, blunt arms hanging rigid in his tight gray suit, buttoned, banging through the low gate to the aisle and glancing back again, livid, to say, "Thanks a lot, you son of a bitch."

Lieutenant Hurd was looking this way. He said, "Walter?"

But Walter was out the door.

Angela closed her notebook, slipped it into her canvas bag. As the homicide cop with the bandit mustache came through the gate she was ready.

She said, "Lieutenant? . . . " As he came over she said, "Bryan Hurd, is it?" Aloud for the first time, wanting to hear herself say his name. He was taller than she had expected. Younger looking, close.

He said, "Well, finally . . . "

They stared at each other.

He said, "You know how long I've been wanting to meet you?"

She said, "Wait a minute. How do you know who I am?"

He said, "I don't." Then said, making a statement, "You're not with one of the papers, are you? You're from somewhere else?"

"I'm on my own."

"That's what I thought. So am I, for the next ten days." He seemed to want to say something else, prevent a silence. "Actually I'm not off till Monday, then I've got the ten days . . . But see, I'm off this weekend, so it's like I'm off now." The silence began and he said, "Just stay with me through this part. I don't want to sound dumb and blow it, but you try too hard that's what happens . . . What's funny?"

"Nothing."

They stared at each other.

She said, "I should've washed my hair."

He seemed uncertain, or hopeful. Then began to smile and said, "You know what I'm talking about, don't you. You know exactly what I'm talking about."

"You haven't really said anything yet."

"That's what I mean. I don't have to say anything. You *know*. And your hair's fine. It's perfect."

She said, "Then I'm all set." And seemed confident again in her long navy blue coat, her jeans and cowboy boots. But she felt the need to say, "Boy, I don't know . . ."

They stared at each other again until Bryan said, "Let's get a drink and talk for a few days."

Neither of them spoke in the elevator going down.

THREE

COMING OUT OF the City-County Building, walking east on Jefferson, they started over and spoke about the weather, looking off at the Ford Auditorium on the riverfront, the fountain misting in Hart Plaza, Bryan saying it was a little too nice, it wasn't like April, April in Detroit was miserable, wet and cold, with dirty snow left over from winter; Angela saying she lived in Arizona, Tucson, and didn't know much about weather, outside of weather in New York when you wanted a taxi; Bryan saying he thought that should about do it for weather, though he could tell her how muggy it got in the summer if she wanted.

Angela said, "Boy . . . " and shook her head in amazement.

"What?"

She said, "We know each other but we don't."

He said, "Maybe we're related. What do you think?"

She said, "I hope not." And was silent.

Bryan glanced at her. She was pulling in. But that was all right because she was still there. Her mouth and nose he had committed to memory and believed he could draw within a couple of tries with clean, simple lines. The awareness in her eyes . . .

"You have blue eyes, right?"

"Sort of blue."

"So're mine."

She said, "I know."

It made him feel good. Walter was a half-block ahead of them and he was pretty sure where Walter was going. Maybe he'd buy him a drink.

She said, "I think I'd like to do Curtis Moore sometime."

"I think Walter would too," Bryan said.

She looked at him now. "You know what I mean."

"I've interviewed him a few times," Bryan said. He told her the only way to get his full attention was to talk about bikes. Curtis had a big tricked-out scoot, a Harley, he kept in the house. He had a cane that telescoped out into a pool cue, with a grass pipe in the grip he smoked going sixty. Curtis painted a white girl brown one time and kept her a week.

Angela said, well, it was a thought.

He asked her how long she'd been writing. She said, making a living at it, just three years.

"You like to write?"

She looked at him. No one had ever asked her that before. She said, "I'm not sure. I've got a couple of problems. I don't know if I'm Oriana Fallaci or Studs Terkel. I'm serious. And I'm about to turn thirty and I'm having a little trouble with that, too."

He said, "I'll tell you how to handle the age thing. But why can't you be Angela Nolan?"

She said, "I don't know if pure Angela Nolan would sell."

He said, "Well, as long as you don't show off. What do you write about?"

"I do interviews. Not the usual type with famous people. Bum Phillips is the only one even remotely famous."

Bryan stopped.

"But why did you say that about not showing off?" Now Angela stopped and had to turn to look up at him. "What's the matter?"

"I read it. It was in *Playboy* and your picture was in the front part, right? With all the pictures?"

"Yeah, in the November issue. You saw it?"

"I cut it out," Bryan said.

"The interview?"

"No, your picture." He held up thumb and index finger about an inch apart. "It's that big."

"Come on—" She was smiling, amazed. "All the naked girls in there, you cut out *my* picture?"

"I'll tell you something else," Bryan said. "It's the first time in my life I ever cut out a girl's picture, naked or otherwise."

"But why?"

He said, "Why do you think? Why do you think we're here, right now?"

She said, "It's getting scary."

He said, "It's not getting scary, it's been. Ever since I saw you." They started walking again.

She said, "It's funny—watching you in the courtroom, you reminded me of Bum Phillips."

He almost stopped again. "You think I look like him?"

"No, I mean something he said." She delivered the line with the hint of a Western drawl: " 'I make decisions according to what's right and what's wrong, not to keep my job' . . . Even the judge was surprised Randall called you."

Bryan said, "Kenneth Randall—you ever get in serious trouble, hire him. He spends most of his time in Recorders Court, that's the criminal stuff; so I see him about once a week."

Angela said, "You didn't give him anything, but you

didn't hold back either. I mean considering Walter Kouza's a fellow police officer. Isn't there some kind of unwritten law, you don't tell on each other?"

Bryan said, "He's not my fellow police officer. I don't need any Walter Kouzas."

Angela said, "He's a bodyguard now."

"Good," Bryan said. "Is that what you're doing, interviewing bodyguards?"

"I was interviewing the body Walter's guarding," Angela said, "Mr. Robinson Daniels of Grosse Pointe and Palm Beach? Daniels Fasteners. They make something for Chrysler."

"They make nuts and bolts," Bryan said. "Yeah, you see his picture a lot, Robbie Daniels. Or you see him at Lindell's with the jock sniffers. Every couple of years he offers to buy the Tigers and in between he buys 'em drinks. I hear he's a pretty nice guy."

Angela said, "That seems to be the word. At least from the gang down in Palm Beach. I haven't talked to anyone up here yet."

"What's he need a bodyguard for?"

"That's the first question I'm gonna ask, if we ever get back together."

"Did you ask Walter?"

"Walter says, 'Why you think? Rich guys need protection from the fucking kooks in the world.' "

"Well, it's not unusual," Bryan said. "Even if it's just for status. But, Robbie Daniels, he *is* pretty well known."

"I know, it's possible." Angela said. "Last week I was gonna drop the whole idea. It wasn't worth all the waiting around. Either waiting for Robbie or waiting to see one of his friends and then getting the same old shit. Rich people don't think, they just assume things. They assume everyone thinks the way they do."

50

"You just said they don't think."

"Don't pick. You know what I mean," Angela said. "Then, when I'd finally get him to sit down and talk, he'd want to play around."

"Make the moves on you."

"No, not like that. The only time—when I met him the first thing he said to me . . . . I'm standing there, I've told him who I am, acting very legitimate and proper . . . he says, 'You know what I'd like to do, Angie?' And that's one thing I can't stand, I don't know why, being called Angie. He says, very straight, 'I'd like to tie you up and fuck your socks off.' "

Bryan said, "No hugs and kisses first, huh?"

"He was being cute. He says things with a straight face, then grins to show he's kidding. You're supposed to think he's a little off the wall but basically cute."

"You don't like him."

They were crossing Beaubien now toward Galligan's on the corner. Walter was already inside.

"I think he's an asshole," Angela said. "But I have a feeling there's another Robbie Daniels inside the cute Robbie and that one could be pretty interesting."

A young executive was holding the door open for two girls going into Galligan's, the girls smiling, touching the door, the young man finally letting go, giving the door to Bryan. He brought Angela past him into the foyer, touching her for the first time. She looked up at him. As the inner door opened, releasing voices and sounds, he said, "What's interesting about the Robbie Daniels inside the real one?"

She said, "I think he likes to kill people."

Walter threw his head back to drain the shot glass. He got his change from the bartender, checked it, picked up a draft beer and a straight-up martini and tried to narrow his shoulder as he came away from the bar, concentrating on the glasses. He looked up and stopped.

Angela was saying, "It's New York. Third Avenue." She saw Walter a few feet away, holding the drinks, staring at Bryan.

Walter said, "You know what you did to me in there? I start to think about it, I don't believe it."

Bryan said, "Walter, I want to ask you something."

Walter said, "A knife is a knife. I don't care it's got blood on it, banana cream pie, what it's got on it. A fucking knife is a knife."

Bryan said, "Just tell me one thing. Who's Norma Zimmer?"

Walter said, "I ever say another word to you, long as I live, I hope I bite my fucking tongue off."

He walked away from them tight-jawed, concentrating on the glasses again as he moved between tables toward the booths against the wall. Now Owen Galligan was coming through the coat-rack hall from the back dining room, stopping at tables, the saloonkeeper officiating, getting the after-work crowd settled in. He saw the homicide detective and pointed to the first table against the brass railing that separated the tables from the bar patrons that were two deep, the young executives and clerks and lawyers who were checking out Angela now, rating her with cool deadpan approval.

"That's yours, Bryan, grab it. Quick."

Bryan said to Angela, "I come in with cops, I don't get this table. As a matter of fact I've never had it." He arranged the chairs so they sat with their backs to the bar and wouldn't have to look at the guys staring down at them. Angela looked the guys over, briefly, as she sat down, leaving her coat on, and that was that.

She said, "Don't you know Norma Zimmer?"

Bryan was looking for a waitress now. "The name's sorta familiar."

Angela said, "How about Alice Lon? Or Ralna English?"

Bryan was shaking his head.

"At one time or another," Angela said, "Norma, Alice and Ralna were all Champagne Ladies. They sang with Lawrence Welk. I tried to interview him once."

Bryan seemed relieved. "In court, I kept trying to think of who she was. Yeah, Norma Zimmer."

"You want to tell me why," Angela said, "or would you rather take a look at Robbie Daniels? He's in the last booth with Walter."

Bryan looked. He couldn't see much of Walter, but there was Daniels lounged against the wall, one foot up on the bench, his knee showing above the table. Daniels was wearing a beige tweed sport coat, white button-down shirt and striped rep necktie.

"He's got a nice tan," Bryan said. "He looks like a tennis pro. The tan and the hair."

"He's forty-one," Angela said.

Bryan's gaze moved to a waitress, tried to catch her eye and missed. "What're you gonna have?"

"I guess Jack Daniels on the rocks."

"Yeah? Is that what you drink?"

"Usually." Angela looked off again. "Robbie claims he runs six miles every day."

"I guess it's the thing to do," Bryan said. "Go over to Belle Isle, even during the week, it looks like they're holding a marathon. I drove around Palmer Park—I live out that way—and measured off a mile. The next day I put on the outfit—sweat pants, one of those knit caps, it was cold that day. I ran the mile, came home and threw up. I said to myself, you were right. It's not only boring, it makes you sick. So I quit jogging."

"When I'm home I like to hike in the mountains," Angela said. "Otherwise, I don't do much."

Bryan couldn't take his eyes off her. He said, "Well, you're five-five, you weigh about a hundred and two. I don't see that you have a problem."

She said, "You could work in a carnival."

"I do," Bryan said. "I guess weights, read fingerprints. Tell fortunes—tell some poor dumbhead he's gonna do mandatory life . . . but at least not the next ten days. I'm going down to Florida, sit in the sun and read."

"Mysteries?"

"No, I don't read mysteries. I'm gonna take the last twelve issues of *National Geographic* and read every word and look at the maps. Fall asleep on the beach reading. I like to wake up about five o'clock, there's nobody around. Then go in and get cleaned up . . . in the evening drink tall rum drinks and look at the ocean. That's the first couple of days. After that I switch to bourbon and go to the movies."

She said, "Alone?"

Bryan smiled at her. He said, "Angela. I didn't think your name would be Angela. I don't know why, I thought it would be Sally or Nancy. I like Angela though, very much." He said, "Yeah, I'm going alone." He smiled at her again. "We have to know certain things, don't we? Before moving ahead."

She seemed hesitant now, getting to it. She said, "It isn't like meeting somebody at school; we've been out for a while . . . I was married when I was twenty, divorced, I was still twenty. It was really dumb. He was with a band and I was going through sort of a groupie period."

"I was twenty-four when I got married," Bryan said. "Divorced at, I was thirty-four or -five."

"How old are you now?"

54

"I'm forty."

"You don't look it. Do you have children?"

"No, but I'd like to. Unless it gets too late."

There was a silence. She said, "I'm gonna be thirty the day after tomorrow."

He said, "That's right, and you're having trouble with it."

She said, "It's not a major problem, I just have to get used to the idea. I know girls who panic and try to revert. They new-wave themselves over and look like clowns,"

He said, "You want to go to Florida next week?"

"Where?"

"Near Boca Raton."

She made a face that was an expression of pain or mild confusion. "I didn't mean *where*. I don't know why I said that." She looked serious now, intent. "I knew you were going to ask me, as soon as you said Florida, and I didn't know what I was gonna say."

"Let me build it up," Bryan said. "It's a nice place, the Ocean Pearl, right on the beach . . . "

She said, "I'm not like this. Why am I nervous? I keep saying the wrong thing."

"Just take it easy. Relax."

"That's what I'm trying to do." Gritting her teeth a little.

He said, "Soon as you *try*—that's what I was talking about before, in the courtroom, and I asked you to bear with me. We have to just get through this first part."

She said, "What I need is a drink."

"You *want* a drink," Bryan said. "You don't *need* a drink. That's like saying you need help, you can't handle it yourself."

"Jesus, you're full of advice, aren't you?" She was loosening up. "What do you read, self-improvement books?"

He held up his hand, looking off, and said, "Marcie, bring us a couple Jack Daniels on ice, please. Doubles." He said to Angela, "You want a double?"

She said, "Yes, I want a double. I don't need one, you understand. I *want* one."

"There," Bryan said, "you got that taken care of. What else's bothering you?"

She said, "I didn't think you'd be a smart-ass."

Bryan said, "Look, if you want, you sit here and I'll sit there. There'll be times when I'm a little tense and you'll give me a poke, straighten me out. It's like when you're taking yourself too seriously, catch yourself becoming indignant over little shitty things. You know what I mean? Or you get very dramatic about something. What do you do?"

"I don't know," Angela said. "What?"

"You give yourself a kick in the ass."

She said, "You're a lot of fun, Bryan."

He said, "You know the first thing I looked at as we came out of court? I looked to see if you were pigeon-toed. My wife was pigeon-toed. She'd walk around the house with this grim look on her face. By the time we knew we were splitting up, all she had to do was walk in the room, I had to get out. See, it wasn't that she was pigeon-toed, I don't mean to make fun of her. It was the tight-assed way she walked that to me represented her personality. She never came up for air."

There was a silence between them, an eye of stillness within the barroom's scattered bits of noise.

Angela said, "I feel a lot better, Bryan. I don't know what you're talking about, but I feel better."

He said, "Good. You want to go to Florida?"

She said, almost sadly, "I thought you were gonna be—this'll probably sound dumb—but I thought you were gonna be, well, romantic. I don't know why."

"I *am* romantic. Why do you think I'm asking you to go to Florida?"

She said, "God, a homicide cop. Why couldn't you be, I don't know, something a little more sensitive?"

"Because," Bryan said, "you came to me with a guy you say likes to kill people. If he likes it, he must've done it. So here you are. You take up with a homicide cop, that's what you get. Not much apparent sensitivity, but all kinds of expert advice."

She was stiffening as he spoke, looking right at him.

"I didn't *take up* with you."

"How about, sought me out?"

"It's not why I wanted to meet you."

"Your indignation is showing," Bryan said. "How many people has he killed?"

"Two that I know of," Angela said.

Robbie said to the waitress, "Darling, don't worry about it. Bring us another draft and a very extra-dry Beefeater and all's forgiven."

Walter said, "Hey, and a ashtray."

"One cigarette," Robbie said to Walter.

Walter looked puzzled. "I thought you meant while we're here. You said I could smoke, right?"

"Walter, you went through an ordeal today. You're a little uptight, okay, I said you could have a cigarette. One. And that's the last one I ever want to see you smoke."

Walter was holding the Camel close to his mouth. Christ, wondering now if he should wait. Drink half the beer first.

"Mr. Daniels, they got me by the balls. I need something like to hold onto. I can't just *sit*."

"I understand that."

"Money I saved, took me twenty years—I'll flush it down the toilet before I give it to a fucking con." He brought out his green Bic and lighted the cigarette.

"Walter, I was there. I saw part of the show."

"You were *there?*" Exhaling cigarette smoke.

"The first thing you have to do is fire your lawyer."

"Eddie?"

"Walter, Eddie's pathetic. He should've objected to everything Randall said. I'm not a lawyer. I know that much. Walter, Randall and the judge play handball together at the DAC. Randall was the first colored guy I ever saw there as a guest. I looked, I thought one of the waiters was taking a shower . . . He even has a tan line."

Walter wasn't listening. "You were in the *court*room?"

"For a little while. I left right behind Curtis."

"I didn't see you."

"I know you didn't." Robbie looked toward the front, to the first table. "That homicide detective had your full attention. What I want to know is, what's he doing with Angie?"

"Mr. Daniels," Walter said, "the trial doesn't come up for a couple months. All right, I got some time. If you got another lawyer, or you have any suggestions at all, that's fine with me."

Robbie was thoughtful. "The mother could probably be bought for a few grand. But you've got Randall to contend with. He'll clean you out, accept a settlement for about a half-million from the city and take a third of it off the top."

"Jesus," Walter said.

"I told you before, your only alternative is to do something about the witnesses."

Walter squinted through his cigarette smoke. "I'm not sure what you mean, *do* something."

"I rode down in the elevator with Curtis. He doesn't say much, does he? Seems very distrustful."

"He's been in solitary half his fucking life. He doesn't know *how* to talk," Walter said, "till you get him in court. Then you can't fucking shut him up."

Robbie was looking toward the front again. "I'm sure a good defense lawyer can handle the STRESS stuff when it comes up. Make it sound like the homicide guy has some kind of a personal grudge. Discredit his testimony. But Curtis—especially if you have a predominantly black jury, which is quite likely—Curtis's something else."

Walter said, "You aren't kidding he's something else."

"What was he in Jackson for?"

"Shit, armed robbery, assault. Grand theft auto, I don't know how many counts they had. He was up for second-degree murder, shot and killed a guy in a bar, they send him to the Forensic Center. He gets cured of whatever suppose to be disturbing him, they let him out. He gets picked up on a gun charge and back he goes to Jackson for two years. He's a fucking nut."

"Now residing at 721 Glynn Court," Robbie said. "Member of the Black Demons, whoever they are."

"How'd you know that?" Walter seemed amazed.

"Walter"—like talking to a child—"I was in the courtroom."

"Yeah, that's right." Walter took a last drag on what was left of the Camel and stubbed it out. "I appreciate whatever you can do for me, Mr. Daniels."

Robbie said, "I've got to take care of you, Walter. I need you for the big one."

"Yeah, that's right." He sounded tired now.

Robbie studied him: heavy shoulders sagging, deep-set eyes staring at his green lighter. "Walter? Would you like one more cigarette?"

Walter looked amazed again, then grateful, little eyes glistening now. "You serious?"

"Hey," Robbie said, "I'm not such a bad guy to work for, am I?"

Bryan said, "Let me get it straight. The burglar was outside the house when Robbie shot him?"

"Yeah, out by the patio," Angela said. "But I don't think you'd call him a real burglar."

"No, I guess he had a few things to learn," Bryan said. He sipped his Jack Daniels. Angela gave him a look but didn't say anything for a moment.

"The second one happened nine years ago—I found out about it while I was researching him, getting some background. At a place called St. Clair Flats."

"That's not far from here."

"Robbie was duck hunting with an executive from one of the car companies, I think Chrysler . . . "

Bryan was nodding. "Yeah, I forgot all about that. Nine years ago, it seems longer. They were in a duck blind and the guy from Chrysler stood up when he shouldn't have and Robbie blew the top of his head off"—nodding again, remembering—"with a Browning twelve-gauge shotgun. Gold-inlaid, it must've cost him seven or eight thousand."

She said, "Were you in on the investigation?"

"No, that's a different county, out of our jurisdiction. I wasn't in Homicide then anyway."

"But you remember details."

He said, "I remember the kind of shotgun, but not the name of the guy from Chrysler." He tried to think of it, but finally shook his head. "Well, you've got justifiable homicide in one case, accidental in the other. What makes you think he likes it?"

Angela held her glass poised, off the table. She said, "Ask him. Here he comes."

Robbie was making his way through the tables, glancing around at first, but now with a whimsical half-smile, head cocked, his eyes on Angela and no one else. Walter trailed behind.

Robbie said, "Could it be? It *is!* How're you, Angie? Good to see you, tiger." Extending his hand and holding hers as he gave Bryan a look of mild concern. "If this lady's interviewing you, lieutenant, let me give you a word of warning. Three words to be exact. Watch your ass." Then the grin. "Hi, I'm Robbie Daniels."

Bryan thought of a television commercial. "Hi, I'm Joseph Cotten." He didn't smile. He gave the handshake enough but not all he had. He liked the guy's sport coat. He didn't like his maize and blue Michigan tie, the way it was tied in a careless knot, the label side of the narrow end showing, *All Silk.* He had met millionaires before, when he drove for the mayor and wore black tie with the black mayor and stayed close to him at functions, Bryan slick and official in his city-bought tux. (A deputy chief called him sir at the benefits and openings until the deputy chief saw him at 1300, on the fifth floor, and found out Bryan was a sergeant on loan from Homicide.) He liked the mayor—enjoyed hearing him shift as smooth as a smile from street talk to official pronouncement—but had been indifferent to the indifferent millionaires he'd met. He would be indifferent to this one, too; though not for the same reason. He resented this one, the uncombed hair, the careless tie, the patter, the same way he resented wavy-haired gospel preachers on television who never stopped smiling.

Robbie was acting but didn't know it, used to playing the role. Making everything look easy. Talking about George Hamilton now.

George Hamilton in town yesterday. Doing a Diamond Mortgage commercial.

George Hamilton's tan that you could kid him about all you wanted but was superb, 100 percent.

"Angie, I wished you'd called."

Angela said, "Why?"

"Hey, I've got to tell you this," Robbbie said. Glancing around, "Walter, come here." Walter edging over, not looking directly at anyone as Robbie put an arm around Walter's rigid shoulders, a possession, though it was meant as an act of fellowship. "My star driver and head of security, Walter Kouza." Standing there in his gray double-knit suit, maroon shirt and tie.

Angela said, with innocence, "Why're you feeling insecure?"

"It's a long story," Robbie said. "I've had a couple of threats lately, in Florida. I didn't tell you about them, I don't think they amount to anything . . . But this is good. Walter's driving, we pick George up out in West Bloomfield where they're shooting—we're gonna have dinner at the Chop House and then drop George off at the Ponch. So we're in the car at least, altogether, forty-five minutes, right? We're talking, he's telling me about his new picture—it's about Zorro, but he plays him as a gay, if you can imagine a swishy George Hamilton who's had to have had more broads than any guy I know of"—his voice dropped—"with the possible exception of one guy." Robbie paused.

Bryan watched him; saw his expression go dead, then brighten again, immediately.

"You know, with the swords and all, the gay blade? We're talking about Hollywood, we're talking about Palm Beach, Dina, Bert . . . Angie, you know. We drop George off at the Ponch, we're pulling away and Walter goes, honest to God, 'Who was that?' " Robbie timed it, giving them a wide-eyed Johnny Carson look. "I said, 'That was George Hamilton.' Walter goes—are you ready? 'Who's George Hamilton.' " Still wide eyed.

Then grinning, looking at Walter fondly as he gave the

rigid shoulders a squeeze. "We're not laughing at you, Walter, it's just an improbably funny situation."

No one was laughing at anything. Walter tried to smile but failed. Bryan watched Robbie raise his arm over Walter's head and bring it down, saying he had to run. "But listen"—looking at Angela—"am I gonna see you?"

"I'll call you," Angela said.

"Okay, but better make it in the next few days or I won't be here. Do you need a car?"

"I'm just hanging out for the time being," Angela said. "At the Ponchartrain. Is that by any chance the Ponch?"

Robbie said, "What else? But if you need wheels, I mean even right now, I'm gonna be with my lawyers the next couple of hours, but Walter's free. He'll take you wherever you want to go. I *can't* see you tonight, Angie, but give me a call tomorrow."

Bryan said, "Would he mind driving us out to my place?" He felt the toe of Angela's cowboy boot poke at his leg. "I have to get my car."

"Sure, anywhere." Robbie gesturing, *why not?* Then frowning, puzzled. "Don't they give police lieutenants cars these days?"

"Not since the price of gas went up," Bryan said. "No more driving home in blue Plymouths."

Robbie seemed interested. "How do you get around?"

"Well, I usually drive my own car down and park it," Bryan said. "This morning, one of my squad picked me up. We had to go to a scene."

Robbie was nodding as he listened. "Fascinating. You mean a murder scene. I'd love to watch an investigation sometime. Is that possible?"

"I suppose so," Bryan said, "if you're interested in homicide."

He felt the toe of Angela's boot again as Robbie said, "I am, indeed."

They rode in his Cadillac Fleetwood behind dark-tinted glass. Walter, silent, taking them north on Woodward Avenue. Angela looking at the city beyond downtown for the first time, not asking what's that or that until they passed between impressive stone structures, the main library and the art institute, and Bryan told her what they were, pointing out Rodin's *The Thinker* in front of the museum, saying that was it until they spotted the golden tower of the Fisher Building. Angela said, well, it's bigger than Tucson.

They didn't ask each other questions or loosen up and say all the things they wanted to say. Walter was right there: rigid, the man never moved, shoulders hunched over the wheel, shark-fin pompadour glistening, stray hairs standing like antennae.

Bryan said, "Walter, you like working for Robbie?"

Walter didn't answer.

"I drove for a guy one time. Followed him around, got to go to parties. You go to parties, Walter?"

No answer.

"I'll bet you see some interesting things, huh?"

Angela was making sad faces, in sympathy. She leaned against Bryan and whispered, "Leave the poor guy alone."

Bryan said, "I want to but I can't." His gaze moved to the side window. "You're in Highland Park now. Coming up on the old Ford plant."

Angela said, "Nice."

Bryan said, "Walter, I was wondering, how come you don't have on your chauffeur's uniform?"

Walter didn't answer.

"I forgot," Bryan said, "you had to go to court today. That the reason?"

Walter's hand moved, mashing the horn to blast a car pulling away from the curb.

Angela hunched her shoulders and Bryan poked her with an elbow. They could see Walter's hands, thick, padded, knuckles like smooth stones, gripping the steering wheel.

"Left before you get to Palmer Park, Walter. You got to go up past the light and come back. Then along the park over to Merton."

"It's looking better," Angela said as they passed Moorish and Art Deco apartment buildings among lawns and old trees, Raymond hunching forward now.

"Up there on the left, Walter, the yellow brick with the front that looks like a mosque." He said to Angela, "Right across from the synagogue. We've got black people and gays of all colors. It's an interesting neighborhood."

Walter braked abruptly and sat looking straight ahead.

Getting out, Bryan said, "Walter, I'm sorry you feel the way you do. But I'll say this. You're a good driver and I think you'll always find work."

Walter waited until they were going up the walk.

"Hey, wise-ass."

Bryan touched Angela's arm. They looked back to see Walter with his elbow on the windowsill, a lone figure in that dark expanse of limousine. Bryan said, "You talking to me?"

Walter said, "I'll tell you something, wise-ass, you think you're so fucking clever. You're bush. Homicide lieutenant, all that goes with it, you're still bush. The biggest thing ever happens to you, some jig on Twelfth Street shoots another jig's been fucking his common-law wife, or you get a twenty-buck hooker slashed to death, tits cut off in some alley, all that street shit. Floater comes up at Waterworks Park, makes your fuck-

65

ing day. That's what you're in, buddy, and that's as class as it gets."

Bryan waited a moment.

"Compared to what?"

Walter hesitated, still aroused, almost eager, but holding back. "Get your head out of the garbage, maybe you'll see how it's done in the majors, wise-ass."

The limousine moved off abruptly, wheels throwing bits of gravel, engine revs rising, then fading down the street. They watched the car until it was out of sight.

Angela said, "I'm beginning to see through you, Bryan. You're not your everyday wise-ass; you use it with a purpose. Put the needle in and get 'em to talk."

They started up the walk again, Bryan taking out his keys. He felt pretty good: his interest aroused to speculate and wonder, without having to worry about it, feel a responsibility. He said, "That's the first time in his life Walter's ever used any restraint, held back. What do you think he was trying to tell us?"

Angela waited as he unlocked the front door and held it open. "I think he was showing off, trying to one-up you. Behind the wheel of his Cadillac limo."

Bryan said, "I hope that's all he's doing."

FOUR

BRYAN WAS GOING through the stack of magazines on the toilet tank in the bathroom. *National Geographic, Smithsonian, Quest, GEO, Law and Order,* there, *Playboy.* But the wrong month. Two more *National Geographics,* another *Playboy.* Too recent. *Car and Driver . . .*

He heard Angela say from the living room, "What're these little marks in the wall?"

He looked out, through the hall and into the living room. She was standing to the left of the front door.

"Bullet holes."

And went back to sorting through the stack. An old *Newsweek, Atlantic, Monthly Detroit . . .*

"*Bullet* holes?"

Smithsonian, another *National Geographic, Esquire, Esquire . . .* another *Playboy . . .* November! He opened it, turned a page.

"Why're there bullet holes in your wall?"

"Somebody shot at me. I came in and turned the light on. Bang—a guy was waiting for me."

There she was: the nice smile, perfect nose, the knowing eyes, soft hair slanting across her forehead, all within the square-inch or so border of the black and white photo. He got a razor blade from the medicine cabinet, sliced the picture out carefully and replaced the magazine, slipping it into the middle of the pile.

As he came out of the hall and crossed toward the kitchen, she saw him: in his shirt sleeves now, the grip of a revolver showing, the gun riding in the waist of his trousers, behind his right hip. It was unexpected and gave her a momentary shock. She said, "Were you hurt?"

"When?"

"When you were shot at."

"No, he missed. I think all I've got's Jim Beam."

"That's fine. What'd you do then?"

"What, with the guy? I took the gun away from him . . . Why don't you put on some music?"

In the kitchen he held the stamp-size photo carefully in the palm of his hand, looked about undecided, then opened the *Good Housekeeping Cookbook* lying on the tile counter and placed the photo inside. There. He turned to the refrigerator and brought out an ice tray.

In the living room Angela was looking through his record albums, a stack of them on the floor next to the Sears hi-fi system.

"All you've got is Waylon Jennings and Willie Nelson."

"No, there're some others. George Benson . . . Earl Klugh."

"You've got a *whale* record." She put on Bob James.

Lamplight softened the starkness of the room, laid flaring designs on the empty walls. The music helped too.

She said, "Did you just move in?"

From the kitchen: "Almost two years ago."

The room didn't reflect him; or anyone. Bare walls and shelves of paperbacks and magazines. A hanging fern, dying; a young ficus that wasn't doing too badly. Chair and sofa slip-covered in faded summer-cottage beige. It looked as though he could move out in less than fifteen minutes.

"When're you gonna fix the place up?"

"What's the matter with it?"

A grocery sack with a red tag stapled to it stood upright on the glass coffee table. It was open. All she had to do, sitting on the edge of the sofa, was pull the sack toward her to look inside. She saw a girl's hairbrush, a beaded purse, a rolled-up cellophane bag that contained marijuana, a packet of cigarette paper and book matches. She saw what looked like pink panties, sandals, a white T-shirt bunched at the bottom of the sack that showed part of a word in black.

She sat back as Bryan came in from the kitchen, a lowball glass in each hand. He said, "You can look at that stuff if you want."

"It belongs to someone, doesn't it?"

"Not anymore. She's dead." He placed the drinks on the table and started back to the kitchen. "I left in a hurry this morning, forgot to take it with me."

The T-shirt was soiled with what looked like coffee stains; black lettering on white that said

DETROIT
IS FOR
LOVERS

She dropped the T-shirt in the sack and sipped her drink, felt the warmth inside her as moisture came to her eyes. "You make a neat one," she called to the kitchen, relaxing, with a good feeling.

He came in with a bowl of dry-roasted peanuts. "I

thought we had some crackers, but we don't." And went back out again.

"What're you doing?"

"We're having a party."

"Are we going to smoke at the party?"

"I quit."

"So did I. Why don't we start again and quit some other time?"

She heard him say, "Okay, but I don't have any."

She went into the sack and brought out the Baggie. The grass looked clean, just a few seeds and bits of stem, dark stuff with a green smell to it. She rolled a cigarette, lighted it and sat back again on the sofa. As Bryan came in, now with a plate of white cheese and celery stalks, she said, "Am I destroying evidence?"

He said, "Not unless you smoke the whole lid." When she offered him the joint he took it carefully. "It's been a while." Drew deeply on it and said, holding his breath, "The last time, I ate about five pounds of caramel corn."

She said, "Well, six feet, about one sixty. I don't see a problem that shows. When do you take your gun off?"

He brought it out, a revolver with a stubby barrel, and laid it on the coffee table. The grip, she saw, was wrapped tightly with rubber bands. He said, "I forgot something." And went back to the kitchen.

Angela drew on the cigarette, staring at the revolver, about to ask him about the rubber bands when he came back in with the *Good Housekeeping Cookbook* and handed it to her.

"You brought me here to cook, is that it?"

"No, look inside. There's something in there."

"What?"

"Just look. It might be in the chicken section."

Angela leafed through pages, came to *Poultry* and began turning pages one at a time, concentrating now, looking for some clue. Then stopped. She seemed awed by what she saw. "I don't believe it." She held up the inch-square black and white photograph of herself.

Bryan leaned over to look at the cookbook open on her lap and nodded. "Under chicken cacciatore."

She said with a softness he had not heard before, "You really did . . . I've got goosebumps."

Bryan said, "It is scary, isn't it?"

Patti Daniels stood against the open door to the study; arms folded, which told Robbie something when finally he pushed the off button on the remote-control tuner, the armed Secret Service agents on the television screen imploding to black and he looked over at his wife. She had asked him yesterday how many times he'd watched it—the video cassette tape of the Reagan assassination attempt—and if she wanted the latest tally he'd tell her: nine times so far this evening.

She said, "I don't get it."

He didn't feel required to answer. Comments would have to be put in the form of a question. He waited, fingering the remote-control device in his hand.

"How many times are you going to look at it?"

He hadn't anticipated that one. "I don't know."

"What're you looking for, blood?"

"There's not much of it to see."

She straightened, brushed at the loose sleeve of her lounging gown, refolded her arms and leaned against the door again. The hip line was provocative; but he knew better.

"Did you have dinner?" Patti asked him.

"Yeah, as a matter of fact, at the Renaissance Club. David and Roger. They're not doing an awful lot of business. I mean the club. All that new-Detroit bullshit—Cartier's moving out, right on the heels of your favorite shop. Walk through the

71

RenCen, the only people you see're working there or wearing name tags. They don't even have full occupancy, they're putting up two more buildings."

Patti said, "I love to talk about economics."

"How 'bout the six hundred grand condo in Aspen? You'd hire an ad agency to sell me on that one."

She said, "The only reason you don't like it is because I do. I'm going back out for Easter."

"Your snooty pals are gonna miss you."

"Tell them I may come down for the polo matches. I'll see."

"The jock," Robbie said. "What've you got out west, another ski instructor?"

She stared at him, posed, pert blonde in folds of champagne silk by Halston, boat-neck design good on her for a few more years, flowing lines to conceal thick legs; in ski pants or tailored clothes, an aristocratic fragility above the waist, a peasant's big-ass sturdiness below: the halves of two different women in one.

She said, "Do you want to compare notes? How about your writer friend—she still around?"

"Angela? Come on."

"I forgot. She must be ten years over the hill."

"Maybe I'll go out to Aspen with you."

"I'm going to bed."

"Jealous husband shoots—what is he, Austrian? Swiss? . . . Jealous husband shoots ethnic ski instructor." Robbie grinned. "Wait a minute. You like that suave foreign type, what about Walter? You could have an affair with Walter, you wouldn't even have to leave the house."

She said, "Are you serious about hiring Walter?"

"Of course I am."

"The servants don't know what to make of him. They don't know which side he's on."

"I like him," Robbie said. "Walter's solid, good Hamtramck stock. Speaking of which, not only Dodge Main is no more, Lynch Road's gone. Chrysler's going down the toilet and Lee Iacocca hangs in there like a hemorrhoid. You see him in the TV ads? He's a fucking storm trooper. Buy a Chrysler product, you son of a bitch, or I'll kill you."

"Good night," Patti said.

"Wait a minute. There're some papers you have to sign, on the desk."

Patti straightened, moved toward the glow of the brass, green-shaded lamp. She seldom came into Robbie's study; it had all the hallowed solid-oak charm of the Detroit Athletic Club, where men in dark suits talked solemnly about ten-day reports and women were admitted through a side entrance. She looked at the pages of legalese and picked up Robbie's gold pen.

"What're we up to now"

"Some more of the liquidation," Robbie said. "Within four days a Jewish auctioneer will have wiped out seventy-five years of nuts and bolts for the automotive industry. And you know what the best part is? The goddamn Japs'll probably buy half the equipment. No more Daniels fascinating fasteners. That's not bad, I could've used that. I see things in headlines lately. Fastener firm finally says fuck it. Daniels—no. Foremost Chrysler ass-kisser closes its doors."

"Sells out," Patti said. "Buying the Cadillac was sort of a tip-off. Rolls and Mercedes don't count."

"Just sign the papers . . . I don't know why I stayed in as long as I did. He'd come down to the plant, his arm hanging, dragging his leg, he'd come down and sit among his bowling trophies and black-framed memories . . . Knudsen, Sloan, Tex Colbert, he even had Horace Dodge up there, Christ, while he stared at me through those fucking glass partitions. Go to Schweizer's for lunch. Dad went every single day for forty-five years. I'd say, let's go to Little Harry's for a change. No,

Schweizer's. I'm never gonna eat another potato pancake as long as I live."

"Poor baby," Patti said.

"What I'm gonna do, sell every machine in the plant except one. I think a Waterbury Farrell Automatic Thread Roller, a big Number 50. Paint it black and stand it out on the front lawn with a plaque that reads: 'It's an ugly fucker, but it sure made us a pile of money' . . . I'd love to do that."

Patti said, "It's too bad you don't have the balls." She signed the papers and left.

"You lied to me," Angela said.

The first thing he thought of: you left the razor blade on the sink.

She had come out of the bathroom and was standing in the hall doorway, holding what looked like a magazine under her arm. "You're not forty. You're thirty-seven or -eight. Which?"

He said, "I'll be thirty-eight in October," relaxing a little but still uncertain, until she held up, not a magazine, his high school yearbook.

"Western," Angela said, "nineteen-sixty-one . . ."

He'd taken it in there one morning weeks ago—saving time, looking up a familiar name, a robbery-homicide suspect he was pretty sure he'd gone to school with—and left the yearbook on the open shelf with the towels.

". . . 'Bryan proved his sterling character both in the classroom and on the Cowboy basketball court where he averaged fifteen points a game,' " Angela recited. "Sterling character, my ass."

"I averaged sixteen points," Bryan said.

"Why did you lie?"

"I'm not quite six foot either."

Angela waited.

He said, "Well, you were having trouble being thirty. So, I thought if I told you I was forty, and looked like I was handling it okay—you know, forty being worse than thirty—it might make you feel better."

"You did it for me?" Angela said.

"I guess so."

She was coming toward him with the warm look again.

"Sometimes," Bryan said, "I tell myself I'm forty. It makes me feel more—I want to say mature—but grown-up, anyway. See, I think you get over forty you're finally there, you're full-grown and it's easier to talk to people. Otherwise, I have the feeling everyone's older than I am."

"I do too," Angela said.

"So I pretend I'm older and it works."

"Are you shy?" She sank down next to him on the sofa and he handed her the joint, the second one she had rolled from the evidence bag.

"No, I don't think I am. Well, maybe a little."

"You weren't shy in court. But it's funny," Angela said. "In a way you seemed . . . not like a little boy exactly, but boyish. Natural. I wanted to make a face at you, like we were in grade school."

"Why didn't you?"

"I didn't know what kind to make."

"So you were feeling like a little girl."

"Yeah, but I wasn't aware of it till I started looking at you. See, I didn't analyze it *then*, at the time."

He said, "Why don't you put that thing down."

She said, "All right," and laid the joint in the groove of an ashtray that said *Carl's Chop House*.

He said, "Are you ready?" Touching her face with his palm as she turned back to him.

She said, "I'm ready."

They kissed for the first time, not rushing it but finally holding on and getting it all, not wanting to let go it was so good.

Bryan said, "That was the best kiss I've ever had in my life."

She said, "God, you're good. But don't say it if it isn't true. Okay?"

"No, I mean it. It was the best one I ever had."

"You're not lying . . . "

"No, it's the truth."

"Please don't ever lie to me, okay?"

"No, I won't. You a little high? I think I'm beginning to feel it."

She said, "It was the best one I've ever had, too."

He said, "Are you having fun at the party?"

Walter was wearing a raincoat over his pajamas because he didn't own a bathrobe. He was wearing black wing tips, too, but no socks.

He knocked and entered the study. It was dark: the only light coming from a green desk lamp on one side of the room and the TV screen on the other, where Mr. Daniels was sitting in a leather chair, his legs stretched out on a matching leather ottoman. The picture on the TV screen didn't move. It was like a color photograph of the Secret Service ganging up on the assassin, who was under the pile somewhere.

Robbie said, "Come on in, sit down."

Walter pulled a ladder-back chair closer to the TV set, sat down and hunched over with his elbows on his thighs.

Robbie said, "See the guy with the submachine gun?"

"Yeah, in the gray suit," Walter said. "It looks like an Uzi."

"That's what it is," Robbie said. "All right, watch." He began clicking the remote-control switch and the pictures on the screen backed up frame by frame. Then changed to another view of action. Then to an earlier, longer view of Secret Service agents and newsmen standing around, waiting. "There," Robbie said, "he doesn't have it." He moved the pictures forward and stopped on the Secret Service agent with the submachine gun angling up from under his right arm, his left arm extended, pointing; he was saying something. Robbie said, "There, he does. Where did he get the Uzi?"

"Out of a case," Walter said. "One latch open, the other one closed, with his finger on it at all times."

"How do you know that?"

"I just know, that's all," Walter said. "That's Quick-draw McGraw, whatever guy has that job, that's what he's called. Keeps within six paces of the president at all times. Maybe eight."

Robbie ran the sequence backward again and stopped on a frame that showed a hand holding a revolver in the right foreground, two bodies on the sidewalk, a policeman's hat, part of the president's limousine.

"What kind of gun is that?"

"No kind," Walter said. "Guy shoots the president of the United States with a fucking Saturday-night special."

"You feel he deserves better. I agree. This is how to do it if you're dumb but lucky," Robbie said. "You want a drink?"

"No, I don't care for anything. I was in bed."

"Two questions," Robbie said. "What did Angie and the cop talk about, the hearing?"

"No, just bullshit. He was pointing out to her some of the, you know, points of interest."

"Okay. The other thing, how do I get hold of Curtis Moore?"

Christ, try and keep up with this guy. "I don't know," Walter said, straightening, sitting back in the chair. "Call him, I guess."

"Incidentally," Robbie said, "you've got a new lawyer, Roger Stedman. He'll get in touch with you when the time comes."

"What do I tell Eddie Jasinski?"

"Tell Eddie he's fired," Robbie said. "I want to try to set up something with Curtis Moore either tomorrow or Sunday, preferably tomorrow. Where does he hang out?"

"You call him at home?"

"Several times, no answer. What about his motorcycle club? You must've dealt with them at one time or another."

"I don't know," Walter said, "they used to always be at a place on Jefferson, across from Uniroyal. Let me think." He looked around the semidark room, a study that was bigger than a parlor, Daniels staring at him, waiting. "Yeah, the Elite Bar, corner of Jefferson and Concord, across from where Uniroyal was. They sit out in front revving their machines. They don't go anywhere, just make a lot of noise, wake up the neighborhood."

"Call the bar, see if he's there."

"You serious?"

"Walter, the proper response is, yes, Mr. Daniels."

Walter sat at Mr. Daniels's desk, called information, then the Elite Bar, said, "What? You don't mean to tell me." Said, "Yeah?" a couple of times and hung up with an amazed look.

"You want to hear something? Curtis don't come in no more, he's working, parking cars at the Detroit Plaza Hotel. I never heard of any Plaza Hotel in town."

"In the RenCen. But why is that hard to believe?"

"You imagine giving your automobile to Curtis, hand him the fucking *keys*? That's what he used to do for a living, steal cars, all 'em for parts."

Mr. Daniels, sitting in the soft glow of the TV picture, didn't say anything for some time. He looked like he was falling asleep, while Walter rolled from one cheek to the other, trying to get comfortable on the straight chair. He said, "Mr. Daniels, you mind if I go back to bed?"

"No, I'll see you in the morning. I want you to pick up some people for me."

"Pick 'em up where?"

Robbie gave him a thin smile. "You've got to be the most, if not impertinent, the most informal driver I've ever had."

"I want to drive," Walter said, "I can drive my own car all I want. I didn't come up here to fucking drive around town. I thought I was hired for a deal you have in mind that I'm the man for it, not driving a limo or living with the help or taking a lot of shit from the cook who's supposed to be Ukrainian and can't even make pirogies, for Christ sake."

"You're tired," Robbie said.

"I'll agree with you there," Walter said. "I didn't hire on to drive any fink cops home to their doors either."

Robbie was pulling himself out of the chair. Without a word he walked past Walter to the desk, took a key from his pocket and unlocked a side drawer.

"Come here."

Daniels was taking a folder from the drawer now. He opened it and laid a large photograph, at least nine by twelve, on the desk beneath the lamp and looked at Walter.

"Here he is."

It was a photocopy, Walter saw, of a photograph that had appeared in a newspaper or magazine, though there was no caption, nothing to identify the man sitting with the small boy perched on his lap, both posed, looking directly at the camera.

The man, who appeared to be about sixty years of age, was dressed in a formal military uniform laden with gold leaf and braid, rows of decorative medals with ribbons, and wore a fore-and-aft plumed admiral's hat.

Walter said, "What's he in, Knights of Columbus?"

Robbie didn't answer, waiting for the right question.

The boy in the photo, with the same hint of Latin coloring as the man, wore a white double-breasted suit with short pants and appeared to be nine or ten years old.

Walter said, "I give up. Who is he?"

"At one time," Robbie said, "one of the world's foremost dictators."

"I don't recognize him," Walter said.

"He died," Robbie said, "exactly twenty years ago."

Walter said, "He's *dead*? Wait a minute. You mean you want to hit the kid?"

"The picture was taken thirty years ago," Robbie said. "The kid isn't a kid anymore. He's a grown man, Walter. The guy we're looking for."

Walter said, "Yeah?" Not too sure. The kid was a nice-looking kid. "This guy, he's pretty bad?"

Robbie said, "Walter, if I told you what a rotten prick this little boy's turned out to be"—Robbie paused—"Well, you'd want to fly down to West Palm tonight."

Walter straightened, eyes catching a gleam of lamplight. "You mean this guy lives down by you?"

Robbie said, "I don't want to get you all worked up too soon, buddy. We've got time."

"I'm ready right now," Walter said. "I'm not doing nothing."

Robbie said, "Yeah, but I am. Let me get some business out of the way, then we'll give it our full attention. How's that sound?"

"I'm ready," Walter said.

FIVE

ANGELA WOKE UP during the night and for a moment didn't know where she was. She had interviewed a woman who used to wake up at least once a week and not know where she was or who the guy was lying next to her; the woman had made a name for herself, subsequently, bringing people into Alcoholics Anonymous. Angela recognized Bryan and went back to sleep. In the morning she used his toothbrush, looked for a bathrobe and couldn't find one. Wearing her navy blue coat over bare skin she made coffee. The morning was bright, trees beginning to bud outside the window; but it was cold in the apartment. She went back into the bedroom, stood looking down at Bryan sleeping and kneed the side of the bed. He woke up, looked at her with instant recognition and a smile, a good sign, and said, "Well, here we are, huh?"

Angela, holding her wool coat closed but not buttoned, said, "I interviewed a Sicilian one time who married a girl in a big ceremony. This was in New York; they both came here from Sicily when they were kids. They're married, they fly down to Orlando, Florida, on their honeymoon to go to Disney World and that night he finds out his wife isn't a virgin. At least he's convinced she isn't a virgin and he has a fit. He calls up the girl's father and her uncle and complains, like they're responsible for giving him damaged goods. The girl, however, keeps insisting she's a virgin. So the guy takes her to a doctor for a virgin test and the doctor says, well, she might be a virgin, but then again she might not. Virgin tests are not all that conclusive. He takes her to two more doctors in Orlando. The first one throws them out. The second one gets the girl up on the table, feet up in the stirrups, takes a look—hmmm, everything looks okay to him; no hymen to speak of, but this doctor's an O.B. and he's not sure he's ever seen a virgin. The husband feels that if it's possible his wife isn't a virgin he isn't gonna go through life wondering about it, picturing her, as he says, with some Puerto Rican or worse. You're not part Puerto Rican, are you?"

Bryan moved his head back and forth, no, on the pillow.

"So the guy sends her home to her father and gets an annulment. The girl, virgin or not, feels the guy has ruined her reputation. Even back in Sicily, the village she left as a little girl, they're talking about it, shaking their heads, see, that's what happens when you go to the U.S. of A. So she brings a slander suit against her ex-husband for a million bucks. She's awarded two hundred thousand and the Appeals Court upholds it. When I interviewed the Sicilian guy he said it was not really her lack of virginity that turned him off. It was the fact on the honeymoon she deceived him. She had brought along a contraceptive device, french-kissed like a pro and had her hand on his joint before he'd even taken his coat off. He said, 'I should give a woman like that two hundred thousand dollars? I wouldn't even if I had it, and I don't.' What I'm getting at is, you can try hard to please somebody and in the end, nobody wins."

Bryan said, "That's an interesting story."

"I'm not a virgin," Angela said. "I was married; but

even if I hadn't been, I still wouldn't be a virgin. I'm not giving up anything or making any kind of claim. I know what I want and I know what I don't want."

Bryan was lying on his back beneath the sheet and blanket, staring up at her, his hands behind his head now.

He said, "We haven't even done it yet."

She said, "Do you know why?"

He said, "I think I was asleep when you came out of the bathroom and you didn't wake me up."

"So it's my fault." Very dry.

"No, I held back, it was out of respect."

"Respect and dope," Angela said, "and a fifth of Jim Beam. I'll tell you what I *don't* want first, I don't want it to be a morning quickie."

Bryan said, "I don't either. I'm hoping it'll last a good ten minutes anyway. Why don't you open your coat?"

She did. Opened it and closed it, giving him a flash of suntanned skin, small pale breasts and slim white panties.

Bryan said, "You want to wait, huh? Little candlelight and soft music?"

She half-closed her eyes, a seductive, bored look, did a little one-two, one-two go-go step and flashed him again.

Bryan said, "Okay, tell me what you want."

Robbie left home at twenty past nine Saturday morning, came out on Lake Shore Drive and had to put his visor down at the spectacle of sun on water.

Both of his homes faced bodies of water. Not so much because he was drawn to the sight, but because people as rich as Robbie who lived in Palm Beach looked at the Atlantic Ocean and if they lived in Grosse Pointe, where there was less frontage, they caught glimpses of Lake St. Clair; one body of water reaching to Africa, the other, beyond the horizon, to Canada;

one a deep blue, the other, green. At least today the lake was a summery green, though it lay flat and empty and it would be a month before the sailboats were out.

Lake Shore became East Jefferson, leaving behind Better Homes for a run through HUD country to high rises on the river and into downtown some twenty minutes later. Robbie turned his black Mercedes into the Renaissance Center—now the glass-towered face of Detroit in travel-magazine shots—bore to the right and came around to the entrance of the Detroit Plaza Hotel.

Now the tricky part.

Spot Curtis Moore. Time it so that Curtis takes the car and no one else.

Robbie nosed the Mercedes into the dim three-lane area beneath the port cochere, hung back to study the people standing around, the traffic flow, the procedure. Then moved up in the outside lane for a closer look. There was more activity than he thought there'd be this time of the morning: maybe a convention leaving or another group coming in. There were two doormen dressed as French policemen. Or redcaps. Two young black guys in red blazers handing out claim checks to the parking attendants who wore drab industrial-blue uniforms and were hard to spot in the half-light. They would give part of the ticket to the owner, jump in the car and take a sharp right down a ramp to the garage level, then reappear some minutes later, coming out a door that was off behind the cashier's window and marked *Authorized Personnel Only*.

Robbie had to leave his car and go over to stand near the door before he was able to identify Curtis.

No cornrows this morning, a moderate Afro. His movement, his walk seemed different too, less studied. He was offstage now doing his work . . . giving Robbie a look as he came past the cashier's window. Do I know you?

Robbie was wearing sunglasses, dressed in a gray suit

and rep tie beneath a buttoned-up raincoat. He held out a ten-dollar bill.

"I think I'm next."

Curtis said nothing. He took the bill, went over to one of the parking maitre d's in the red blazers, got a ticket and came back.

"How long you be?"

"Couple of hours."

Curtis tore a stub off and handed Robbie his claim check. Now Robbie watched him slide into the Mercedes and take off as he slammed the door closed; gone.

Robbie waited near the cashier's window where several people stood with their backs to him. It would take a few minutes. There were no more than four or five parking attendants working, so three or four should come through the *Authorized Personnel Only* door before Curtis appeared again.

Well, you never knew. The door opened, a blue uniform appeared. The door closed and opened again within a few moments and there was Curtis. Out of order, out of character. It bothered Robbie, gave him a mild tug of alarm. Even a minor miscalculation would not do in this business; or else several dozen popular novels had given him the wrong information. But he had to proceed right now or throw out the plan and start over.

He held up his parking ticket, caught Curtis's eye.

"You just took my car down. I have to get something out of it."

Now the lassitude, the slow move, the look of indifference as Curtis shifted and got back into character, pleasing Robbie more than Curtis could imagine.

"What do you do in a case like this?"

"Want me bring your car back?"

"That doesn't seem necessary," Robbie said. "Why not take me down, show me where the car is?"

"Ain't allowed. Just the people work here."

Robbie showed him the folded ten-dollar bill he had ready. "What if I stand over there by the ramp? No one will see me. The next car you take down, stop for a second and I'll hop in."

"I don't have the key."

Robbie felt instant irritation. "You just took the car *down*." It couldn't be this complicated.

"I put the key over in the cashier place"—Curtis pointed—"see, then I come out."

Robbie said, "Well, then get the key."

"I don't know I can do that."

Robbie brought his billfold out of an inside pocket. "I'll bet you twenty bucks you can."

Curtis went back in through the *Authorized Personnel Only* door. Robbie waited. Christ, complications. Curtis came back out.

"I get in a car," Curtis said. "Wait till you see the man owns the car goes inside the hotel. Or you see the dudes in the red coats looking? No deal, man. You understand what I'm saying to you?"

Robbie waited. He watched Curtis go over to pick up a gray four-door Lincoln Continental, watched him get in before he moved to the ramp opening, timing it, hearing the car coming and then a faint squeal of brakes. Robbie opened the door and slid in, the car moving as he slammed the door, down the right-curving chute, Curtis cranking the steering wheel, nicking the Lincoln's bumper along the cement wall.

Robbie said, "Where's Carlos?"

The flat tone was just right.

Curtis was holding the steering wheel cocked, tires squealing on the pavement. Now they were down, rolling along the aisle past rows of cars gleaming in fluorescent light.

Robbie said again, "Where's Carlos?"

Curtis braked abruptly. He said, "I seen you someplace. Else I don't know the fuck you talking about." He twisted around to look past the seats, backed the Lincoln into a space in one effortless move and pulled the keys from the ignition. He got out. Robbie got out.

Robbie said, "Whether you admit it or not, I know you're with Carlos." Staring at Curtis deadpan, the way it was done.

"I know I'm in deep shit you don't get out of here," Curtis said, handing Robbie his keys and then pointing. "Your car over there."

"You gonna wait for me?"

"I don't know you or what you talking about—fucking Carlo, whatever you saying." Curtis started to walk off. "I be back."

Robbie liked the way the Mercedes was parked, front end out. He got behind it and lifted the trunk lid. The canvas tool kit lay to one side of the spotless luggage compartment. He rolled it open, took out the frame of his High Standard Field King, then the ten-inch suppressor tube and grooved it onto the frame, hearing the click of the lock mechanism. The target pistol was ready, the clip fully loaded. He ducked down as a Seville came off the ramp and swept past. Robbie remained low. Another car came down. He listened to doors open and thunk closed. He listened to footsteps on the cement floor, heard voices yell back and forth, words that sounded to him like some Gullah dialect echoing through the concrete level, then laughter. Another car came down. He raised enough to watch the parking attendant get into a Buick Riviera and squeal off toward the exit ramp, following an arrow.

A green Chevrolet station wagon came down, Curtis Moore behind the wheel. Robbie unbuttoned the top half of his raincoat, slipped the target pistol that now measured close to sixteen inches in length inside the coat and held it there, like

Napoleon. A car door slammed. Footsteps approached the Mercedes. Robbie moved past the side windows to the hood of his car. Curtis was across the aisle, coming this way.

Robbie said, "Curtis?"

Curtis looked up. "You got what you need?" Then stopped, looking right at Robbie. "Hey—how you know my name?"

Robbie wanted to hurry, but he had to play it out. Or else why bother? He said, "Because I know you work for Carlos."

Curtis was scowling, giving him a mean look. "Man, I work for the hotel's who I work for."

Robbie brought out the pistol, extending it like a blue-steel wand and began shooting Curtis, aiming high and seeing Curtis throw his head from side to side doing a backstep dance, the snout of the gun giving off hard punctuations of muted sound, casings ejecting, while off beyond were metallic pings and pops in the cement confines and the windshield behind Curtis sprouted spiderwebs. Robbie jammed the gun under one arm, got to Curtis, who was turning red, smearing chrome and sheet metal red, slipping off the red car fender, got to him and eased him down—eyes glassy, sightless—between the cars, careful not to get any of the red on his raincoat, then shoved Curtis with his foot, hanging onto a door handle for leverage, and got most of him hidden beneath the car. A sporty Chrysler LeBaron. Robbie liked it. It seemed an act of loyalty, the least he could do.

Driving up the exit ramp in his Mercedes he became inspired and saw a billboard statement in his mind, lettered in red:

> *"When it comes to hiding victims*
> *I'll take a Chrysler every time! "*

With his name beneath it in neat black type. *Robinson Daniels, well-known sportsman.* Hey, yeah.

Less than a minute later, at five past ten, the Mercedes turned the corner and pulled up in front of the main doors to the Renaissance Center, the area far less congested than the hotel entrance around on the side. Robbie, in his gray suit, maize and blue striped tie laid across his shoulder by the river breeze, stepped out of the car, stood in the V formed by the open door, waved toward the entrance and yelled out:

"Mr. Cabrera? . . . Here!"

The buyer from Mexico. A gentleman in a dark suit, followed by a young, darker-skinned gentleman in a dark suit, came out from the entrance shade nodding, smiling all the way to the Mercedes.

"Sorry if I'm a little late," he said now. "Hi, I'm Robbie Daniels."

"I hope there's a moral to this," Angela said. "I mean I hope you're making a point." With her dry tone.

"If I don't forget what it is," Bryan said. He was sitting up in bed now with his coffee, the covers across his waist. White skin, dark hair on his chest.

Angela sat in an unfinished rocker he'd brought back from Kentucky years ago, Angela still in her navy coat, legs crossed, letting him have a glimpse of tan thigh.

"Go on."

"Where was I? Yeah, Donnie and—I want to say Marie—Donnie and Lorie finally get married. But Margo won't leave."

"Why didn't they throw her out?"

"Well, for one thing it's Margo's house. The three of them're trying to get along the best they can, but Lorie says she can't take it anymore."

"Why didn't Lorie and Donnie move out?"

"Because nobody was working. They're living on food stamps. Donnie says you can't work full time and disco at night, it can't be done. See, his one ambition, he and Lorie, was to get on 'Dance Fever.' So he doesn't like Lorie working either. Margo goes out and hustles a couple nights a week and that's the only money they've got coming in. But, as you can imagine, Margo isn't too fond of the setup. She became, Donnie says, hateful and inconsiderate. And Lorie, meanwhile, every time she gets Donnie alone she tells him she can't live this way. If he doesn't get rid of Margo she'll leave him."

"I don't believe this," Angela said.

"It's true, every word." Bryan sipped his coffee. "Well, they finally work out a plan. They borrow enough money from Margo, like a hundred and fifty bucks, and take out a life insurance policy on her life, Margo's, for ten thousand. That part was Lorie's idea. Lorie keeps telling him, if you really love me you'll do it. Donnie would tell *me*—he'd get a sad, faraway look and tell me, 'I love that girl. I love her more than words can say.' "

Angela said, "Yeah," meaning, go on; interested.

"So finally one night the three of them have a party. They get Margo drunk on Scotch, Donnie takes her in the bedroom, gives her a last jump—"

"Come on—"

"It's what he told me. Then he holds a pillow over her face until she's dead."

"They murdered her?"

"They murdered her. Wait. Then they tie her to the bed, arms and legs outstretched. They ransack the house to make it look like it's been robbed. Then they set the house on fire, tie each other up quick and start yelling for help. Their story's gonna be a bunch of bikers broke in, robbed them, raped and murdered Margo. But Donnie gets trapped in his own fire. In fact he probably would've died if a cop hadn't come in through a window and saved him. The cop got a citation. We investigate—right away we don't like the looks of it. The way drawers have been pulled out evenly, left open. The sofa's ripped all to hell with a knife—for what? Who hides anything in a sofa? Nobody in the neighborhood heard any motorcycles that night . . . Well, Lorie confessed first, then Donnie, and both were convicted on first degree. But here's the thing. Donnie writes to me about twice a year. He's worried about what I think of him, my opinion. In the last letter he says—"

The phone rang in the living room.

"He says, 'I know there are a lot of ill feelings toward me—' "

The phone rang.

" 'So all there is left to say is, God help us fools.' " As the phone rang again he said, "Would you get that?"

Angela said, "It's gonna be for you, isn't it?"

Bryan said, "I don't have any clothes on."

Angela went into the living room in her navy coat. Bryan came out a few moments later with a bath towel around his waist. She handed him the phone and he said into it, "I'm on furlough." He listened for almost a minute, sitting down on the sofa, his tone subdued when he said, "What time did it happen? . . . You sure? . . . Who's on it, Annie? . . . See if you can get Malik, he's probably out on his boat. Doug'll be home in bed, Quentin, he'll be in bed too, somewhere . . . Good, Annie, I'll see you later." He hung up.

Angela was standing, hands in pockets holding the coat closed.

Bryan said, "So Donnie's in Jackson doing mandatory life and worried about what I think of him, all because he loved Lorie *more than words can say*. I finally wrote to him, I said, Donnie, why didn't you just give her some flowers and candy?"

Angela said, "Your compassion spills over, doesn't it?" She came to the sofa, sat down close to him and put her hand on his knee, moving the towel to touch his bare skin.

Bryan said, "So the moral is, when you love somebody

you better be able to say how much, in words, or you could get your ass in some deep trouble."

Angela said, "I'm not sure I'd kill for you, Bryan, but I'll buy breakfast."

"Is that what you want more than anything?"

"I guess at the moment. It's not however the *big* thing I want more than anything."

Bryan looked at her and moved his eyebrows up and down, twice.

"Macho man," Angela said. "Guys kill me." She slapped his thigh, then leaned on it to get up. "Let's go get some breakfast."

"I'd like to," Bryan said, "but I can't. Curtis Moore was shot and killed about an hour ago."

SIX

HE TOLD ANGELA Police Headquarters was referred to simply as "1300" because it was at 1300 Beaubien and there the numbers were, in gold, above the entrance. Nine stories of Italian Renaissance gone to grime and without a vantage as the old Wayne County jail closed in from one side and a new jail facility rose in cement forms on the other.

He asked her if she was hungry yet, nodding to the Coney Island across the street where the fry chef in the window was grilling hot dogs. Angela said no, thanks. She could still see the blood smears on cement and chrome; all that blood from one person. They had stopped at a Koney with a *K* in the Renaissance Center and she smoked cigarettes, sipped black coffee, while Bryan had two with everything. Brunch. He told her outside Police Headquarters it was almost two-thirty. She said she still wasn't hungry.

Construction dust hung in the air, the sound of high-steel riveting and transit mixers grinding out cement for the new county jail addition going up behind 1300. Bryan said they

93

wouldn't have to advertise, the new building would have full occupancy within a week of completion.

In the lobby past the snack bar were the names of police officers killed in the line of duty, memorialized in marble wall sections on both sides of the elevators. They had to wait, Bryan holding the grocery sack with the red tag. Police personnel came and stood by them. They moved into the elevator and Angela was aware of the size of the men; they reminded her of professional athletes.

Fifth floor. Directly off the elevator was Room 500. Bryan told her they had moved recently because they needed more space and got maybe an additional ten square feet. He kept talking to her. There was a hole in the laminated door panel that looked as though someone had tried to kick it in. Angela wondered about it. Why anyone would want to break into a Homicide Section squad room? Unless, on the other hand, the person had been brought in kicking.

There were sounds in the empty room. A phone ringing. A portable radio tuned softly to classical music. A walkie-talkie reciting code numbers, getting no response.

Bryan picked up a phone. Angela looked around, neither disappointed nor surprised, not expecting much in a sixty-year-old building that belonged to the city. Metal desks and file cabinets and a coffee maker against municipal green walls. About four hundred Polaroid mug shots mounted on a sheet of wallboard. A map of the city. Two windows that looked down on Beaubien and the Coney Island place. But an adjoining room the size of a walk-in closet that held a table with a type-writer and three chairs was painted pink. Bryan hung up the phone. He told her it was their interrogation room and the color was to relax suspects, make them more receptive to questions. Angela wasn't sure if he was kidding or not. She had questions of her own but saw they would have to wait.

Jim Malik came in. Back from the morgue.

94

Bryan seemed surprised. "They do a post on Curtis already?"

Just starting. But Malik had been there for someone else. A little girl, from what Angela could gather. Perhaps a previous murder. She realized they didn't finish one and pick up another, like piecework; the murders came in unscheduled. Malik seemed frustrated; a muscular forty-year-old with sandy hair and a Guard's mustache. Cordial, smiling as he was introduced to her, but on the hunt; a man who appraised women openly, making plans on glimpses of fantasy. Then it was time for Angela to listen and observe these people whose business was murder:

Malik saying, "The M.E. went all through her, twice. Peeled her throat, no sign of ligature. Laid open the lungs, nothing. No sign of hemorrhage, no indication of restraints on wrists or ankles. I mean he didn't find shit outside of some maggots ready to pop."

Bryan said, "Toxicology doesn't show anything?"

Malik said, "We don't have it yet. But no sign of trauma and they think she's too young to've O.D.'d. So they're making it indeterminate pending toxicology. If nothing shows up in the blood, they'll call it exposure."

Bryan said, "Her panties were rolled down."

Malik said, "I know they were."

The phone rang and Malik answered it. He said, "Squad Five, Sergeant Malik . . . Yes, ma'am . . . No, he's on the street right now." He hung up and said, "You know what I think?" The phone rang again. He picked it up and began talking to someone about a shooting.

Angela listened.

Bryan took off his sport coat. Gray tweed with cord pants that almost matched. She wanted to ask him about the rubber bands on the grip of his gun, but she wanted to listen to Jim Malik.

"The one in the bar? . . . Yeah, the thing is, Terry, usually that kind of a situation you ask who saw it and thirty people were out in the can at the same time taking a piss . . . Right, all at once. But this time they all go, yeah, they saw it. Was the big dude come at the little dude . . . "

Bryan asked her if she wanted a cup of coffee. Still listening, Angela said yes and watched him cross to the coffee maker that was next to a strange-looking box that held walkie-talkies in slots with small indicator lights on. She had the feeling Malik was aware of her listening to him. The soft strains of classical music were still coming from the portable radio sitting on a file cabinet.

"That's the way every one of 'em tells it. They go, yeah, the big dude—guy weighs about two fifty, two sixty—he comes at the little dude with a knife and the little dude gets this pistol from somewhere and pops the big dude through the left eye, that's it . . . Yeah. Terry? The evidence techs're through, the morgue guys, they have to get help the son of a bitch's so big. They lift him up to get him in the body bag, there's the knife. Pearl handle . . . "

Bryan was coming back with coffee in a Styrofoam cup. He said, "Tell him to forget it."

Malik was saying, "Well, that's up to you. *Maybe* manslaughter. But nothing you say is gonna stick with thirty eyeball witnesses looking at you . . . Seventeen, whatever. All you need's one . . . Terry, if you're hot for the guy try and stick him with the gun . . . Yeah, okay. Let me know." Malik hung up. "Prosecutor's office."

Bryan said, "They'll dismiss it at the exam and the gun'll never come up. Somebody shoved it at him. All of a sudden he looks down, there's a gun in his hand and this giant asshole's coming at him."

They spoke quietly while Angela felt excitement.

Malik said, "That's what I told him." He paused a

moment. "Anyway, I think she pushed her panties down and put her hands in there to keep warm. I'm serious. Lividity shows she was lying on her left side on the back seat and she died that way, man, without any sign of a struggle, in that position."

Bryan said, "Her panties were rolled down, not pushed down." He began to tell Angela about the little girl, eleven years old, who had been dead two months when they found her in the back seat of an abandoned car inside an unused garage with *Somebody Please* written in the dust on a window.

Angela, nodding, trying to picture the little girl, said, "What did you mean about her panties?"

But the door opened and he was looking away.

Doug Parrish and Annie Maguire came in, both holding manila envelopes.

Bryan said, "Doug, Annie . . . Angela Nolan." Brief, but without trying to appear anxious.

A courteous pause. Nods. Glad to meet you. Annie Maguire somewhat shy about it, but a beautiful smile. That was done and Parrish was opening his envelope, dumping small shell casings and several bits of misshapen lead onto Bryan's desk.

Parrish said, "Curtis was done with a twenty-two. Guy hits him at least four times. Cracks a windshield, two slugs still in it. Ruins the finish on five cars. But, I would say professionally done." The old gray wolf speaking, adjusting metal-frame glasses that matched his full head of hair.

"But he wasn't close," Bryan said. "He didn't stick it in Curtis's ear, did he?"

"Look at the rounds," Parrish said, offering evidence. "What do you see?"

Bryan picked up a flattened chunk of lead.

"Stingers."

"Stingers and yellowjackets," Parrish said. "Hyper-velocity, hollow-nose expanders. The guy knew what he was doing."

Malik said, "Kanluen, he took one look inside Curtis—they're just starting to do a post on him. He says it looks like Curtis was hit with forty-fives. The head, the face, in the chest, they tore around in there like in a pinball machine. The one in the head very much like that Reagan's secretary, what's his name."

"But he didn't get close," Bryan said. "What was he afraid of?"

"Well, nobody heard it," Parrish said. "What does that tell you? The guy used a silencer. And you don't get a silencer down at the corner."

"You have car noises in there," Bryan said.

"He fired ten rounds we know of," Parrish said. "He had a good suppressor it wouldn't been any louder'n a B-B gun."

Malik said, "I understand Annie isn't watching the autopsy 'cause Curtis didn't get hit in the privates. They still strip the guy down, Annie."

Angela watched Annie's reaction. A nice smile, not a trace of malice or resentment; probably used to Malik, something that went on between them.

Annie said, taking a handful of claim checks from the manila envelope, "I was busy learning the valet-parking business."

Bryan said, "Oh shit." Tired. He appeared to be dealing with several different thoughts at once, looking into the future as Angela watched him and smoked cigarettes. He asked when the parking guys were coming in.

Annie said around five-thirty.

Parrish said, "We're gonna have to run after one or two of 'em. I know goddamn well."

Malik said, "Or they walk in and start copping. Say homicide, they'll cop to whatever they think of first. Things we don't even know about."

Annie laid the claim checks on Bryan's desk and was

taking out more as Bryan said, "Okay, we talk to everybody who parked there around ten o'clock. Hotel guests, visitors . . ." He picked up one of the claim checks. "It's on here. Time in, time out." And then said, "Shit, we have to find anybody who left about that time."

Malik said, "Get the license number off the ticket, the receipt."

Bryan said, "It isn't on here," and looked up. "Annie, how do they find a car if there's no license number written on it?"

The ticket indicates the section the car is parked in, Annie explained. And the ticket number corresponds with the other half of the ticket in the car, by the windshield. She said, "We do have the license numbers of all the cars that were there when it happened."

Bryan said, "Except there was an empty parking space, wasn't there? Right across the aisle from where he was shot. Is that the section we're talking about?"

Annie said, "I'm afraid so. You'll see all the ticket numbers are consecutive. The cars that came in after nine-thirty and were still there. And you're right, one ticket's missing and there's no receipt for it in the cashier's office."

Bryan said, "So a car was in that empty spot and there's no record of it. Did the guy drive down himself? That's against the rules, isn't it?"

"No one's allowed down there but the parking attendants," Annie said. "I don't know how he could've gotten down."

Malik said, "The guy wanted to drive down, who's gonna stop him?"

Bryan said, "Someone'd chase after him and not necessarily Curtis. We're not talking about robbery. If the guy wants Curtis he doesn't want to get in an argument first, with somebody else. He wants to deal with Curtis and only Curtis."

Parrish said, "Which gets us around to motive."

Bryan said, "Not yet."

Saving it, Angela thought. The motive in killing a black-leather-jacket ex-convict parking attendant.

"Let's look at what we've got first," Bryan said. "We get on the computer to Lansing with the license numbers, get the owners of the cars that were there when it happened. Narrow it down. Ask when they arrived if they saw a guy drive down on his own, or if they saw anything strange, guy getting into a car *with* a parking attendant. Okay. But what about the cars that *left* about the same time the guy who was in the empty parking place arrived, I mean upstairs at the entrance and might've seen him? Anybody waiting for their car to come up—how in the hell do we contact *them?*" He said, "Jesus." And then said, "All right. We find out from the hotel who checked out between nine-thirty and ten and left in a car. That'll give us a few more names."

Annie said, "I think we'll have about thirty or forty counting check-ins and check-outs. But some of these aren't valet parking, they're people who're staying at the hotel. We won't need Lansing for them, the claim checks tell us who they are."

Bryan said, "How many parking attendants?"

"Four," Annie said. "I have their names and addresses if they don't show up."

Bryan said, "Okay, we start with them. First question. Did anybody see a black Fleetwood Cadillac over there any time this morning? Next question. If the answer's yes, then you ask if a black Fleetwood Cadillac occupied that empty space for any length of time. And if they say yes to that, we might have an arraignment first thing in the morning."

He had their attention: Angela, Malik, Parrish and Annie Maguire all looking at him, the three detectives with expressions of mild expectation, surprise.

"Or," Bryan said, and paused. "Where's Quentin?"

Malik said, "He's still at the morgue. Kanluen's opening Curtis up, Quentin goes, 'I wouldn't miss this for the world; the mother tried to shoot me one time.' "

"Maybe we can save ourselves a few hours," Bryan said. "Call Quentin and tell him to pick up Walter Kouza. I'll give you the address."

Malik said, "*Wal*ter? Jesus Christ, that's right. He might be dumb enough."

Parrish said, "Walter's never used a twenty-two in his life."

"I hope not," Bryan said. "But let's pick him up anyway."

SEVEN

BRYAN FINISHED OFF a pail of mussels, ordered crab-legs and potato skins and was content to wait with his glass of beer, believing he felt as good as he had ever felt in his life. Keyed up but in no hurry. It was his favorite time of the day.

Angela was working through a Greek salad with Jack Daniels on the side and whitefish on the way, no longer restrained. She had not seen the body, only the red traces that remained, but it had been enough to subdue her through the afternoon. She seemed aware again rather than preoccupied and would look around Galligan's at the after-work crowd with interest, then would look at Bryan again and ask a question. She asked a great many questions.

"Do you eat a lot?"

"I've had what, two hot-dogs all day."

"I just wondered. You don't look like you eat much."

"I wondered if you ever ate anything," Bryan said.

"I do when I'm not on police investigations," Angela said, "and have to go to murder scenes."

"I shouldn't have taken you."

"No, I wanted to go. In fact I'll go whenever you ask me." She took a big bite of feta cheese and tomato and made the act seem dainty. "I like to watch you, Bryan. I loved it in the squad room, watching you putting pieces together. You think the little girl was murdered, don't you? Even though there's no evidence to go on."

"Yeah, I think she was."

"What if you don't learn anything more?"

"Then I put it away," Bryan said. "Forget about it."

"Just like that."

"Well, try to forget about it."

She said, "I worked for a newspaper when I started out, but I never did police stories. What's a post? A post mortem?"

"Yeah, an autopsy. They have to determine the cause of death. Even when a man's been shot four times."

"It's so different than anything I've ever experienced—just listening to you," Angela said. "Everyone seems calm, but you know they're keyed up and they don't want to miss anything." The warm look was in her eyes again and she seemed keyed up herself. "You're a pretty earthy bunch, aren't you? Especially Malik."

"We work in the street, the street rubs off," Bryan said. "Malik has sort of an indifferent, tough-cop style, but you put him in the Pink Room with a suspect he'll get a statement. I don't mean with intimidation, Malik'll bullshit the guy, put him at ease."

"And Doug Parrish," Angela said. "Very firm in his convictions."

"He surprised me today," Bryan said. "You're right, Doug's set in his ways. He usually takes a more conservative approach. But if he's convinced the guy used a silencer then you can be pretty sure the guy used a silencer. He doesn't wing it very often. Annie's much the same, but her manner's entirely different. Annie, you don't even know she's there."

Angela said, "She seems too nice to be a homicide detective. I mean she doesn't seem the type."

Bryan said, "Well, you don't need muscle really, you don't have to smoke cigars . . ."

"The guys aren't inhibited by her?"

"No, Malik tries to shock her, but how's he gonna do that? She's seen everything. No, Annie smiles. She's a very easy person to be with."

"Have you ever . . . had a feeling about her?"

"No," Bryan said. "I've never kissed a cop or gone to bed with one. I kissed a girl writer once and went to bed with her, but nothing happened. She didn't want to rush into anything."

"I heard you blew it."

"Well, I know she didn't."

"Don't be crude."

"Can't I say anything I want to you?"

"I have another question," Angela said. "You don't really think Walter's the one, do you?"

Bryan looked at his watch. "Well, I'm gonna ask him in about an hour. Then let the parking guys take a look at him."

She said, "But he knows you'd suspect him. It would be so *dumb*."

"I keep an open mind," Bryan said. "That way I never get too surprised. But yeah, I can see Walter doing it. I don't think intelligence is a factor. Look at what's her name, the head of the girls' school who shot the diet doctor. Jean Harris. She isn't dumb. You read the poems she wrote to him? Well, they were kinda sappy, I guess. But if anybody was *dumb* it's that skinny doctor. He didn't see it coming."

"I forget you're a psychiatrist," Angela said. "You read people and advise them."

"Only certain ones."

"You advise me, help me look at myself."

"You're easy."

"Okay," Angela said. "Do you know what I'm gonna do this evening?"

He felt a warning he didn't understand and now wasn't sure what to say. The waiter arrived and gave him time, serving Angela's whitefish, his crab-legs. A polite waiter in a black vest, anxious to please. He left them.

Angela said, "Well?"

He said, "For some reason I don't like the sound of it."

The waiter returned with potato skins, giving him a few moments more. He ordered another draft of Stroh's and a Jack Daniels for Angela. He liked the way she sipped it and seemed to enjoy the taste.

"All right. What're you gonna do this evening?"

"I'm going home."

He said, "You don't mean to your hotel."

"No. All the way home, to Tucson." She seemed to smile, a crafty look. "I thought you were never surprised."

"I was wrong," Bryan said. "Why're you going home?"

She said, "Well, I haven't seen my folks in a while, since last summer. I was away for Christmas and tomorrow's my birthday. So, I think it's a good time for a visit. I want to get a picture of you though, before I leave."

Bryan frowned, all this rushing at him at once. "Wait a minute. Are you coming back?"

"Sure. I'm still working on Robbie."

"Yeah, but he might be somewhere else."

"Well, you might be too. You're going to Florida, aren't you?"

"Not right away . . . You sound different. How long're you gonna be gone?"

"I don't know. A week maybe."

"And then what?"

He saw her shrug one shoulder in the navy blue coat and tried to remember her without the coat on.

She said, "I have to finish the piece for *Esquire*. That's Robbie. Then, there's a publisher wants me to do a whole book on rich people. But I don't know if I can handle it, or want to. Then, who knows?"

He said again, "You sound different."

"I'm not. Are you different?"

"No."

She said, "Aren't you hungry?"

"I don't think you're coming back."

"If I say I am but you don't think I am," Angela said, "then *I* think you're starting to choke up, Bryan. Maybe taking yourself a little too seriously. And you know what you do when that happens. Right?"

He said, "There a lot of things I want to say to you."

She said, "Good. Save them."

She took a picture of him outside, against Galligan's painted brick wall. She kissed him and said, "Don't I get a hug?" before she got in the taxi. He walked back to 1300.

In the hallway by the elevators Annie Maguire said to Bryan, "We had them down at Squad Six when Walter arrived, so they haven't seen him yet. They don't know what's going on. Walter doesn't either, for that matter. He's ready to go through the wall."

"Who's with him?"

"Quentin." Annie waited a moment. "Do you think this is a good idea?"

He said, "You want to wait for probable cause? Or you want to find out right now? Tell me how many times we get clear-cut probable cause?" Bryan entered the squad room.

Three of the valet-parking attendants were sitting next to desks like job applicants. The cashier was at Malik's desk and Malik was trying to get her to pose for a Polaroid shot. "Come on, smile now. Big smile." The girl was laughing, moving around. "I'm not shitting you," Malik said, "we're gonna send it in, Miss Black America contest." Parrish was watching, not saying anything.

Bryan opened the door to the Pink Room partway. Quentin Terry said, "Here's the man now, Walter. I told you he be here. You want cream and sugar?"

Walter said, "Cream, two-and-a-half sugars."

"Two-and-a-*half*," Quentin said, getting up from the folding chair to edge past Bryan, rolling his eyes as he went out. Bryan closed the door. He could hear the girl, the valet-parking cashier, laughing.

Walter sat in the corner between the table with the typewriter and the wall, wedged in there and looking mean, heavy shoulders hunched, ready to come out of the chute.

Bryan said, "How do you like it?" Meaning the room, nodding then to the Miranda sign on the wall. "Your rights. There they are. Nobody can say we don't give you your rights. Read it, Walter."

"The fuck you think you're doing?" Walter said. "Bring me down here."

"I got to ask you some questions, Walter. Somebody did Curtis Moore."

In the silence that began to lengthen Walter said, "Come on," with reverence. "Come on, don't shit me."

"I'd never do that, Walter."

"Jesus Christ, you mean it? *Curtis?*"

"You didn't hear about it? It was on the news."

"How'm I gonna hear about it? I'm driving around the fucking limo all day. Pick these guys up, take 'em the plant. Pick 'em up again, take 'em out the airport. Listen, you find the guy did it let me know. I want to shake the fucker's hand."

"What plant?"

"Daniels. He's selling all his equipment. Got these

buyers in from Cleveland, Indianapolis, Christ, Mexico, Japan.
Couple Japs, they come all the way over here to buy some
machines that turn out nuts and bolts. Big fuckers—I mean the
machines, like drill presses. Another guy don't speak nothing
but Kraut, he comes all the way from West Germany."

"How about around ten this morning, a little before?"

"I left home quarter to ten, from Grosse Pointe. Eight-
nine-nine Lake Shore. Ask the cook, he'll tell you. Fucking
Ukrainian."

"Who'd you pick up at the Plaza?"

"What's that, the one at the RenCen? I never picked
anybody up there."

"Didn't go near it, uh?"

"No, first thing I picked up these guys out at the airport.
Fly in, fly out. Daniels had riggers there right at the plant. Some
guys from the Teamsters, two-nine-nine. Give the buyers an
estimate right on the spot, how much to haul the shit out. The
auction isn't suppose to be till Monday, but Daniels, he can't
fucking wait to get out of the nuts and bolts business. It was
okay for his old man but Robbie, see, he's a friend of George
Hamilton, whoever the fuck George Hamilton is. I met him, I
still don't know."

"You drove the Cadillac?"

"What do you think I pick 'em up in, the fucking Omni?"

There was a yellow legal pad next to the typewriter. Bryan
said, "Write the names on there and the approximate time you
picked them up."

"I don't know their names."

"You can get them, can't you?"

"I don't know. I'll see."

Bryan opened the door several inches, glanced out and
closed it again.

"Coffee's not ready yet. You want to wait?"

"You mean," Walter said, "do I want to leave now or do

I want to wait till the *coff*ee's done? Jesus Christ," Walter said, getting up off the folding chair.

Bryan pushed the door open all the way, caught Malik's eye and saw one of the valet-parking attendants look over his shoulder.

"Quentin's gonna drive you home."

"Tell that dinge I don't need any conversation this trip. Fucker never shuts up," Walter said, pulling down the sleeve of his gray suit, brushing at invisible dirt. He followed Bryan through the squad room now and out into the hallway to the elevators. Here, Walter narrowed his eyes, turned back to the squad room as Quentin came out putting on his suit coat, Walter catching a glimpse of the three valet-parking attendants looking this way. The door closed.

"Wait a minute," Walter said. "What's this shit going on?"

Bryan pushed the elevator button again. Quentin was adjusting his suitcoat.

"You brought me up here to get eyeballed, didn't you? Who're those guys. You try and put me in the Plaza today—that where they're from?"

"They park cars," Bryan said.

"Hey, I used to pull this kind of shit too, you know. You bring me up here, not a fucking shred of probable cause, hoping one of those monkeys'll cop on me, huh?" Walter stopped. He looked at the door again and said in a much quieter tone, "What'd you say they do?"

"They park cars," Bryan said, "at the Detroit Plaza Hotel. Where Curtis Moore used to park cars till somebody took him out."

"How?"

"We don't know yet."

"Bullshit—was he shot, stabbed, what?"

"Shot. Four times."

"What kind of gun?"

"That's what I meant, we don't know yet."

"The guys up in Firearms know," Walter said. "You telling me they haven't given you the ballistics yet? Bullshit."

Bryan said, "Thanks for coming, Walter."

When Quentin Terry got back from Grosse Pointe he met them at the Athens in Greektown, the cop bar. Parrish had gone home to watch "Hill Street Blues." Bryan, Annie and Malik were about ready to leave, having a last beer, picking over the information they got from the valet-parking attendants and the cashier, which amounted to almost nothing.

One of them didn't know Curtis had been working this morning. The others saw him, yeah, but didn't notice anything funny going on or Curtis talking to anybody in particular. The one who found Curtis's body said the blood led him to it; he thought at first somebody had spilled paint. The cashier remembered Curtis coming in, getting some keys from where they hung on hooks, Curtis saying a man needed something from his car; but people were at the window, she was too busy to notice anything. Except when the police came and she heard about Curtis, she remembered him getting the keys. No, there was nothing unusual about the keys that she remembered. Wait now—or did it have some kind of a charm or good-luck piece on it? She'd try to remember and let them know.

Quentin Terry said, "Walter didn't hardly open his mouth in the car. I told him a couple Polish jokes, the man didn't even smile."

Bryan said, "He ask you about the gun?"

"Yeah, he tried different ways," Quentin said. "Especially interested if the gunshots were through and through. Wanting to find out the caliber."

"He was surprised when I first told him," Bryan said. "Couldn't believe it. The guy that did it, I think if he'd walked in Walter would've put his arms around him and kissed him."

Malik said, "Kissed him, he'd have blown him."

"But out in the hall," Bryan said, "he was different. You notice?"

Quentin said, "Like something begun to bother him."

"Not so much that we'd set him up," Bryan said. "It was when he found out those guys in there parked cars. Why would that bother him?"

He walked with Annie Maguire to the parking structure on St. Antoine, past the Saturday-night lineup waiting to get in the Hellas Cafe. She asked him where his girl friend was.

"I just met her yesterday, at Walter's hearing."

Annie said, "You have to start somewhere." She said, "I bet she's from a big family."

"I don't know. She didn't say."

"Haven't gotten into all that yet."

"Well, I don't know if we will," Bryan said. "She went home. Tucson, Arizona."

"She told you she'd be back, didn't she?"

"That's what she says, I don't know."

"Come on, don't play dumb, Bryan."

"I mean it. I don't know what she's thinking."

"Well, this afternoon," Annie said, "she took her eyes off you maybe once."

"Is that right?" Bryan said. "I didn't notice.

Annie stopped and looked around. "Isn't that your car back there?"

They had walked past Bryan's seven-year-old BMW. It was faded gray with rust spots along the chrome like sores. He said, "It looks like mine."

Annie said, "You need to get away, Bryan. Soon."

Daniels wasn't in his study when Walter got home and he couldn't go up the front stairs to look for him. He had to go through the pantry and the kitchen to the goddamn back stairs and go up that way if he was going to his room. The bathroom door was closed. Walter knocked. He heard the sound of the cook's voice give him a grunt. "Wash your hands when you're done!" Walter called through the door. Fucking Ukrainian. He went downstairs again to use the other john, the powder room in the front hall.

The black Mercedes sedan was gone from the garage. The yellow Mercedes convertible that Daniels called a drophead was there. The Cadillac was there and the Dodge Omni that nobody used was there. So Daniels could've taken the big Mercedes or his wife could've. Walter hadn't said two words to the wife. It was a fucked-up house. Nobody talked to anybody. Nobody even argued. The place was like a hotel where you passed people in the hall and everybody was polite but nobody seemed to give a shit about anything.

Walter heard a car; somebody dropping Mrs. Daniels off. She came in to find him sitting on the Queen Anne bench in the front hall, cocked a hip as she looked at him and smiled, sort of half-closing her eyes.

"You've been waiting for me, haven't you?"

Walter said, "Pardon?"

Mrs. Daniels seemed a little high. No question about it—all at once sinking down next to him in her lynx fur that Walter remembered from Robbery would run about eight, nine grand. She smelled of booze, but she smelled good too, leaning against him now. He didn't know what was going on. Her hair was in his face, but he'd have to touch her, hold her up if he tried to move. Now she was raising her face to look at him. He felt her hand on his thigh, trying to squeeze it but not able to get any purchase. He didn't know what was going on.

Mrs. Daniels said, "Can I ask you a question, Walter?"

He felt her hand crawl to his fly—Christ!—and probe until she found his member.

"What do you call one of these in Polish?"

Walter sat as straight as he could, not moving. "It's called . . . it's usually they call it a *hooyek*."

"A *hooyek*." Mrs. Daniels spoke the word lovingly. She let go, got up and crossed to the stairway, weaving just a little. A hand on the balustrade, she looked back at him. "A *hooyek*?"

"That's correct," Walter said. "H-u-j-e-k, *hooyek*."

"Thank you," Mrs. Daniels said. She went upstairs.

Walter fell asleep. He opened his eyes and thought the woman was back and got a shock when he saw it was Mr. Daniels sitting next to him now, in his raincoat. Daniels said, "What time's the next bus?"

It wasn't like a hotel, it was like a fucking state hospital—Ionia or the Forensic Center. It was in Walter's mind to go upstairs and pack, right now, get the hell out.

Daniels said, "You awake?"

His voice sounded all right. Walter was sure he'd been drinking though; he could smell it.

"Yeah, I'm awake."

"You don't have to wait up for me, Walter."

"I got to ask you something. In the study."

"There's nobody around."

"Your wife was here." Walter looked at his watch. "Jesus, almost an hour ago."

"Come on," Daniels said, getting up.

He poured himself a cognac from the portable bar next to the television set, rolled amber reflections in the snifter glass, raised it to his face, then seemed to remember Walter, fidgeting, moving about by the desk.

"You want one?"

"I want to know something," Walter said. "I want to know if it was you did Curtis Moore."

Daniels said, "The guy who was gonna testify against you and was shot and killed in the parking garage of the Detroit Plaza with a High Standard Field King twenty-two? No. It must've been someone else."

Walter sat down. "I knew it. They pick me up, bring me down to 1300, I'm wondering what the fuck's going on—it was you. I knew it, but I don't believe it."

"Good," Robbie said. "No one else will either." He sipped the cognac and rolled it around in his mouth now before swallowing. "Goddamn raw fish and seaweed. I should've taken them to the Chop House."

Walter said, "Mr. Daniels, I was a police officer twenty, almost twenty-one years. There is no way you can commit a homicide at a place like that, all those people around, and get away with it. There's no way in the world."

Robbie said, "Are you relieved, I mean that he's dead?"

"What I feel—yes, I am," Walter said. "But what I happen to feel has nothing to do with it. I appreciate your, well, your doing it for my sake. But, Mr. Daniels, I'm afraid you're gonna be in the worst trouble in your life. I can't believe it." He looked at Daniels with a vacant expression that said there was no hope, it was all over.

"Yes or no," Robbie said, "did Curtis deserve what he got?"

Walter nodded. "There's no question about that. Yes."

"You're enormously pleased he's out of the way?"

"Sure I am, but—"

"You were questioned by the police?"

"Bryan Hurd. The guy at the hearing."

"Did my name come up?"

"No, it didn't."

"Then I'm not a suspect, am I?"

Walter looked up. It did not occur to him until this moment that Daniels could possibly get away with it.

"Where did you tell them you were?" Daniels asked.

"At the time? Here. Or picking up the buyers."

"He believe you?"

"Yeah. I think he knows I didn't do it."

"Then what're you worried about?"

"What'm I worried about? *You.* What's your story?"

"What do I need a story for if I'm not a suspect?"

"Because it can get around to you," Walter said. "One thing leads to another. Pick up something here, pick up a piece of information there. Somebody saw a car. Next fucking thing they're knocking on the door."

"Well, I was with somebody too, if it ever comes to that," Robbie said. "I picked up some of 'em didn't I? The Japs."

"What time?"

"Walter, I just put the little guys on the red eye to San Francisco."

"They can be contacted by telephone, can't they?"

"I'm not gonna concern myself," Robbie said, "with something that's not likely to happen. We've got the big one coming up. Soon as I get those fucking machines out of there we head for Palm Beach and get on it."

"When?"

"Next week. And once we start—I forgot to tell you, you get an extra grand a week combat pay."

"Yeah? You never mentioned that."

"I think it's only fair. Pros get top dollar, don't they?"

"Hey, if you say so. I'll tell you, I like the idea of getting out of town. It can't happen too soon."

"How about a cognac?"

"Yeah, I'll have one." Walter was feeling a lot better. He said, "You know, they get somebody like Curtis as a homicide victim, they got to go through the motions. But they're just as happy as we are the fucker's out of the way. It's not like they got a hard-on to get a conviction, you know, where they're hot to get somebody. You understand what I mean?"

"Yeah, I can see that." Robbie came over with a snifter and handed it to Walter. "Seventy-five years old. You've never had a cognac like that in your life."

Walter took the glass, put his head back and drained it. "Yeah, that's all right. Very good."

Robbie stared at him.

"But tell me the truth," Walter said. "Did you really do it for me, on account of the lawsuit?"

"Well, not entirely."

"I didn't think so. I figured there had to be some other reason, take a risk like that," Walter said. "You mind telling me why you did it?"

"Practice," Robbie said.

EIGHT

SUNDAY, BRYAN SPENT part of the day at the Detroit
Plaza talking to the doormen, the parking supervisors and
several of the guests that had checked in Saturday morning. All
it did was tire him out. He wondered if he was coming down
with something, a virus. Very seldom did he feel this tired. He
went home and watched a tennis match televised from Boca
Raton. The weather looked good down there; though maybe
boring, the sameness of it. He watched McEnroe put on one of
his temper tantrums. The crowd booed and Bryan found himself siding with McEnroe, resenting the spectators in their
sunglasses and resort outfits; outsiders looking in, not knowing
shit what it was like. It surprised him, because he usually
thought McEnroe was an asshole.

The phone rang and he thought of Angela.

He said, "Oh, hi, Peggy."

She said, "Well, what's the matter with you?"

"I was sleeping."

It was his former wife, who had got the house in Indian
Village and was getting twelve hundred a month alimony,

because at the worst possible time he had felt sorry for her: seeing her enter the lawyer's office, decoupage purse held in both hands, tiny pigeon-toed Capezios bringing her to the conference-table meeting that was as solemn as a Good Friday vigil; he would not have been surprised to see her genuflect and make the sign of the cross. His offense, his petition for divorce, was treated as a matter of faith and morals—even though there'd been no other women, no fooling around—while the settlement, like an atonement, was strictly in bucks.

Peggy said, "Well, I guess you've been hearing a few things, considering how people love to talk."

He told himself to sound concerned. "No, I haven't heard a thing. What about?"

"Well, I've been seeing someone," Peggy said.

"You mean a guy?"

"A man, yes. What did you think I meant?"

"Well, that's fine . . . Isn't it?" He wasn't sure yet what attitude to have. "He's not married, is he?"

"*No,* he's not married," Peggy said. "But people love to talk and they always will. I suppose it's human nature."

People. As in "People Will Say We're in Love." She had been cute Peggy Doran in her Junior Miss outfits, a little Doris Day doll who had turned Adult almost immediately following the ceremony. Serious. Responsible. Proper.

He said, "Well, Peggy, how you doing otherwise?"

She said, "I'm doing very well, if you'd like to know. Much better than I'm sure you ever expected."

Bryan said, "That's great."

"As a matter of fact, I'm getting married in August."

Bryan waited, cautious. Did she actually say it?

"I'm sorry. You're gonna do what?"

"I said I'm getting *married*."

It was true. He heard the words clearly and they could mean nothing else.

"Are you still there? What's the matter with you?"

She always said, What's the matter with you? She had said he'd ruined her life, thrown away everything they had. (A world of Early Americana.) She had said she'd never marry again. Ever. Now she mentioned a name.

"In August, huh?"

But she was saying now, "You don't know him. He's in the insurance business. A very kind, considerate person."

"Peggy," Bryan said, "I think it's great and I want to wish you all the best." It was true! Christ, it was true! "And a lot of happiness." He couldn't think of what else to say. "I don't know him, huh?"

"No, and he's never heard of you. His name's Paul Scallen. He lives in Dearborn."

"That's great, Peggy. In August, huh? That's a good month, one of the best." Christ, only four more payments. May, June, July—maybe three.

She said, "I'm sure you're relieved. You won't have to pay alimony anymore."

Bryan said, "Hey, that's right . . ."

Later on he kept expecting Angela to call because he saw his luck changing right before his eyes. When she didn't, he pictured her mom and dad, nice people, asking questions about all the interesting places she'd visited. Maybe brothers and sisters around too. She had to have time with her family. She hadn't given him a phone number. He didn't even know their name, or if she was using their name or her married name or how many Nolans there were in Tucson. Well, he didn't feel tired now. Not at all.

Sunday turned out okay.

Monday was something else.

In the morning Bryan stopped by his inspector's office

and brought him up to date with Case Assigned Reports, looked out the window at the county jail while Eljay Ayres skimmed through the yellow pages.

Ayres said, "Looks like you can close the little girl and the guy in the bar. They'll never bring him up."

Bryan said, "Let's keep the little girl open. We might learn something."

"Well, it's your time we talking about," Ayres said. "I thought you were on furlough."

"I'm supposed to be, yeah."

Eljay Ayres looked at him and then at the yellow pages again. "Curtis Moore . . . no big surprise to anybody."

There was an easy edge of authority in his tone. Eljay Ayres had been Bryan's counterpart, lieutenant of Squad Six until his recent appointment to inspector of the entire Homicide Section. He wore three-piece suits and a Smith and Wesson automatic tight in the waistband of his trousers, a street-hip black man who seemed wary of Bryan and addressed him at arm's length. Bryan wanted to tell Eljay he didn't resent his appointment, that he had no desire to move up into administration; in fact, if he had to stay at 1300 all day he'd probably find something else to do. A talk over drinks would come in time and both would feel better and relax. Right now it was business.

"How do you feel about Walter Kouza?"

"He didn't do it," Bryan said.

"The Polish Gunslinger. I don't know," Ayres said, "he could've been stewing over it, drinking booze. You check him out good?"

"Soon as I leave here," Bryan said. "Get the names of people he was with."

"Who else you got?"

"Nobody. You know Curtis, the people he ran with. One of his friends could've got tired of him. We inquire who he's been hanging out with; they ropa-dope you, tell you yeah, he's tight with Bicky, Micky, Kicky—nobody's got a real name."

"You don't close pretty quick," Ayres said, "who's gonna take the case?"

"Annie Maguire. She's got a few more people to talk to. There weren't any bikes around, nobody in club jackets. All we've got are a few hotel guests we haven't talked to yet. Ones that checked in about that time."

"Then I think," Ayres said, "you ought to forget Curtis, take advantage of the time you got coming."

Bryan said, offhand, a mild tone, "You trying to get rid of me?"

Ayres remained solemn. "I don't want you to overwork yourself, Bryan. There be plenty more when you get back."

The auction was underway at Daniels Fasteners: buyers and aides in business suits standing around with riggers in hard hats while the dressed-up auctioneer and his podium were moved along on a hand truck by assistants in red blazers. The procession passed beneath tired fluorescent lights to a machine that seemed to have no beginning or end and the auctioneer said, "Lot Number 35. We've got here, in excellent condition, a National three-quarter-inch double-stroke, solid-die and open-die, long-stroke Universal cold header. Who's gonna give me twenty thousand to open?"

Bryan said, "What I've always wanted." He stood in the dead factory with Annie Maguire, watching.

Robbie Daniels, followed by Walter, came up from somewhere behind them, Robbie saying, "And if you don't like that one I've got a Peltzer and Ehlers hot-nut former you'll flip over . . . Hi, I'm Robbie Daniels," offering his hand to Annie as he glanced at Bryan. "Lieutenant, good to see you again. But don't tell me this young lady's a policeman, please."

Both Annie and Bryan smiled. He said, "Well, I can't lie to you, Mr. Daniels," and immediately felt foolish. What was he doing? He caught Walter's eye, his serious expression staring back at him. Tense? It was hard to tell. In his tight suits Walter always looked a little tense. Daniels was saying to Annie, "It's a pleasure. Do you know I've never met a policewoman before?" As though it was almost impossible to believe. "Come on, let's go up to my office. There's no place to sit around here."

Bryan said, "We just want to ask Walter something. Get some names."

"Hey, that's right," Robbie said, "you're investigating a murder, aren't you? Walter told me about it last night. Fascinating." He looked at Walter then. "My attaché case?"

Walter said, "What?"

"Remember? I left it in the car?"

Walter walked off. Bryan watched Robbie shake his head and thought he would comment but didn't.

He took them up a wooden stairway to the administrative offices that were divided by wood-framed glass partitions, the offices dark, empty except for bare desks and file cabinets, a few old-model typewriters under plastic covers. An oak desk and chairs remained in the spacious corner office that looked down on Franklin and Riopelle, on railroad tracks and warehouses and old brick factories extending to the riverfront, a setting left from the Industrial Revolution.

"Anyone who asks me why I'm selling," Robbie said, "I tell them, would you rather come down here every day and look at this mess"—with a sweeping gesture, sport coat open, rep tie askew—"the backside of a dying city, or get down to the sunbelt where it's happening and invest in the future?"

Bryan thought, I got to get out of here. He said, "I don't

want to take up any of your time. If we could just have the names of the people Walter picked up . . ."

"That's right," Robbie said, "you want some names." He turned to a thick file on the desk, opened it and began looking through company letterheads. "No—I thought so. These are today's. Saturday's are in my case." He walked to the windows now and looked down on Riopelle. "Come on, Walter, you're holding up the Police Department." Then said, "I can vouch for Walter. But from your point of view I can see why he's a suspect."

Bryan looked at Annie. He said, "Well, he isn't, really. We have to fill in some holes in the report."

Annie said, "He must've told you about Curtis's brother, the shooting."

"And a few others," Robbie said. "Walter doesn't know it, but he's a very entertaining guy."

Bryan looked at Annie.

"Here he comes," Robbie said, turning from the window now. "The ones he picked up Saturday had made firm offers. So I invited them in before the auction. Got rid of half the equipment. Guy from Mexico—he couldn't speak a word of English—even bought office fixtures. Right, Walter?"

He came in carrying an alligator attaché case. "What's that, Mr. Daniels?"

Robbie took the case and laid it on the desk. "I was telling them about the guy from Mexico who couldn't speak English."

"Only talked Spic," Walter said. "Used his hands all the time."

Robbie snapped open the case. He took out a High Standard twenty-two target pistol with a five-and-a-half-inch barrel and laid it on the desk without comment.

Bryan looked at Annie. Then at Walter, who was staring at the gun.

Robbie was taking out company letterhead sheets now, glancing at them, handing them to Walter. "These are the buyers you picked up, right?"

Walter looked at the first two or three. "I don't know, Mr. Daniels. I can't tell from just the names."

"Look at the cities, where they're from."

"I don't know," Walter said.

"Well, they're quite likely to remember you, Walter." Robbie glanced at Bryan. "Call 'em, if you want. But I'll take an oath Walter left the house at nine-thirty and picked up these particular buyers."

"Quarter to ten," Walter said.

"All right, a quarter of ten."

"I didn't pick up any Jap. I know that."

Robbie said, "Sure you did. Namura. Little fella with horn-rim glasses and buck teeth." He looked at Bryan and grinned. "No, I'm kidding. He wasn't especially oriental looking."

Walter said, "I know I didn't pick up any Jap."

"Well," Robbie said, "I could be wrong. We were coming and going all day."

"I saw those two Japs here," Walter said, "but I know goddamn well I never picked 'em up."

"All *right!*" Robbie said.

Bryan looked at Annie.

"I think you've made your point," Robbie said. "Fine. You remember the ones you didn't pick up but not the ones you did. Anyway . . . take the letters and have 'em Xeroxed somewhere. I'd appreciate it."

Bryan said, "We can copy the names and addresses. Save some time."

It was all right with Robbie. "Fine, since you brought your secretary . . ."

"Miss Maguire's a sergeant." Bryan said, "A homicide detective."

Robbie grinned. "Well, Miss Maguire can get on my case anytime."

Annie said, "Okay," with a shy smile and looked at the twenty-two target pistol on the desk. "Do you keep that loaded?"

"Sure," Robbie said. "It's been lying around the office—I was taking it home. Since we're closing down. It's a nice little weapon."

Annie said, "It's a gun till you shoot somebody with it. Then it's a weapon."

"I never thought of it that way," Robbie said. He picked up the target pistol, touched the safety with his thumb to release it.

Bryan thought, It's a show. Why he brought us here. He watched the way Robbie held the gun.

Robbie was saying, "This was dad's office for something like a hundred years. He used to sit here and stare through the glass partitions at me. Past his secretary's office, his sales manager's office, to the one at the end, without the window. That was my office when I started out. In fact it was my office until he died, nine years ago." Robbie raised the target pistol as he spoke. "Dad would sit here and stare. He was partially paralyzed from a stroke and never seemed to move. Just stared, wondering what was gonna happen to the business, I guess. I couldn't read a newspaper unless it was the *Wall Street Journal*." He was sighting now through the glass partitions to the bare wall in the last office.

Bryan watched him.

Robbie fired.

Bryan saw the first glass partition drilled, cracks flowering out from the bullet hole. He saw Robbie fire again and fire again and all three partitions dividing the offices exploded, collapsed in the sound of shattering glass to leave jagged ends in the wood frames.

Bryan looked at the ejected casings on the carpet, green with a worn floral design. He wanted them.

Robbie said, "There." Then grinned. He said, "Before you call for an EMS wagon let me tell you I've been wanting to do that for as long as I can remember. There's something about those glass walls I've always resented . . ."

Bryan watched him stoop, pick up the ejected casings and drop them in his coat pocket.

"Like living in a goldfish bowl, someone watching you all the time." Robbie blew into the barrel of the target pistol for effect. "Well, they're gone now. In fact this whole goddamn place is gone, but I had to do it." Smiling. "I feel a lot better."

It was not something Bryan had to accept or believe at this moment. He nodded in sympathy and let it go at that. The man was putting on a hell of a show. They would review it later—once they got the spent cartridges, the bits of lead that would be flattened and imbedded in the plaster wall. But as he thought this he was startled by a realization that was as sharp and clear-cut as the broken shards of glass.

He wants you to have the bullets.

But not the casings.

It was a game that both sides had to play, or pretend to play. Walter was not involved. Walter seemed lost.

Annie said, "I wonder if you damaged anything. I noticed some office machines . . ." Annie knew something. Her eyes made contact with Bryan and moved away.

He said, "You've been looking for a used typewriter, haven't you, Annie?"

Robbie said, "We still have a few around. If the Mexican didn't get 'em." He was looking out at the empty offices,

128

cooperating. "You see one you like, Miss Maguire, it's yours. But listen. I got to get back down to the auction and look interested. Okay? I'll see you a little later."

He's going to say *ciao,* Bryan thought.

"*Ciao,*" Robbie said and headed for the stairs.

Annie walked out, began to roam after Robbie left. There were a few moments of silence before Walter said to Bryan, "The fuck you looking at me for?"

In the medium-blue unmarked Plymouth, moving up Riopelle to Jefferson, Annie opened her hand. Bryan looked from the windshield to the flattened bits of gray lead, three of them, in Annie's palm.

She said, "What do you think?"

He said, "I haven't finished yet. Ask me later."

She said, "You must know something I don't."

He said, "Well, I think you'd be safe in throwing those out the window. But let's get a comparison anyway."

"So you're sure it's not the same gun. Even though it's a twenty-two."

"No, but I'm pretty sure it's not the same barrel," Bryan said. "We could still make the gun if we had the casings, but he didn't let us have the casings, did he? He knows a few things about ballistics."

Annie said, "Wait a minute. Who are we talking about? I thought our guy was Walter. Like maybe he borrowed the gun and put it back and Daniels is a little weird but basically harmless."

"That could be," Bryan said, "but let's think it through again. After I make a phone call."

In the squad room he spoke to the Palm Beach chief of police, spoke to him for several minutes asking polite questions.

He hung up and sat staring at nothing. Then rose to stand at the window, looking down at the Coney Island across the street, and began to feel tired again.

When Annie came in he knew by her expression what she was going to say.

"You're right. It's not the gun that did Curtis."

"At least not the barrel," Bryan said. "Though it probably doesn't make much difference. I just saw a hunch fly out the window. Palm Beach says the gun Daniels used on the Haitian burglar—justifiable homicide, the chief underlined that—was a Colt Python, three-fifty-seven."

"Maybe he has a collection," Annie said.

"That's a nice idea," Bryan said. "I like it."

She said, "I still think we should stay close to Walter. I'll call some of the people he picked up Saturday, if you want me to."

"Call the Japanese guy too."

"Walter said he didn't pick him up."

"But if the guy came halfway around the world—you know what I mean? Went to all that trouble, then somebody picked him up. And if we don't ask, Inspector Eljay Ayres is gonna want to know why, isn't he?"

Annie brightened. With her nice teeth and complexion she always looked clean, healthy; she responded to what she felt and looked you right in the eye.

"Maybe what's his name, the Japanese guy, stayed at the Plaza and Walter doesn't want us to know he was there."

"Maybe," Bryan said. If she wanted to bet on Walter he'd let her. In fact, he'd give her a little more to make it interesting and said, "I'll tell you something else. Down in Palm Beach, guess who investigated Robbie shooting the Haitian?"

Annie said, "No!" She loved it.

"Yes. And right after that Walter goes to work for Robbie. What does that tell you?"

Annie thought about it. "Not much, really."

She had a nice mouth too. Very expressive blue eyes. Bryan said, "Angela asked me if I'd ever made the moves on you."

Annie smiled but seemed embarrassed. "Did she? Why?"

"I think seeing us working together, the way we get along."

"Has she called you?"

"No."

"What're you gonna do about it?"

"Nothing. I'm going to Florida tomorrow. You guys are on your own."

Annie began to smile again. "But not the Ocean Pearl in Boca Raton this time?"

NINE

||||||||||||||||||||||||||||||||||||||||||||||||||||||||

IN THE EARLY morning old people walked the beach looking for shells left by the tide. The women, in sleeveless shirts
and kerchiefs covering their hairdos, studied the sand and
seemed to have purpose. The men followed, looking for
something to happen. They wore adjustable nylon golf caps,
many of them cocked in a recollection going back to world
wars, sporty old guys who seemed lost. They poked at blue
translucent balloons among the even line of seaweed washed up,
dead Portuguese men-of-war, and that would be a high moment
when nothing much was expected. There were people from
Michigan, from Ontario, from Ohio and New York State.
They wiped the sediment from their Buicks and big Olds-
mobiles and talked about mileage; they went to the Early Bird
dinner at five-thirty. There were not as many families with
children as there used to be. Once in a while a girl with a nice
body would appear way off coming along the sand and Bryan
would wonder about her; but not long, not interested enough to

put the *National Geographic* aside and push up out of the beach chair and go through the ritual of making the moves. Not this trip. He would look from habit or because the sight of a girl with the nice body was an element of pleasure in his picture of a beach on the Atlantic Ocean in season.

He went to sleep in the sun, lying on his side on a Woolworth blue and white beach towel and woke up in shade, his shoulder cramped, looking eye level at sandpipers running on their stick legs, nervous, afraid of everything. He would rather be a seagull and dive for fish. He wondered where birds went to die. There were billions of birds but you didn't see many dead ones. He was reading an article about cranes and egrets getting messed up in the oil along the Texas coast. It was cool in the shade; late afternoon now.

The lone figure way down the beach was still in sunlight. A girl coming along the edge of sand left glistening by the surf. A girl in twin strips of red cloth. She came gradually away from the waves rushing at her ankles and as she reached the shade the gleam left her body, her slender arms and legs turning a dusty copper, the patches of red cloth faded, though highlights and something white remained in her hair. She came across the empty sand looking at him through round sunglasses, past the line of seaweed and up the slight rise to his chair. The low chair with aluminum arms was all that separated them.

He pushed up to prop his cheek on his fist, looking at her sideways. The white thing in her hair was a barrette.

"I was gonna come up behind you," Angela said, "but you caught me."

He said, "What were you gonna do then?"

There was time to play around. No hurry now.

She said, "Lie down next to you. Blow in your ear. Feel you up. Have my way with you."

"Then what?"

"Have a cigarette. Did you bring any?"

"In the room."

"I didn't see them."

Bryan said, "Come on—really? What'd you tell Mr. Ocean Pearl?"

"I said I was your missus, what do you think?"

"You put your things in there and changed?"

"I was afraid you were gonna come in. Yeah, I changed and then walked down the road. Came back up the beach and made my entrance. Did you like it?"

"Soon as I saw you I knew it was you."

"Yeah—you thought it was some young girl. I mean you were hoping it was."

"Happy birthday. How're you handling it?"

"Well, four days into it, not bad. You're getting tan."

"How're your folks?"

"Okay."

"I thought you were gonna stay a week."

"I couldn't."

"Why, what happened?"

"Nothing. I missed you too much. So I called your office . . ."

"Well," Bryan said, "here we are."

They smiled, almost shy with one another. It was going to be something.

He said, "You want to be civil for a while or go crazy right away?"

She said, "Let's see what happens."

"Will you go with me to meet somebody at six?"

"Of course."

"Just for a drink. Then we're on our own."

"Fine."

He said, "Are we in the neighborhood of what you want most?"

She said, "We're right there. I think we've always been

there, but I have to feel it. You don't have to say a word if I feel it."

"Start feeling," Bryan said.

They were in Number 1 facing the ocean, away from the rest of the units centered around the swimming pool and patio. Living room, bedroom, kitchen and the whole Atlantic right outside the windows.

Angela showered and he showered. She stood in the bedroom in white bra and panties. Every boy's dream. He got a glimpse as he poured bourbon over shaved ice packed in smoke-colored glasses. She came in to have her drink in a terry-cloth robe and that was fine. They'd see how long they could keep their hands off each other.

Gary Hammond, the Palm Beach squad-car officer, couldn't believe it when he saw them coming. The same girl, the house-guest; in a white sweater and slacks. She looked better than she had last month when it was cool and she wore the dark tur-tleneck. The Detroit homicide cop, Lieutenant Hurd, looked in shape. Not the big-city beer-gut dick he expected. Gary stood up, bumping the table and grabbing his glass of beer. He was glad he'd cleaned up, put on a sport shirt. The girl was smiling at him as they came in past the hedge to the sidewalk tables.

She said, "Well, it's nice to see you again," sounding like she meant it, and introduced him to the homicide lieutenant. Up close the homicide lieutenant made Gary think of a major-league baseball player; something about him. He looked like he should have a wad of tobacco in his jaw. Though he seemed very polite, soft-spoken. One of those quiet guys who looked at you and seemed to know things.

He asked if Gary would mind telling about Daniels shooting the Haitian, the circumstance and the investigation. Gary said, "Well, I'm glad *some*body's interested, except it's a closed issue." He told the story and the homicide lieutenant listened and did not interrupt once. Then he began asking questions. Good ones.

"You believe the Haitian—what's his name?"

"Louverture Damien."

"You believe his intent was burglary?"

"Yes sir, I'm pretty sure now."

"Why didn't you think so at first?"

"Well, it wasn't I thought he come for any other reason, it was just nobody looked to see if he might've."

Lieutenant Hurd seemed to like that. "Do you know where Daniels got the gun? Where he kept it?"

"No sir, nobody asked that either."

Angela said, "When I saw him in his study with Walter, the day I left, he had a gun in his hand. But it wasn't the one he used."

Lieutenant Hurd said, "Do you know if he has a gun collection?"

"Now that could be," Gary said. "I asked Detective Kouza if the Python was registered, the one Daniels used, and Detective Kouza made some remark like, you want to check him for priors, too? But at the hearing Mr. Daniels was asked that and he said yeah, he'd bought the gun from a reputable shop where he was known and often used their target range. See, like he'd been dealing there a lot."

Lieutenant Hurd said, "You think Daniels might've had the gun on him? Is that what bothers you?"

"No sir, it was his story about the Haitian coming at him with a machete."

"Whose machete was it?"

"There you are." Gary Hammond grinned. "The guy didn't come all the way from Belle Glade carrying a machete. His wife says he never had one in his hands. The first he heard about it was in the hospital, dying. So I say to myself either the

Haitian's lying or Mr. Daniels, one. It turns out the machete was from the tool shed on his property. See, but how would the Haitian know to go in there and get it?"

"Was it locked?"

"I asked the gardener, he says no. I asked him was the machete, could it have been left out? He goes, hell no, I take care of my tools, put them away . . . and all like that."

"Was the machete checked for prints?"

"No sir. See, I got there—there was the Haitian on the ground, shot twice, bleeding all over the place, with the machete lying close by. But it wouldn't do no good to check it now. The gardener's probably been cutting scrub with it anyway."

"Did you ask Walter why he didn't have it dusted?"

"No sir, it was his investigation. I was mostly waving at traffic on South Ocean Boulevard . . . Hey, don't you all want a drink?"

Lieutenant Hurd said, "How about ballistics on the gun?"

"There was no need for it, nothing to prove."

"You keep the two slugs or did Walter throw 'em away?"

"No, they're in a envelope, in the file."

They sat back and talked about Palm Beach and the season, sipping bourbon, looking at the outfits in the cafe, trying to tell the tourists from the regulars, those who had money and those who didn't; Gary saying there wasn't much excitement other than stopping drunks and then you had to be careful who you pulled over. Palm Beach was a playground for the rich people and they okayed the rules. Place swung from Christmas to Easter, then rolled over and went to sleep.

Lieutenant Hurd said, "What do you think of Walter Kouza?"

Gary had to give that a few moments.

"Well, to tell you the truth, I thought basically he was

dumb. I mean I don't think he was any good in school, if he ever went. But he knew things. We'd pick some guy up for vagrancy—Detective Kouza seemed to *know* if the guy had any priors and he'd usually get the guy to cop. We have a problem with vandalism, broken windows, something like that, I can't even get twelve-year-old kids to cop. Detective Kouza, he has 'em in the room there a couple minutes, they tell him whatever he wants to hear."

"What about when he left?" Lieutenant Hurd asked if Walter had said anything about what he'd be doing.

"He did and he didn't," Gary said. "He made it sound like foreign intrigue, like he was going to work for the CIA. But he really didn't say anything you could put your finger on. So I just figured, you know, it was bullshit."

"Trying to impress you."

"Yeah, he was always laying a trip on you, his twenty years experience," Gary said. "Like he had seen it all. I guess more than anything, Detective Kouza wanted you to think he was important."

Looking at the stars she said to Bryan, "I'd walk out in the desert—it's all open land back of their house, up in the Santa Catalina foothills. I'd go out just to be alone for a few minutes. And then I'd hear my dad. I mean I could sneak off, leave him asleep in his chair. The next thing, I'd hear his voice. 'See those lights over there?' " Her voice lower, a more serious tone. " 'That's the new Las Palmas condo development. Then over there you got Casas Adobes and Vista del Oro.' " She stopped and then said, "I'm putting you to sleep, aren't I?"

Bryan said, feeling as content as he could feel, having her right there and knowing she would be there for a while, "You were gonna tell me why you went home. The real reason."

She said, "All right. I didn't go home because it was my birthday."

He said, "You went home to see an old boyfriend. Look him over one more time."

"I don't have an old boyfriend."

"Since your divorce—what, ten years, you've never had a boyfriend?"

"You don't have boyfriends anymore. And I was never anyone's old lady."

"And nobody *dates*," Bryan said.

"No, you don't date. I went with a guy who played with Frank Zappa and had known my husband. In L.A. It was kinda fun, but he was spacy."

"Not serious?"

"Never . . . You want to hear some music? I could go in and turn the radio on, open a window."

"I'd rather listen to you," Bryan said. "You can tell me anything you want."

He liked her voice, quiet and close to him, with the sound of the ocean breaking out of the darkness. He liked to sit and follow the specks of amber light that were ships in the Gulf Stream and seemed as far away as stars. People out there staring at shore lights. He looking at them and they looking at him, with fifteen miles between them. She got up and went inside. But no music came. She returned with glasses of cold Chablis, sat down in her deck chair—the arms of the chairs touching—and raised her legs to the low cement wall.

"Thank you . . . So you didn't go home to see your old boyfriend."

"No. I went home to see my dad."

When she paused he said, "Rich people don't say my dad. They say dad, like their dad is the only dad."

She thought about it and said, "You may be right. If I do the book on rich people I'll check it out."

"Go on about your dad."

"Okay. You reminded me of him quite a bit, as soon as we met. And I wondered if that's why I thought I knew you and felt good with you right away. I mean not only comfortable, I felt protected. Which could be a big mistake. Like giving me a false sense of security."

"Right. I'm not your dad."

"You sure aren't. And you're not anything alike, either. That's the amazing part. You might sound alike, a little. But your attitudes are so different."

"Does this turn out good?"

"There. That's the difference right there. He's serious about dumb things and you aren't. Of course it turns out good, because I think you're right. The way you look at things. You're not cynical especially, you're . . . I can't think of the word."

"Objective."

"No . . . Well, partly."

"Carefree."

"No."

"Romantic?"

"No!"

"Straightforward."

"Come on—"

"Erect."

She said, "Macho man returns." She looked off at the pinpoint glow of stars and running lights. She said, "Are you? Really?"

In the big double bed in darkness in the middle of the night she said, "God, I love you."

They could hear the surf through the open windows. No other sounds.

He could tell her. He could tell her a few things about how he felt. But he couldn't *hear* himself telling her. Not yet. He said, "We're there, aren't we?"

She moved her hand down to touch him and said, "You're not only not romantic you're not too erect anymore either."

He said, "Keep your hand there. Pretty soon we'll hear violins."

TEN

IT WAS THE next morning Annie called Bryan. She asked him how the weather was. Perfect, he told her. She asked if Angela had got hold of him. She certainly did, he told her.

Annie said, "The valet-parking cashier came through. Remember, she thought there was a good-luck piece or something on the keys Curtis took? She saw another one just like it, a circle with three spokes. A Mercedes insignia."

Now you're moving, Bryan told her.

Annie said, "Wait. I talked to the last of the hotel guests that came in that morning around ten or before. One of them was very friendly, I liked him. He checked into the hotel with his wife." Bryan said, yeah? "But he lives in Bloomfield Hills." Bryan said, oh. He said, well, the guy probably took his wife down for the weekend. Annie said, "He's a talkative type, sort of a bullshitter. At least he was at first. But as soon as he found out what it was about, he shut up." Bryan asked, then what was it she liked about the guy.

Annie said, "Before he shut up he remembered seeing a dark-colored Mercedes sedan. It was in front of him with the door open and he couldn't pull up to get past. But there was no Mercedes down in that area of the garage, near Curtis. So the question is, where did it go?" Bryan said, maybe the car only picked somebody up. Annie said, "That's possible. But I checked to see if anyone we know owns a Mercedes. And you know who does?"

Robbie Daniels, Bryan said.

Annie said, "You rat."

Bryan told her if she wanted him to be her straight man she'd have to set it up better. Or not sound so eager. What else?

Well, she'd finally got hold of the Japanese buyer. "But he didn't stay at the Plaza and Walter didn't pick him up."

Then why did Daniels make an issue of it? Why did he keep insisting Walter picked the guy up? Unless he wanted to confuse them, throw them off.

"I don't know," Annie said. "I did talk to a couple of buyers who remembered Walter, but they came in later in the day. I'm having trouble getting hold of the guy in Mexico City. Carlos Cabrera. Nobody at his company seems to speak English. But I'll keep trying if you think it's really necessary."

Bryan asked her how you could tell what was necessary from what wasn't until you did it.

Annie said, "As long as you're having a good time, Bryan, don't worry about it."

They hung up. About twenty seconds later Annie's phone rang.

"Annie, go out and have a talk with Daniels. Ask him who he picked up, if anyone. Fish around, see if he's hiding anything. Okay? And take somebody with you . . . Annie? What's the name of the guy's company in Mexico City?"

She told him Maquinaria Cabrera, S. A. And asked if he wanted her to spell it.

He said, "Maquinaria? If I can say it I don't need to be able to spell it." He wrote the name *Carlos Cabrera* on an Ocean

Pearl postcard that showed the resort with palm trees on a perfect day. Then asked her for the phone number.

Anything else?

"Yeah," Bryan said. "Set Robbie up if you can. Look him in the eye and ask him if he was at the Plaza Saturday morning."

Angela, in the terry-cloth robe, sat at the breakfast table with the *Miami Herald*. She watched Bryan, in his bathing trunks, get up from the phone and begin to move around idly, looking out the windows, deciding something.

She said, "What's maquinaria mean?"

"Mah-kee-*nah*-r'yah." Bryan stopped to look at her. "Machinery." His bathing trunks, that he'd been wearing for ten years, were dark blue sun-faded to a washed-out purple. They reminded Angela, she had told him, of an old junk car, though she wasn't certain why.

She said, "You didn't learn to say it like that in Spanish class."

He said, "You go to Holy Trinity grade school for eight years with Chicanos and Maltese you learn how to pronounce all kinds of words. Some pretty good ones, too."

She said, "Let's get dressed and do our shopping now instead of later on."

"If you want."

"You need some outfits desperately," Angela said.

He didn't like the sound of that. He didn't like articles of clothing put together to make "outfits." He liked shirts and pants, sweaters, combinations that came together and didn't seem to mind, but were not thought out in advance.

"First," he said, "you have some pictures of Daniels, don't you? That you took?"

"Dozens."

"You have 'em here?"

"Yeah, in my case."

"I wonder if we could send a few to Annie," Bryan said. "Something she can show around."

Angela nodded, seeing some of the shots flash in her mind: Robbie in his thin sweater over bare skin scratching his stomach, Robbie grinning, Robbie gesturing; he could be a male model. She said, with hesitation, "Do you think he killed Curtis?"

"It's possible," Bryan said.

"But why would he?"

"You're backing off." Bryan said. "You told me, not too long ago, you think the man likes to kill people."

"Is that what I said?"

"Those were the words."

"Yeah, but . . ." It was different now, looking directly at the possibility. "Robbie seems so . . ."

"What, charming?"

"No—"

"Fun-loving?"

"Are we gonna play that again?"

"You're the writer," Bryan said. "What's the word? Robbie seems so . . ."

"Harmless," Angela said. "But weird."

"You were there when he shot the Haitian. You said there was something strange about it and you tried to talk to him after, later on."

"I did. I asked him, did you have to shoot the poor guy? It was the first thing I said to him after the police left. And Robbie said, very serious, 'You're writing about me and you have to ask that?'"

"Maybe blowing smoke at you," Bryan said. "I think he goes for dramatic effects."

"Or maybe telling the truth," Angela said. "As though

he was saying, 'If you know me, then you'd know I had to shoot the guy.' After that, for the next few days, I tried to corner him to find out what he meant. But he avoided me—I mean to the point of being rude. He made excuses, never had time to talk. And he was strange. Off somewhere in his mind." Angela said then, "Do some people—have you ever met anyone who shot people for the fun of it? For kicks?"

"Whatever the reason," Bryan said, "yeah, there're people who like to shoot people. There're cops who look for an excuse. There're guys who get into armed robbery, I'm pretty sure, hoping they'll have to use their gun."

Angela was quiet for a moment. "At the hearing, the plaintiff's lawyer asked if you'd ever shot anyone."

"He asked if I'd killed anybody lately," Bryan said. "He knew. He was making a comparison, with Walter."

"Well, have you?"

"What, killed anybody? No, I never have. Or had the desire."

"What if you did have to, sometime?"

"Then I'd do it." Bryan said. "If there's no choice, I guess you do it."

Annie Maguire said to Robbie, "You've got an awfully nice house. It reminds me a little of where they signed the Declaration of Independence. The outside."

"It's comfortable," Robbie said. Leading Annie through the front hall to the study, his sneakers squeaked on the marble floor. He let her go in first, then rated her as she looked around the study. Nice can filling out the skirt of the beige suit. She wore a dark blue button-down shirt with it; a well-worn brown-leather bag hung from her shoulder. He wondered what kind of gun was inside. She wasn't bad looking at all: the clean, wholesome type. He imagined a spray of freckles over motherly breasts. There was that to be said of some older women: they offered a comforting, maternal sexuality that could be a nice change. Annie, he judged, was about thirty-four.

"You know who you remind me of? Julie Andrews."

Annie said, "Jim Malik—he's the one I told you on the phone was coming out with me? But something came up he had to do. Jim says I remind him of her too. Except I'm fatter and I don't talk funny."

"I certainly wouldn't call you fat," Robbie said. "In fact, the first thing that came to mind when I opened the door—you know what I wanted to do?"

Annie smiled. She said, "What?"

"Tie you up," Robbie said, deadpan, "and fuck your socks off. I've never slept with a cop before." He maintained his bland, almost melancholy expression, waiting for her reaction, ready to break into a grin.

Annie said, "Someone else said that to me one time." She walked past the big chair facing the television console and sat down on the couch of soft brown leather. "When I was working Sex Crimes."

Robbie didn't get a chance to grin. He said, "Sex Crimes?"

"We handled criminal sexual conduct. Rape, in varying degrees," Annie said. "That was before I got into Homicide."

"Sex Crimes," Robbie said again. It had a ring to it. He dropped into his chair, swung his sneakers, laces untied, onto the ottoman. The policewoman showed up very well against the rich brown leather. "How about a drink?"

"No thanks," Annie said. "Anyway, there was a guy we were after who came to be known as the Weekend Rapist. He'd go into a house Saturday or Sunday night—we'd find cigarette butts out by the garage where he watched the house until the lights went out. Then he'd go in. And always with a gun. He wasn't a cat burglar, the kind that sneaks in and out. This guy stuck the gun in their face, whoever was home, and took what he wanted. Mostly jewelry, valuables, things like that. Cash. And if there was a woman in the house he'd rape her. Actually he forced the woman to perform fellatio and then he sodomized her."

"Wow," Robbie said.

"Anyone else in the house—the husband, kids—he'd make them lie on the floor in the same room and cover them with a blanket so they couldn't see him. But they could hear, and this guy would give a blow by blow—"

Robbie grinned. "If you'll pardon the expression, uh?"

"—of whatever he was doing. Though mostly what they heard was the poor woman crying. Then he'd *thank* her, take the stuff and leave."

"What'd he wear?" Robbie asked.

"Watch cap, dark sweat shirt with a hood and aviator sunglasses. He had a beard too."

"Fascinating," Robbie said.

"But he didn't always say please and thank you," Annie said. "Twice—and the women were alone both times—he put a pillow over their face, pressed a twenty-two revolver into the pillow and shot them in the head."

"Unpredictable," Robbie said.

"In some ways," Annie said. "In other ways, no. He always used his girl friend's car, as it turned out, and that led us to our suspect. A guy who was out on parole following a B and E conviction—there had been an attempted rape in that case too, but it was dropped in the plea bargaining. Anyway we brought the guy in—Dennis Kenzie, I'll never forget his name—and I handled the interrogation. Well, right away he started to come on to me, making sly remarks, saying what you said about tying me up."

"Really?" Robbie sounded disappointed, upstaged.

"We were pretty sure Dennis was our Weekend Rapist, just from little things he'd let slip. But we couldn't get a positive I.D. from any of the victims and we didn't have nearly enough to bring him up. But then," Annie said, "he started calling me, asking me to go out with him. And he started hanging around. Twice I ran into him in Greektown. And finally I was pretty sure he followed me home. A few days later I came in the house—there he was waiting for me in his knit cap, his sunglasses, pointing a gun at me. He took my purse, pushed me in the bedroom and told me to take off my clothes. He'd even brought a rope to tie me up."

"Jesus," Robbie said, "what'd you do?"

"I reached under the mattress, pulled out my spare thirty-eight Chiefs Special and told Dennis to drop his gun," Annie said. "And when he didn't, I shot him."

Robbie liked it and began to smile. "Just like that. Did you kill him?"

"No, he survived. He's doing mandatory life," Annie said, "with a limp." She smiled back at Robbie now with that sweet-girl way that opened hearts and said, "Mr. Daniels, were you at the Detroit Plaza Hotel any time Saturday morning?"

His smiled remained, part of it, the smile becoming vacant with the effort to maintain his composure, giving himself time.

He said, "You know who picked up the Japs—after I accused Walter and we almost got in an argument over it? *I* did. We had so many buyers in that day . . . Well, everything's gone now, all the equipment . . ."

"Did you pick them up at the Plaza?"

"No, it was the Ponch. I'm quite sure."

"Did you pick *any*body up at the Plaza?"

He appeared to give it some thought. "I don't think I did. I know I dropped some people off there, later."

"What kind of car were you driving?"

"Saturday? . . . I had the Mercedes."

"What color is it?"

"Well, we have a black one and a yellow one, to go with whatever mood you're in. Saturday I was in something of a funereal mood, the end of an era, seventy-five years of nuts and bolts . . . ." Robbie gave her a sly look and began to smile again. "You know, you're quite attractive. Were you ever a model?"

Annie said, "Are you serious?"

"Were you ever on television?"

"On the six o'clock news a couple of times," Annie said. "Walking a prisoner from 1300 to the Frank Murphy Hall of Justice."

"That's not all," Robbie said. He pushed up the remote-control box from the table next to him and pushed a button. "Watch."

Annie was looking at him and wasn't sure what he meant until he nodded toward the television console. She turned and saw herself on the screen, in color, walking toward the couch. She saw herself and heard her voice saying, "Someone else said that to me one time. When I was working Sex Crimes." She heard Daniels's voice, offscreen, say, "Sex Crimes?"

Angela had walked down to the beach while Bryan was on the phone again with Annie. She felt him near and opened her eyes. The hair on his chest moved in the wind.

He said, "Walter left yesterday with the Mercedes. Robbie's coming down tonight. How does he usually fly?"

"He hitches a ride on some company jet," Angela said. "Or he charters one. He very rarely flies commercial."

Angela waited. Bryan was looking off at the ocean.

"I think we ought to move to Palm Beach," he said. "You know of any places?"

"I know a Holiday Inn," Angela said. "I know many Holiday Inns, all over." She waited again.

"Robbie told Annie I should give him a call. He wants to play golf with me. You said he was weird," Bryan said. "I believe it."

"I also said he was harmless," Angela said.

"Yeah—we're not so sure about that part," Bryan said. "I would like to get to know him better."

Angela said, "Can I watch?"

The rental car was a Buick Century he could not say anything for or against. It was dark shiny brown in the hot sunlight. It took them north out of Boca on 95 while he told Angela about Annie's visit with Robbie.

"He doesn't *think* he picked up anyone at the Plaza," Bryan said. "Does that sound like him?"

"No," Angela said, "if anything he's Mr. Positive. But what he'll do, he'll look you right in the face and lie. Then have that little-boy impish grin ready in case you call him on it."

"The weird part, Annie said he videotaped her. He has hidden cameras mounted in the study and showed her a *movie* of herself on TV."

Angela was nodding. "The first time I interviewed him he played back the whole scene in living color."

"You saw the cameras?"

"Well, they're not exactly hidden, but they're not as obvious as the ones you see in banks or stores. He has the same setup in Palm Beach, also in his study."

"What is it, he likes gadgets?"

"That's what he claims," Angela said. "It's a toy. He had a surveillance system installed in his plant, got interested in electronics and bought much more exotic equipment for his homes. But just in his studies—I mean they're obviously not for surveillance. He doesn't touch a thing—the cameras pan with you when you move, zoom in for close-ups—I don't know how it works."

Bryan said it sounded like a pretty expensive toy. Angela said there was something like a hundred thousand bucks worth of videotape equipment in each home; but that was beside the point. Did Robbie play with his toy or use it for some other purpose? Bryan said maybe to keep from being misquoted. Angela said, or to record what some people might confide and then hold it over their heads . . . The son of a bitch.

"You don't like him," Bryan said.

"It's funny, I dislike him even more since I met you," Angela said. She was silent for several miles and then said, "Get off at Southern Boulevard. I'll show you where he lives."

They crossed the bridge over Lake Worth and came to Palm Beach. "Now right on South Ocean Boulevard," Angela said. "Just a little way. There. Pull into the drive."

Bryan could see only part of the house through the iron gate and the palm trees lining the drive. "Is that a house or a hotel?"

"Hacienda Daniels," Angela said. "Now we go north."

They backtracked, crossed Southern Boulevard on the beach road and Angela pointed to the Bath and Tennis Club. "From here up to Worth Avenue, about a mile or so, is the very *in* section, between the Bath and Tennis Club and the Everglades Club. If you know how much money you have you don't belong here. Robbie's a little pissed off because he's about two hundred feet *south* of being, quote, 'between the clubs.' The architecture is all either pseudo-Spanish or Mediterranean Mausoleum."

"I don't think you should write the book on rich people," Bryan said.

"Why, because I have a point of view?"

Bryan nodded toward a colossal, ornate structure with a slim minaret pointing to heaven. "What's that?"

"It's somebody's house," Angela said. "Shelter."

Bryan said, "I'd hate to have to vacuum and dust the place."

Angela said, "One old broad used to maintain a staff of

fifty—count 'em—fifty servants. She also has eighty-six phones. One for each room. You have to know whose money it is, hers or his. See that house? *She* was once a baton twirler on the Sealtest Big Top Circus. But as the society writers say, 'She left show business behind.' That one, coming up, the old gal was a silent-film star who happened to marry John Paul Getty."

"You could be a tour guide."

"Yeah, stop the bus and everybody gets out and throws tomatoes."

Bryan said, "You don't sound upset, but you really are. I don't get it."

"I can point out a few hotbeds of fascism too," Angela said. "They're not all fascists, but when Jack Kennedy was shot some of the Old Guard actually threw parties."

"Who told you that?"

"A very reliable guy I know here. He writes for the local paper, the *Post*."

"Well, that was a while ago."

"Nixon was here last month. Greeted like a savior . . . That's Worth Avenue, where all the expensive stores are."

"Where the rich people shop?"

"No, where the tourists shop. Rich people don't spend their money, they invest it in real estate. That's the *in* thing to talk about at the clubs, real estate."

Bryan said, "Why do rich people make you mad?"

"They don't," Angela said. "I just feel that the way they live, their entire life-style, is irrelevant, it has nothing to do with reality."

"Because they have money and you don't?"

"No. Because their whole goddamn life is based on real estate. Owning things."

"You said that's all your dad talks about. Real estate. Is he rich?"

"No, he wears a string tie and a cowboy hat with his

gold-frame glasses, drives a Cadillac, lives in Country Club Estates with a guard, a *guard*, Bryan, at the entrance and tries hard to sound rich. But he doesn't know how. That's what's wrong with them," Angela said, with her cool edge. "The rich people make their life look so goddamn good we all bust our ass trying to get the same thing."

Bryan said, "If the poor people suddenly became rich would they do it any different?"

"Probably not."

"Are rich people fun to watch?"

"Not especially."

"Fun to talk to? Interview?"

"Not at all. They don't *say* anything. They don't *know* anything that's going on outside their own walled-in life. They're completely out of touch with reality."

"I'll talk to you," Bryan said. "Soon as I think of something. But first, tell me where the Holiday Inn is."

"The one we're going to is in Palm Beach Gardens," Angela said. "About ten miles north of here."

"Palm Beach Gardens?" Bryan said. "I've never heard of it."

That was the first thing Robbie Daniels said, too, the next morning when Bryan opened the door of Room 205 and there he was, boyish as ever.

"Palm Beach *Gardens*? I've been here practically all my life, I've never even heard of it . . ."

ELEVEN

THE SECOND THING Robbie said, looking over the room, the double beds, one made with its spread intact, the other torn apart, was, "You want to know something? This is the first time I've ever been inside a Holiday Inn. It's not bad at all."

Angela said to Bryan, "See? What did I tell you?"

She sat at the room-service table in her terry-cloth robe having breakfast.

Robbie said to Bryan, "Go ahead. I'll have some coffee with Angie while you get dressed."

"I am dressed," Bryan said.

"I mean for golf," Robbie said.

"I am dressed for golf," Bryan said.

Robbie looked at Bryan's dark blue T-shirt that had the words SQUAD 5 HOMICIDE stenciled on it in white. He looked at Bryan's faded gray corduroy pants and tennis shoes with four blue stripes on them—not three, *four*—and said, "Oh."

As they left Angela said, "Don't worry about me. I'll find something to do."

They drove off in Robbie's silver Rolls. Robbie said, "How is that, pretty nice stuff?" Bryan told him to be careful and Robbie shut up.

What Bryan did, he noted things he would tell Angela about later.

The Seminole Club. "Ben Hogan once said if he had to play one club all the time it would be Seminole," Robbie said. "Where do you play in Detroit?" Bryan said, "Palmer Park, mostly." A public course. "Oh . . . What do you shoot?" "Low eighties." "How about if I give you twelve strokes?" "Fine." Robbie gave him an entire yellow golf outfit. Yellow pants, yellow shirt with the little alligator on it, yellow silk sweater. ("I looked like the Easter Bunny.") White shoes with tongue flaps. Robbie gave him the twelve strokes—the son of a bitch, the sandbagger—and beat him by twenty-six. Bryan tried to cheat, moving his ball around in the rough, but the caddy kept watching him. He lost six golf balls, one in the Atlantic Ocean, but took a penalty on only two of them or else his score would have been one-oh-six. He wouldn't tell Angela too much about the game.

He'd tell her about the gingersnaps in the locker room. Strange. And the macaroni and cheese special for lunch; all the rich guys eating the macaroni and cheese they didn't get at home, eating it like they'd discovered it. He'd tell her about some of the rich guys he met—Angela was right—who talked about real estate in places he'd never heard of. And how he'd met the Chicano-looking guy named Rafael Fuentes who re-sembled Rudolph Valentino—he seemed to pose—and had a dry, almost bored way of talking with his Chicano accent that had some other accents mixed in, but seemed like a nice guy. Very well mannered. Robbie called him Chichi or Cheech and seemed on familiar terms. The thing was, the guy didn't seem to know Robbie. Robbie asked him, "How's the coke business, Cheech?"

Chichi said, "I no longer have the bottling plant. It was confiscated."

(Confiscated?)

And Robbie said, "Señor Slick. You know what I'm talking about, Chichi. A little *dulce nariz*, perhaps?"

Trying to show off. Literally translated, candy nose, but meaning nose candy. Cocaine.

Which Chichi smiled at in his bored cultured way, then snapped his fingers. "A party—where was that? Everyone wanted to escape, to fantasize."

Robbie said, "And you got caught in a cabana, I think it was, going down on the hostess."

"A lovely lady," Chichi said. Bony features creased in a smile of recognition. "Ah, Robbie"—pronouncing it Robie—"now I remember you. The Detroit industrialist with the delicacy of a drill press. Are you still seducing little girls?"

"Only when your sister's in town," Robbie said. "Nice seeing you again, Cheech."

"Nice seeing you, too," Chichi said. "By the way, I met your wife yesterday at Wellington . . ."

Got him. Bryan caught Robbie's instant look of surprise.

"Ah, you don't know she's here, uh? With that Polish count, what's his name? From Colorado. The one who dyes his hair white and wears the fringed jackets."

Robbie said, "What difference does it make?"

"I don't know," Chichi said, "Patti is your wife, not mine. She and the count flew in for the polo. I wouldn't worry about it."

Robbie said, "Do I look worried?"

Chichi Fuentes took the question literally and studied him. "No, you look more confused, I think. I told them, you want the best polo, go down to Casa de Campo; you want only to fuck, well, Palm Beach is all right."

They *ciao*-ed each other with cold smiles and that was that.

Bryan would remember it as pussy time at Seminole: two grown men spitting at each other in the locker room. Was this the way rich guys had it out? He'd have to ask Angela.

But the most interesting part of the day came later. Robbie said why didn't they go to his place, kick their shoes off and have a few? Fairly offhand about it. Bryan said fine. He was already sure Robbie had something in mind and wanted to talk.

Bryan thought of a nun he had in the sixth grade at Holy Trinity whose favorite word was *gawk* and was always telling the class to quit gawking at the ceiling or gawking out the window at the new freeway excavation. Sister Estelle. She would not have been proud of Bryan Hurd as he walked through the Spanish mansion, through the living room that was larger than the Holiday Inn lobby, and gawked in every direction. Christ. People lived here. Two people. And some servants. He saw a maid in a white uniform and then a guy with his hair slicked back wearing an apron, in the kitchen talking to Walter. Arguing about something. Robbie entered and they shut up—Walter looking past his boss now to Bryan waiting in the hall. Walter staring, with almost a balloon coming out of his head that said, "What's he doing here?" Robbie spoke to Walter for several minutes, holding onto his arm; then came back apologetically, "I'm sorry—" and took the homicide detective upstairs to his study and unlocked the double bolts.

"I was interested—during Walter's court hearing that colored lawyer asked you if you'd killed anyone lately, you told him no," Robbie said, "and I wondered if in fact you *have* ever killed anyone."

Bryan said, "I remember reading about one of yours."

It caught Robbie by surprise. "The Haitian? That wasn't in the Detroit papers, was it?"

"The guy from Chrysler, in the duck blind." Bryan made a quarter turn on the bar stool, giving the room a glance. What looked like covered light fixtures high on the walls could be video cameras; he wasn't sure. The room was dim except for track lighting directly overhead. He wondered if there was a camera up there. He wondered when Robbie Daniels would get to the point.

"I forgot about Carl," Robbie was saying, standing behind the bar, a sneaker up on the stainless sink. "That was a shocking experience. But the Haitian, that was something else. Guy came at me with a goddamn machete."

"What'd you use?"

"Colt Python. It's my favorite, so I grabbed it. You want to see it?"

It didn't matter if he wanted to or not. Robbie went over and got it, left the cabinet open and came back hefting the big, three-and-a-half-pound revolver with the ventilated barrel. He seemed to enjoy holding it. When he offered the gun Bryan took it.

"What do you carry, lieutenant?"

"Regular thirty-eight Smith, Chiefs Special. I had a Colt automatic once, but I had to get rid of it," Bryan said. "I found out it wasn't authorized by the department."

"You found out?"

"Well, I didn't carry it much and I didn't keep up on all the regulations." Looking the Python over, extending it now, Bryan said, "He had a machete, huh?"

"Came at me swinging," Robbie said.

"So you had no choice but to shoot."

"None," Robbie said. "You've never been in that position?"

Bryan seemed to smile. "Not lately."

"I'm surprised, you don't seem interested in guns."

Bryan gestured, a small shrug. "No, not especially." He laid the Python on the bar and picked up his vodka over ice. Robbie hadn't asked him what he wanted to drink; he'd started pouring and that was it: a guy who had been drinking socially, semiprofessionally most of his life and probably felt he could outdrink an Athens Bar city cop any day of the week. Maybe he could. The imported vodka was all right though. Bryan felt pretty good, his mind sharp and clear.

Robbie said, "You see this guy coming at you who obviously means business—what would you have done?"

"I wasn't there," Bryan said. "I guess nobody was but you. But if you say you had to shoot him, well . . ."

"All right," Robbie said, "how about—a different situation. You don't *have* to shoot, but you feel justified."

They were getting to it now. Bryan said, "Like some really bad dude, or somebody you're pissed off at?"

"Think of an individual," Robbie said, "you know the world would be a much better place without."

Jesus Christ, Bryan thought. "Like who?"

"Come on, you know the type I mean. An international pure-bred asshole of the first order."

"I don't know any," Bryan said.

"There are some fairly obvious ones."

"Well, I don't know how international he is," Bryan said, "but how about Howard Cosell?"

"Come on, I mean a real one."

"Two for one," Bryan said, warming up to it, "Cosell

and George Steinbrenner. Or, I know a couple Recorders Court judges—but I think I'd rather catch 'em crossing a street and run over 'em with a car. Does it matter how you do it?"

"I'm serious," Robbie said. "Consider someone like—have you ever heard of Carlos?"

"Carlos," Bryan said. The name was familiar.

"Number one terrorist in the world today. Hijacks planes, kidnaps, murders—"

"You had a buyer from Mexico named Carlos," Bryan said, holding Robbie's gaze. "Carlos Cabrera."

It stopped Robbie. His smile was tentative, with a hint of suspicion. "How'd you remember that name?"

"I spoke to him on the phone," Bryan said. "Asked him if he remembered who picked him up that Saturday. He said you did." Staring at Robbie, not letting him look away. "I asked him where he stayed. He said the Detroit Plaza."

Robbie moved around behind the bar again, giving himself something to do. "If Mr. Cabrera says I picked him up . . . Come to think of it I guess I did. But not at the hotel. No, he was waiting at the main entrance of the RenCen with his assistant. Right out in front." Now remembering details. "Did he tell you that?"

"He might've. But it's all the same general area, isn't it?"

"We're talking about an entirely different Carlos," Robbie said, breaking free and beginning to run now. "A Venezuelan educated in Moscow, trained in PLO *fedayeen* camps. Carlos has worked with both the Red Brigade and the Baader-Meinhof gang. He's the ultimate professional terrorist—kidnapped those OPEC guys in Vienna, he's murdered who knows how many people. His operating principle is from an old Chinese saying, 'Kill one, frighten ten thousand.' "

Bryan said, "You'd rather do Carlos than Howard Co-sell, huh?"

"I'm serious, goddamn it!" Robbie took a drink to settle down and managed a weak grin. Serious but still boyish. "Sorry about that. Sometimes I get a little carried away."

Bryan, with all the time in the world, said, "You want to go out and shoot Carlos, is that what you're telling me?"

"Look at it this way," Robbie said. "All over the world people are shooting each other. Iranians and Iraqis, Russians and Afghans, Christians and Moslems in Lebanon. Look at Angola, Uganda, Cambodia, Chad—"

"Chad . . ." Bryan said. He had not thought too much about Chad lately.

"Ethiopia, Guatemala, El Salvador . . . People are shooting each other and most of the time they don't even know what side they're on. We look at those places, it's hard to tell the good guys from the bad guys. But there are other areas where we know goddamn well who the bad guys are."

"Wait a minute," Bryan said. There was something he wanted to do. He got off the stool, went over to the open cabinet and looked in.

The display of handguns was impressive, interesting: most of them high-caliber, high-velocity models that would be selected with serious intent. The twenty-two target pistol Robbie had fired in his office wasn't on display. He tried the door below the open cabinet but it wouldn't budge.

"I showed Walter my collection," Robbie said. "Walter goes, 'Christ, you could invade Cuba.' "

Bryan came back to the bar. "I don't know about Cuba, but it might get you through downtown Miami."

Robbie raised his eyebrows. "Speaking of which. You know the Cuban boat people, the ones that came from Mariel? Just in the past year something like eighty-five of them have been shot and killed."

Bryan settled into the stool. It was comfortable and things were moving right along. He didn't have to urge Robbie or lead him now.

"There's an outlet in Miami sells a half-million dollars worth of handguns a month, and that's only one place. We're into guns, man. Everybody is, the good guys now as well as the bad guys. And you know what it comes down to, the bottom line? Who shoots first."

Now he was trying to sound hip. He didn't know who he was. Or as Angela said, there was an interesting other Robbie inside the cute Robbie. The one in there was dying to pull the trigger and the present world climate was inspiring him, bringing him out on stage.

"You can wait for an intruder. Somebody breaks into your house, which happened right here. Or, if you have the wherewithal, the purpose, the ability, why not go out after the same sort of game? Only bigger?"

"Like Carlos," Bryan said.

"Like any number of individuals on the other side," Robbie said. "Carlos is an example. Maybe someday, down the road. A more realistic one might be . . . say, a big-time drug dealer that none of the government agencies can touch. A guy who's fucking up lives, kills people who get in his way and lives like a king."

Bryan said, "Well, you're looking for action you could join the Marines."

"Listen, a hundred and twenty years ago," Robbie said, "during the Civil War, gentlemen of means raised their own regiments. 'Bring your horse, a shotgun and a pistol and ride with Nathan Bedford Forrest.' You put a sign on a tree in the front lawn. Now you don't fight with armies; the sides aren't clearly enough defined. But, you don't have to raise a regiment to take out some of the bad guys."

He was serious. Listening to him was not exactly embarrassing, but close to it. The man didn't hear himself as he was. He was picturing himself in a role. With a sword. Born a hundred years too late. Maybe that was it.

Bryan said, "I notice you read some pretty exciting stuff. We can get all kinds of secret thrills from books, can't we? Especially in a nice comfortable study. Quiet, air-conditioned . . ."

"The star German terrorist Ulrike Meinhof," Robbie said, "refused to hide out in an apartment that didn't have central heating, or the usual comforts of home. He complained about the primitive conditions in PLO training camps, raised quite a stink about Al Halil, in Libya. Which incidentally got Qaddafi very pissed off."

"I guess what you're saying," Bryan said, "you don't have to be poor to want to kill somebody."

"You don't have to be a cop, either."

Bryan waited, letting the silence lengthen. "What's the matter, you bored?"

"Usually."

"Golf doesn't do it, uh?"

"There's very little competition."

"Well, now you're into a game I know something about," Bryan said.

"I'm aware of that." Robbie sipped his drink. "Except you haven't told me if you've ever killed anyone."

"Does it matter?"

"I don't believe you have," Robbie said, "and I think that's odd. I mean if I've killed and you haven't, who's the authority?"

"I think it might depend," Bryan said, "on who you've got in mind."

The curly haired smiler who owned a half-dozen cars, a couple of million-dollar mansions, property in seven states and was sometimes mistaken for a movie star looked at the thirty-grand-a-year homicide cop with the solemn mustache.

He said, "It's funny. You go to a club for a round of golf, you're asked what you shoot. But this kind of game you're asked *who* you shoot, or would like to. It's considerably more exciting, isn't it?"

"Only if you win," Bryan said. "You lose, you don't get off buying a round of drinks."

TWELVE

HE GROANED AS he worked sore feet into his loafers, sat back and rested, then groaned again as he got up out of the Holiday Inn chair.

Angela said, "Sometimes you sound old."

She stood at the mirror over the bank of dressers, looking at his reflection across the room, the glass door to the balcony behind him in flat light.

He said, "I told you, I like to sound old."

"Not creaky old."

"I played eighteen holes on a ball buster. That'll do it to you."

Angela was adjusting the neckline of her dress, pulling it out and looking down inside. "But did he tell you *who* he wants to shoot?"

"He talks around it." Bryan moved to the closet, came out with his blue polka-dot tie. "If you could get rid of anybody you feel doesn't deserve to live—or the world would be a better place without—who would it be? I think some girl told him one time he's 'real deep' and he believes it."

"You know who might be a good one," Angela said. "Robbie."

"I thought of that," Bryan said, "after." He came over to the mirror to tie his tie, standing obliquely behind her. Angela's eyes raised to his reflection, his face already deeply tanned.

"Who did you suggest?"

"I gave him Howard Cosell. I didn't mean it though. I like Howard, he's all right."

"You like everybody."

"No, but when I think about it, I don't dislike as many people as I thought. I decided I like John McEnroe, for example. I'd take him for backup any time."

"How about Walter?"

"Walter's Walter. I think Daniels played the game with him and signed him up. Walter, I can see him, makes out a list of prospects and licks his thumb going through the pages. But I guess I didn't play it right. It was funny, I had the feeling, it was like I was waiting to get a bribe offer. If I said the right thing, showed some interest, he'd have offered me . . . I don't know. Shows me the exclusive club, his home—it was like, all this can be yours if you play along."

"The temptation of Bryan Hurd."

"Except he didn't offer me anything; so what was he doing? He tells me about an international terrorist as a likely target, a guy named Carlos. That rang a bell, so I told him I'd called that Mexican buyer, Carlos Cabrera."

"Did you?"

"No, I took a shot. I told him the Mexican said Mr. Daniels himself had picked him up. At the Plaza. And Robbie said, that's right, I guess I did. No argument. So he was there Saturday morning."

They thought about it separately, staring at their reflections, tieing a tie, pinning the front of a dress, wondering about a man who talked about killing people. She said, "Are you always this detached?" And thought of him in the squad room. "No, you're not. But you don't seem interested."

"I'm used to working from some kind of possible motive, and I don't see it," Bryan said. "Why would he kill Curtis Moore?"

Angela moved to the chair by the balcony and sat down, erect, knees together, as though practicing. She said, "You discussed it with him in the abstract, didn't you? When he talks about killing people, does he show any kind of emotion? Does he get excited?"

"He rationalizes. But when you begin with bullshit the conclusion you reach is still bullshit."

They were dressing to meet Robbie at the Everglades Club for cocktails and dinner. Angela had brought one dress, the beige wraparound cotton knit she wore. She wondered if it was dressy enough for the Everglades and had asked Bryan several times if he thought the neckline was all right. He'd said, "If you hold rich people somewhere below you, how're they gonna see down your dress?" She'd said she was asking what *he* thought, not anyone else, and made him feel like a smart-ass.

She would sit stiffly erect now, then bend forward from the waist, testing her moves as Bryan got into his dark blue Sunday suit.

"Did Curtis Moore come up at all?"

"No, but that's an idea," Bryan said. "Offer Curtis as a guy you'd like to shoot if someone hadn't already. See if he lights up."

"Would we be meeting him tonight if you weren't a cop?"

That was a good question. Or, would they have been invited? He sidestepped it and said. "I thought you want to see the Everglades Club."

"I do," Angela said. "How about when I bend over?"

"Nice . . . You don't have a bra on."

"Sure I do. See? But there's not much to it."

He said, "We've got a little time, haven't we?"

She said, "Now wait a minute. You know how long it took to get this pinned?"

He said, "We sound like we're married."

They looked at each other and then looked away. But there it was.

Walter got back to the house at ten minutes to seven, looked around and found Daniels out on the patio, all dressed up in a tan suit and red-striped tie, like he was going out. Except he was reading a book. Walter started his report: "You know how many Rolls—" But Daniels raised his hand, not looking up from the book. Walter had to wait for Mr. Cool to finish the page and bend the corner over.

"Now then."

"You said the guy had a Rolls. You know how many fucking Rolls are parked out at Seminole?"

"I told you it was a dark blue sedan."

"Well, it turned light tan since you seen it."

"Walter, did you follow him or not?"

"Yeah, I followed him. He went down to Hillsboro. That area there before you get to the inlet where you can't see the houses? It's all trees. He turned into a drive. I parked down a ways, came back. It's a big house made of like shingles. Right on the beach but back, you know? With all these sea-grape trees around it."

"Hillsboro." Daniels seemed mildly surprised, then pleased. "Go on."

"He picked up a broad. Skinny, but with great big ones, stuck out to here."

"How old?"

"Young broad, early twenties. Reddish hair with gunk around her eyes. Had on a lavender dress with little straps."

"What kind of shoes?"

"Sandals, like wedgies."

"Just testing you, Walter." Robbie was in a good mood now.

"They got in the Rolls, took Sample Road over to the Interstate and went down to Miami, all the way to the end. Got off in Coconut Grove, that area there and drove over to a high rise on Brickel Avenue just north of the Key Biscayne Causeway. The place's got not only a fence around it, it's got bob wire on top the fence and a sign says beware of guard dogs. Fucking Miami, I'm telling you, the fucking natives're taking over."

"Between Brickel and Bay Shore," Robbie said. "You know what you can see from the penthouse of that condominium looking east?"

"I imagine you can see the whole bay," Walter said.

"Yeah, but in particular," Robbie said, "from twenty-six floors up you've got a clear shot of Government Cut."

"Yeah, I imagine you would."

"And the Coast Guard base."

"Now you're talking," Walter said, raising an arm as though he were making a muscle and pulled his shirt out from his armpit. "I was wondering what we're playing here. So the guy likes to watch the Coast Guard boats and he's not with the DEA, I know that, driving a fucking Rolls. So what's he handle, weed?"

"He doesn't *handle* anything," Robbie said. "He arranges for the importation of marijuana and cocaine, staying well above the action, and makes approximately, part time, two hundred thousand dollars a month . . . when he isn't inspecting embassies."

Walter said, "Wait. This is the same kid we been talking about? The kid sitting on the old man's lap with the Knights of Columbus outfit on only grown up now?"

Robbie paused, deadpan. He said, "Amazing," staring at Walter. "I'm the only person in the world would have any idea what you just said. To answer your question, yes, it's the same kid on the guy's lap with the Knights of Columbus outfit only grown up now."

"I think it was, with the Knights of Columbus outfit *on*. You left out *on*," Walter said and thought, Fuck you, too . . .

"Walter, why don't you sit down."

"Yeah, I think I will. Thanks."

"Okay. He went up to the penthouse, stayed about a half-hour. Right?"

"You followed him before?"

"Many times. Go on."

"He was in the building twenty-three minutes," Walter said. "The broad waited in the car . . . This kid comes along—listen to this. This kid comes along looking for his dog. He's calling, 'Here, Piper! Here, Piper!' "

Robbie stared at Walter.

"The kid goes up the street. In a couple minutes here's this dog, this little white scottie comes along. The broad sees it, she opens the door, goes 'Here, Piper!' The dog hops in the car and she starts playing with it. The guy comes out, gets in the car—now you could see *him* petting the dog, playing with it. The broad goes to open her door, too late, he drives off, the dog's still in the car. The dog's got this little red collar on, you know, with the license hanging on it? Probably has the name and address. No, the guy drives off. He don't care if the dog belongs to the kid and it's gonna break the kid's heart, fuck no, take it. They drive off with the dog."

Robbie waited, making sure there was no more to the story. He said, "Walter?"

"Yeah?"

"Then where'd they go?"

"They went back up to Hillsboro, the broad's place."

"How do you know it's hers?"

"I call the Broward County sheriff."

"Walter, don't tell me that—"

"Mr. Daniels, what was I doing the past twenty-one years? I identify myself as an officer with Palm Beach County, give 'em a phony name, a badge number they don't know from shit and ask 'em to look up in their directory who lives at the address in question. I talk to a clerk, it took maybe a minute and a half." Walter dug into his back pocket, brought out a notebook that was limp, curved to fit his hip; he opened it, licked his thumb to turn a few pages and said, 3524 Ocean Drive. The deed to the property and the lots on both sides are registered in the name of Doris Marie Vaughn.

Robbie said, "*Dorie?*" Amazed. "She's a polo groupie."

Walter said, "I don't know what she does for a living, but she's got dough. That property in there with the lots'd be worth a couple million."

"Jesus," Robbie said, "Dorie Vaughn. Well, you know what he's doing, what he's using the house for."

"I got a pretty good idea what he's doing when I left," Walter said. "Even with the gunk on her eyes, that's a tasty broad."

"She's a good kid, but flaky."

"Well, nobody says you got to talk to 'em."

"I want to see the house," Robbie said.

"I thought—you're all dressed up you're going out."

"I've been waiting a long time for this kind of a setup," Robbie said. "Jesus, Hillsboro. It's perfect. Come on, I want to see the house."

Walter said, "I hope she knows how to take care of Piper. Knows what she's doing."

Robbie paused getting up from the chair, hands clamped on the arms. "Who?"

"Who we been talking about?" Walter said. "The broad."

Angela thought of an image. The tourists stroll past the expensive Worth Avenue shops. Near the end of the street they see any ordinary entrance gate, no sign, a pink facade, the unadorned back of a building. The tourists barely notice it. But its the rear end of the Everglades, one of the world's most exclusive clubs. And Worth Avenue is the *alley* that runs behind it.

"I thought of it coming in," Angela said.

Bryan said, "Then what happens?"

"Boy, are you a smart-ass."

"No, I think you should write your rich people's book. Get it out of your system."

"If I can do it without the usual knee-jerk attitude. It would have to be straight impressions without cute asides. And no adverbs." Speaking as her eyes wandered.

"You'd better close your mouth then, quit staring."

"I'm not staring."

He watched her gaze slide over the lounge that was like a formal living room. They sat in upholstered chairs, their drinks on a glass-top cocktail table.

"You are now."

She said, "My God. You know who that is?" Nodding to point. "The three ladies sitting together."

"That's all're in here. It's like a woman's club."

"The one with the pearls. That's Mary Sanford. Very close friend of Rose Kennedy. If you're putting on a charity you'd better have Mary Sanford or you're dead. I hear she's nice though."

"Are you from a big family?"

"Two sisters and two brothers. All older."

"And you had to wear your sisters' hand-me-downs."

"For about ten years. How'd you know that? . . . Damn it, I should've brought a copy of the *Social Pictorial*. Or the *Shiny Sheet*. The one's Mary Sanford. And I think the one next to her is Anky Johnson. That's Revlon money. But she usually wears a turban."

Bryan said, "How come you don't see any guys here?"

Angela's gaze began to move again, inching over the lounge. "They're all dead. Or they're upstairs playing dominoes. Or both . . . I hope we eat in the Orange Garden. I mean dine. That's *the* room here."

"We're gonna eat at McDonald's if Smiley doesn't show up."

"He's always late."

"Well, I read one time, a prompt man is a lonely man," Bryan said, "and it's true." He sipped his Wild Turkey. When they came in and sat down he was going to order their favorite, Jack Daniels, but he had said to the waiter, "While we're waiting for Mr. Daniels we'll have—" and paused awkwardly and changed the brand. Not wanting to call attention to himself. The homicide cop trying to act as though he belonged. Angela hadn't noticed.

She said, "Oh, my God," in a hushed tone. Then, without moving her mouth: "The one in pink, just coming in. The middle-aged Barbie doll. That's Robbie's wife. With the bald-headed guy with the white hair. And you know what? Robbie won't think a thing of it."

Bryan said, "The wild-west jacket and the hair, the guy looks like Buffalo Bill. I understand he's a count."

"He is? How do you know?"

Got her. "You hear things," Bryan said. "But how

come, if his wife's here he doesn't know it?" He thought of his former wife, Peggy.

"Because," Angela said, "as Robbie puts it, 'Patti and I do our own thing.'"

"Why are they married?"

"Because it's too much trouble to get a divorce. Split up the fortune. If they can both do what they want, why bother? One of his girl friends—here's an example, a girl who thought he was serious about her came to the house one night. She got right to the point with Patti. 'When're you gonna give him a divorce?' Patti doesn't even know who she is. They go in and confront Robbie. He looks up from his book and says, 'Don't get *me* involved in this . . .'"

He thought of Peggy again. "My wife—I mean my former wife called last week . . ."

But Angela was watching the proceedings. "Now they're paying their respects to Mary Sanford Telling her how wonderful it is to see her. Little hand-kissing there . . . Gushing now, it's always good to gush a little."

"You better not write the book," Bryan said. Then said, "Does Robbie have a girl friend now?"

"I don't know. He picks girls up." Angela thought of something and looked at him now. "It's funny, he talks about it, but he's not what you'd call a dedicated chaser."

"Maybe he likes guns better," Bryan said.

Robbie came out of the trees to the dead-end access road where Walter was waiting by the car, its front end pointing toward the beach, the silver Rolls ghostly in the early darkness.

Walter said, "He still there?" The words came louder than he'd expected and he half-whispered, "In the house?"

"His car's still there," Robbie said.

"You didn't look in a window?"

"When I get that close," Robbie said, "it's gonna be done. But we're not quite ready yet. Two things. I want pictures of the place—"

"What kinda pictures?"

"I'll show you the camera when we get home. I want movies. And I want you to watch the place for a few days. If he's bringing stuff in and out, and I'm sure he is, then I want to hit him when the stuff's here. You understand what I'm getting at?"

"You want the place put under one-man surveillance for a few days you say," Walter said. "*I* understand what you mean, but I don't think you do, if you don't mind my saying. The fuck'm I suppose to do, I camp here twenty-four hours? Who relieves me? Right now a squad car comes along, we're parked here in the fucking trees, two guys, the first thing they think of, somebody's copping somebody's joint. This whole area, any place you got houses worth a million bucks you got more security'n in a fucking bank, and I'm not kidding."

Robbie said, "Walter, look at the house."

"I think I saw it closer'n you did."

"I mean—consider where it is. You can barely see it, even from the beach. Empty lots on both sides full of trees. You come out the driveway and walk across the road, there's the Intracoastal right there, almost in your backyard. And a dock. You notice the dock?"

"Yeah, I notice the dock?"

"Now we know little Doric Vaughn didn't buy the house."

"All I know it's in her name."

"Walter," Robbie said, "a guy who makes two hundred thousand dollars a month on the side bought the house. Because it's exactly the house he wanted. He can take deliveries in front, right out of the ocean. Or he can come out the back door and pick up something left on his dock. A little watertight package that's worth around a million bucks. But *he* doesn't pick it up, the girl does; she's got to be good for something. Then, I'll bet you anything, you see a yellow van stop by the house. The same van you'll see down in Coconut Grove. The same guy driving it who lives in that high rise on Brickel Avenue. It's all coming together, Walter. All the work I've been doing on this project is finally paying off. But now we get to the tricky part. I don't want to have to buy some stuff and plant it on him. Christ, not when he's dealing in it. I want to get him, ideally, when he's in the house and there's a delivery sitting there. The police get an anonymous call, they find the son of a bitch, he's dead and it's obviously a dope-related hit. That's the way I want it to work and that's why I brought you in, Walter. Because you're a pro. You've forgotten more about surveillance than I could ever learn."

"Yeah, well I know surveillance," Walter said, "I've been on enough stakeouts in my life I should. But you got other people around here working not exactly surveillance but close to it. Security."

"Who, the police?"

"The police."

"Walter," Robbie said, "if you can buy a house, pick out a house and buy it because it's ideally situated for what you're doing—no matter what it costs—then, Walter, you can buy any fucking thing you want. Including police. A couple a bills a week to see that no Haitians break in . . . and not see anything else."

Walter rubbed his hand over his jaw. "You're talking about a lot of surveillance."

"Bring a cooler of beer and a pack of Camels." Robbie winked in the darkness. "Come on. I'm late."

They were on their third drink. Wild Turkey over ice.

Angela said, "Having fun at the club?"

Bryan didn't answer and they were both silent for at least a full minute, comfortable together if not with the waiting, neither good at small talk so not trying too hard.

"Would you rather belong here or Seminole?"

"If I had to play the same course every day, Seminole," Bryan said. "I like the macaroni and cheese."

"Did you try the gingersnaps?"

"I've never been in a locker room before where they serve cookies. Palmer Park doesn't have a locker room. You finish a round in the evening you walk across Woodward and have a drink with the hookers. Seminole, you talk about real estate."

"I told you."

"I met one guy who doesn't fit the mold. Chichi Fuentes. I figured he was either a golf pro, a gigolo or an orchestra leader."

"I know him," Angela said. "In fact, if I do the book Chichi said he'll give me all kinds of trivia, for color. He knows everybody and everything that's going on in Palm Beach."

"He didn't seem to know Smiley."

Angela stared at him.

"Your mouth's open again."

"I just had a thought." One that seemed to disturb her. "What did Robbie say about him?"

"Nothing."

"He didn't tell you anything? Who he is?"

"No, but Chichi told Smiley a few things about his wife. That's why I know the bald-headed guy with long hair's a count. A Polish count."

"Chichi," Angela said, hunching closer, "is an international playboy from the Dominican Republic. You see him in *W* all the time."

"Wow," Bryan said.

"Listen. I'm serious. You remember Trujillo?"

"He was a dictator. Kind of a fat guy."

"God and Trujillo, that was his motto," Angela said. "Supreme ruler of the Dominican Republic for about thirty years, until he was finally assassinated in, I think, '61. Well, Chichi's one of Trujillo's illegitimate sons. He married a sugarcane heiress first, then a very rich American woman and then an Italian movie actress. Women adore him."

"Why?"

"Because he's charming. He's a lover." She groped and came up with another one. "He knows what women like."

"Did you read that or did he tell you himself?"

"Bryan—he's rich. He plays polo. He used to drive sports cars. He's held diplomatic posts all over the world. Chargé d'affaires in Paris, a lot of places. In fact, right now he's inspector of embassies for the Dominican Republic . . . I'm *serious*. He's single . . . probably the most eligible bachelor in Palm Beach."

"Robbie doesn't like him."

"You know why? Robbie would like to *be* him."

"Or George Hamilton. What else does he do?"

"Well, he's broken up a few marriages, once was named corespondent of the year. Let's see—over like a three-year period he collected seventy-seven parking tickets in Palm Beach County and was stopped something like twenty times for speeding. My friend at the *Post* did a story about it, how Chichi flaunts his diplomatic immunity and tears up tickets." Angela paused, thoughtful. "There was something else," she said and paused again and began to nod.

Bryan watched her, used to waiting for answers.

"Yeah—he was called before a Dade County grand jury that had something to do with dope-related murders, I think in Miami. I read it when I was researching him, but I don't remember when it was."

"What happened?"

"He refused to waive immunity, so they couldn't talk to him."

"They didn't ask him to leave the country?"

"I don't think they wanted to indict him. Chichi was called as a witness. He had business dealings, I think, with whoever it was they were after."

"Maybe he's a high-class smuggler," Bryan said. "Uses his diplomatic pouch."

"Cheech? I doubt it. He doesn't need money."

"How do you know?"

Angela didn't answer.

"At the club, the first thing Robbie said to him was how's the coke business?"

"He did?"

"Then at his house," Bryan said, "we're playing his game, who would you like to shoot? Robbie goes, well, there's Carlos the terrorist. Maybe someday. And then he said, 'But a more realistic one might be—' and paused like he had to think of one before it came to him— 'How about a big-time dope dealer? Somebody who's messing up people's lives and the law can't touch him.' "

"I can't see Chichi as a dealer," Angela said. "He's the great seducer. He told me he hasn't slept alone since he was fourteen years old."

"Maybe he's afraid of the dark."

"I can't see him bothering with something like that, smuggling. He's not the type."

"Maybe not," Bryan said. "But Robbie didn't offer the drug dealer as an example. I think the idea appeals to him. Somebody bad who's close by."

Angela said, "Does Chichi look like a bad guy to you?"

Bryan said, "Does Robbie? . . . When I first mentioned Chichi you got a funny look on your face and you said, 'I just had a thought . . . ' "

"I wasn't thinking about dope."

"No, it was before we got into that."

"Oh—" Angela came alive. "You said he didn't seem to

know Robbie and I thought—right away I thought, what if Chichi's the one he wants to kill?"

"Why would he?"

"That's the trouble, the motive's so flimsy—"

"Because he doesn't like him?"

"Sort of, but more because Chichi never remembers Robbie's name," Angela said. "Does that sound dumb?"

Ruth May Hayes, thirty-seven, was tied by the neck to the rear bumper of her boyfriend's car and dragged in circles over a field until she was dead. Robert Jackson, thirty-four, and James Pope, thirty-five, died in a gunfight that developed when Jackson put his cigarette out in a clean ashtray. Sam James, thirty-five, told his wife their twelve-year-old daughter's shorts were too tight; an argument followed and James was stabbed to death. Paul Struggs, twenty-nine, was shot to death by his girl friend. Richard Scott, twenty-three, was shaking hands with people he'd been arguing with at a party when someone struck him from behind with a baseball bat and killed him. Myros Cato, forty-seven, was shot to death by his wife following an argument. James Ware, sixty-five, was shot to death by his son, a psychiatric patient at Veterans Hospital. Charles Roby, thirty-two, got in an argument with his girl friend over a pack of cigarettes and she stabbed him to death. Gloria Glass, fifty, told James Lindsey, fifty-six, they were through; Lindsey shot and killed her. Betty Goodlow, thirty-two, was beaten, doused with paint thinner and set on fire by her boyfriend. Michael Kirby, twenty-five, got into an argument with the babysitter, who stabbed him in the head, then shot him with a rifle. Geraldine Phillips, thirty-five, told her boyfriend she was going to jog around the block; he became enraged and stabbed her to death. Marvin Rife, nineteen, was throwing bottles at a neighbor's house when the neighbor came out with a shotgun and killed him. Benny Vann, forty-one, was shot to death by his girl friend because he'd dated her sister. Larry Young, sixteen, pulled a toy gun on his friend and said, boom; his friend, twenty-three, pulled a real gun and killed him. George Peterson, fifty-one, came out of a bar and mistakenly got in someone else's car; he was pulled out by the car's owner, identity unknown, and kicked to death. Cecil Castner, twenty-five, swiped at Delois Tanksley, twenty-one, with a knife; she hit him with a chair, got a handgun from the bedroom and shot him in the back of the head; she was convicted of careless use of a firearm resulting in death and drew eighteen months probation. Joseph Vennie, fifty-five, was angry when L. C. Ford, forty, locked out of his car, woke Vennie up and asked him for a coat hanger; Vennie struck Ford over the head with a gun; Ford took the gun away from him and killed him with it.

There were approximately six hundred seventy additional homicides, not unlike these, that had taken place in the Detroit area during the past year and were familiar stories to Bryan Hurd.

He said to Angela, "I can tell you how people kill each other and sometimes why and you tell me if any of the motives make sense."

She said, "So it doesn't matter if the reason sounds weird."

He said, "To tell you the truth, killing someone who doesn't remember your name makes more sense than most."

She said, "What do we do now?"

He said, "Let's get out of here and have a Jack Daniels someplace."

THIRTEEN

BRYAN MADE PHONE calls most of the morning with the yellow pages open in front of him and by two that afternoon they had moved from the Holiday Inn in Palm Beach Gardens to the Villas Atlantis in Lake Worth, on the beach and only about five miles south of Robbie's home on South Ocean Boulevard.

"I didn't come thirteen hundred miles to sit by a swimming pool," Bryan said. "I like the ocean."

Angela said, "Uh-huh." She was sure they'd moved to be closer to the action, to keep an eye on Robbie.

Except that Bryan didn't contact Robbie. He wasn't kidding, he sat on the beach. He did make phone calls home from their Atlantis villa that was actually an efficiency and talked to Annie Maguire or Malik, keeping in touch. But most of the time for the next two days he was out there in the sun with his *National Geographics*. He told Angela interesting facts about owls, kelp life and jackals.

She said, "Nobody even knows we're here."

He said, "Good."

"Aren't you gonna *do* something?"

Bryan said, "You asked me—I told you I was going to Florida to sit on the beach and read and you asked me if I read mysteries? I said no. I don't read mysteries for the same reason I don't involve myself in homicide investigations when I'm on furlough. That's the whole idea of a furlough. Get away from it."

"But if you know someone's gonna get killed . . ."

Bryan said, "I know of, I bet, five hundred people in Detroit who could very likely kill each other or somebody else in the near future. I don't know how to prevent homicides. I go in after and clean up."

She said, "At least tell him you know what he's doing."

"Who, Robbie? He told *me*."

"Then we should tell Chichi . . . *some*thing."

"If he's in drugs he's watching his ass very carefully. You don't have to tell him a thing."

"But we don't know he is, for sure."

Bryan closed the *National Geographic*, got up from his beach chair, went into Villa Number 16, the third one back from the beach in the line of cement bungalows and made a phone call while Angela stood watching him in her red bikini and he watched Angela. He called young Gary Hammond of the Palm Beach Police.

Angela could hear the sound of Gary's voice but not what he was saying. When Bryan hung up she pounced on him. "What did he say?"

"Wait."

They had a glass of orange juice in the air-conditioned efficiency. Gary Hammond called back and Bryan listened; he said uh-huh several times, he asked Gary how he was doing, asked what was a good place to eat on a cop's pay, said great, I appreciate it and hung up.

He said to Angela, still waiting, "Chichi's the source for the Palm Beach crowd, the swingers who've moved up from Cuba Libres to just plain coke. He passes out weed gratis. He's small potatoes locally but a name in Miami. He's sort of an importer-broker. He doesn't deal directly, he makes phone calls and goes to Bogotá or Santa Marta a few times a year. And because he's in the diplomatic corps they can't touch him."

"Exactly the guy," Angela said, "that Robbie proposed to you. The untouchable asshole, the ideal target." She was silent for several moments, thoughtful. "You know what? I'm doing the wrong story."

Bryan watched her move to the closet now and come out with white pants that were like string-tied pajama bottoms and a T-shirt.

"Where you going?"

"Do some research," Angela said.

Walter spent the first day thrashing around in the scrub without getting even a glimpse of Chichi Fuentes. Hotter'n a son of a bitch in there. He could hardly breathe. Trying to swat bugs and work the goddamn Jap camera, the goddamn equipment, the videotape recorder and the battery pack, hanging by straps around his neck, either strangling him or banging his knees or getting tangled up in the brush.

"That's right, I forgot to tell you," Robbie said. "Afternoons Chichi's either at Seminole or Palm Beach Polo in Wellington." He said, "Sorry about that, Walter."

Walter said, "You know how many different kinds of bugs're in there, just counting the fuckers you can see and maybe you can kill if you're fast enough?"

"How many?" Robbie said. "No, I'm kidding, Walter. I'm sure you're doing a hell of a job. You do have something on the tapes though, don't you?"

"Yeah, I got him, finally. I got something else too."

"What?"

"Let me wash up, put something on these bites. My wife's got some stuff—she's always getting bit. I don't know why—I mean I don't know how a bug'd land on her, Jesus, and want to take a bite. Or maybe there're more bugs over in West Palm than come to the beach."

"I'll give you something," Robbie said. "Come up to the study."

He had the ointment sitting on the bar next to an ice-cold vodka and tonic with fresh lime. Walter came in and drank it down. Walked in wearing a clean shirt, new Bermudas that covered his knees, new sandals made of straps and buckles and brass rings that couldn't be much lighter than combat boots, put that frosted glass to his mouth and didn't take it down till he was sucking air. Robbie made him another one while Walter dabbed ointment on his arms and legs and they were ready.

"Showtime," Robbie said, sitting down before the television console. Walter remained at the bar, the bottle of vodka handy.

The picture came on.

"Okay, there's the house from the north side," Walter narrated. "Notice there's no doors. The only doors're in the front and in the back . . . Okay, there's the dock . . . Boat going by on the Intracoastal . . . Another boat . . . There's one going the other way . . . Okay, this is approaching the house from the other side. Notice, as I said, there's no doors."

Robbie said, "Christ, Walter, it's a four-thousand-dollar camera. Couldn't you hold it a little steadier?"

Walter said, "You try it. The fucker sitting up there on your shoulder."

"I gave you a tripod."

"How'm I gonna use a tripod? I get set I got to move. I look like those assholes on eyewitness news except I'm in a fucking jungle, fucking bugs eating me up, the VCR, the battery pack, the fucking cables—try lugging all that shit around and hold the fucking camera still."

"That the patio?"

"Okay, that's the patio. That's—see, there's Piper over there chasing something. Look, driving him crazy. Probably the fucking bugs . . . Okay, here she comes. Bugs don't bother this broad."

"Dorie," Robbie said. "Very nice tan. Well, hey . . ."

"Hang onto your pecker," Walter said, "the show's just starting . . . Takes the top off . . . You ever see anything like that in your life? Defy the laws of fucking gravity. Look at that . . ."

"No tan lines," Robbie said.

"You aren't kidding no tan lines," Walter said. "Now, hooks her thumbs in there . . . You got any music? We should have some music go with this. Boom. Da-da da-boom. Off comes the little panties. Look at that, the red hair and the black bush. She could have quails in there, hiding."

"Hasn't started to sag yet," Robbie said.

"That's how you tell if a broad dyes her hair, look at her bush."

Robbie said, "Is that right?"

"What I can't figure out," Walter said, "the fuck she put the bathing suit on for she's gonna come outside and take it off?"

"Why didn't you zoom in?"

"I zoomed. You think I didn't zoom, for Christ sake? Wait up. I almost zoomed out of the woods and jumped her . . . There's your zoom."

"Very tight."

"How would you know?"

"Your zoom . . . You're pretty steady now, Walter. You're getting better."

"You bet your ass I'm steady. I got it homed in now.

Locked. You'd have to break my arms. That broad can't move, I'm on her. Look at that, scratching her puss . . . Now she gets on the lounge. I kept thinking, like trying to give her mental telepathy, roll over, roll over, you don't want to burn your buns."

"What's this?"

"We're in the woods again. I heard a car so I moved a little toward the back of the house . . . Okay, there's his Rolls Royce. You notice it's light tan? The Datsun Z's the broad's. Okay, the guy's already inside."

"Chichi?"

"Yeah, it's about five o'clock now. But the day before it was closer to six."

"What's he do when he comes?"

"The fuck you think he does? . . . Now we're in the woods again . . . Coming out . . . I'm almost on the beach now. Notice the level, I'm practically lying down."

"There he is."

"Yeah, he comes out on the patio. See Piper? . . . Look at that, runs over to him . . . The broad rolls over . . . there she is, her puss winking at the guy he's playing with the fucking dog. I like dogs, don't get me wrong, but Jesus Christ . . . Now they're chatting. You have a hard day at the office, dear? About right there I had something hard I could've showed her . . . Playing with the dog again. Hi, Mr. Piper. You're a good little doggie, aren't you? You miss Coconut Grove and your little friend? Tough shit. Now they're looking out at the ocean. I thought maybe something was gonna happen here . . . There, shot of the ocean. Nothing. Back to the show . . . Broad gets up, stretches, he goes right on talking. Stands there like a pimp. I mean he doesn't even *touch* her."

"That's about what he is," Robbie said, "a pimp. He uses women."

"Well," Walter said, "if you use 'em for the right thing and they like it, that's different. She bends over now to pick up the suit. Look at that. Taking my picture with her brownie . . . They bullshit for a minute or so and go in the house. That's it. Beginning of the next tape'll show him coming out with the broad about twenty minutes later, then some more boats going by. No boats stopping, no yellow van."

Robbie didn't move, staring at the empty television screen.

"You want to see it again?"

"I think so," Robbie said with a thoughtful tone. "I want to study the layout a little closer."

"I know what you want to study," Walter said. "But hey, it's okay with me. You're the boss, Mr. Daniels."

Angela believed the shiny brown thing that had run out of the bathroom was a palmetto bug. Bryan told her she didn't want to think of it as a roach because of the connotation, but that's what it was, a cockroach.

They were in the Buick Century driving north into Palm Beach; seven-thirty and still bright, though the sun was gone, off somewhere behind condominiums.

"It was probably a German cockroach," Bryan said, "but it could've been a Madeira. They're both that shiny light brown. They'll eat anything, soap, paper   glue. I saw two of them when I went in there to take my shower. I thought it was one long one at first, but they were like butt to butt. I think they were getting it on."

"Palmetto bugs fly," Anglea said, bringing it up from some early recollection.

But no match for Bryan. "A lot of different species have wings, they're still cockroaches."

"I like your owl facts better."

"Roaches're ugly but you got to admit they're quick," Bryan said. "You know how quick an American cockroach is?"

"You're gonna tell me anyway," Angela said.

"An American cockroach—you roll up a newspaper and try and hit him with it, the American cockroach can take off in fifty-four thousandths of a second."

"Almost as quick as Chichi Fuentes," Angela said.

"So you didn't just buy a new dress today. Where's the place we met Gary?"

"Go up Royal Palm to County and turn right. It's on Poinciana."

"I'm glad you know your way around."

"That's not all I know," Angela said.

They sat back of the hedgerow, outside but in shade, among the tourists in their resort outfits, everyone drinking, finished with one part of the day and beginning the fun time. Bryan said, "You see cowboy hats all over now, don't you?" Angela told him the polo crowd was gradually going western; you saw cowboy hats at Wellington, even more at Royal Palm and Gulfstream. He told her he missed her today. She looked at him with her warm glow and said, "Did you, really?" He said, "I miss you when you leave the room to go to the bathroom."

She said, "When you were reading about roaches, was there anything in there about the Santo Domingo variety La Cucaracha Fuentes? I'm finding out what a beauty he is."

They sipped bourbon collinses from tall frosted glasses, Bryan in a blue-orange-yellow Hawaiian shirt, playing the role of tourist, enjoying it; Angela crisp in a white linen sundress, brand new, more conscious of an image.

"He procures girls for stag parties on yachts."

"I was in Vice," Bryan said, "but I never raided a yacht. I hung out mostly in public toilets."

"You're in Palm Beach now, boy," Angela said. "The toilets are Italian marble and Chichi will get you anything you want for a price. I talked to my friend at the *Post* and he sat me down with a society writer who's got a chart of who's sleeping with whom plus a list of the young single girls. The ones that come up from the minors and hang out at the polo clubs and the *in* bars. Chichi is hot right now for a girl named Dorie Vaughn. He's supposed to have her set up in a house somewhere."

"You mean a whorehouse?"

"No, for privacy, to get away. She's not in the phone book. I checked the County Clerk's Office and there's nothing registered in her name, so I tried Broward County. Drove all the way down to Lauderdale and what do you know? Dorie Vaughn has a home in Hillsboro."

"Where did that get you?"

"To Hillsboro, where do you think. I drove past and took a peek, just from the driveway. Little Dorie's got a place that's worth at least a million, maybe more."

Bryan said, "I mean where does it get you in the end? You know the guy's in dope. What else you want to know?"

Angela said, "I want to know about the scene here. I want to know if rich people get high like everyone else."

"Talk to the feds, they'll give you all the information you want."

"I don't want facts, Bryan, I want color. I want to get next to Chichi and get him to tell me some stories."

"I think you should stick to your rich people's book."

"Should," Angela said. "Do you say *should* a lot? I hadn't noticed."

"I don't know, but I think we should eat," Bryan said, "before I take a bite out of you."

They drove to Chuck's Bar-B-Que Pit on Federal Highway, a place Gary Hammond had recommended, where the light fixtures were wagon wheels and Charlie Russell prints hung on the walls. Angela said, "Oh, my God—never ask a cop where to eat." But it wasn't bad. They had ribs and a pitcher of beer in the rustic lounge and would remember Linda Ronstadt singing "It's So Easy to Fall in Love."

Bryan saw familiar cowboy hats come in. Two of them. The same two that had walked past the sidewalk cafe and eyed them.

Angela said, "Why don't you want me to do one on drugs?"

"It's been done."

"What hasn't? If cockroaches've been done, everything has."

The two cowboys came to the table that was between the bar and the booth where Angela sat close to Bryan, eating ribs with her fingers, busy talking and not worrying about her new white sundress. The two cowboys made a production of standing at the table and surveying the room, their gaze coming around to Bryan and Angela before they eased down and drew chairs up for their boots. Their big scoop-brim cowboy hats remained squared over their eyes. Angela was saying it was the point of view that was important; you could still make it interesting with a fresh slant. The two cowboys were telling the waitress they wanted a pitcher of beer.

Bryan felt tired. He asked Angela if she'd bought her new dress on Worth Avenue.

She said, are you kidding? She said the idea would be to describe the traditional Palm Beach setting, the island of conservatism, the last bastion of Old Guard ideas, beginning to gently sway to a new wave, the groovy Young Guard making its move.

"Cowboys at the polo clubs," Bryan said.

"Exactly. That's one indication. A shit-kicker informality seeping in."

Both scoop-brim hats were funneled this way. One of the cowboys said, "What did she say?"

Bryan said, "Where else did you go today?"

"Well, I had lunch at Two Sixty Four, very lively place, with my newspaper friend and the society writer. She works for the *Shiny Sheet*."

"And you were discussing Chichi . . . "

"Yeah. I told you that. Then I stopped by his apartment—it's at the corner of Worth and South Ocean Boulevard, the ultraexclusive condominium. But he wasn't home. The doorman said he was playing golf."

"You talk to the doorman a while?"

"For a couple of minutes. Doormen like to gossip."

"You asked him a few leading questions."

"A few."

There you are, Bryan thought. She talked to Chichi's doorman and the doorman picked up the phone and called somebody. His fingers were greasy. He glanced up to catch the waitress, get some clean napkins and took a look at the two cowboys staring at them: giving them their tough-hombre movie-cowboy stares that wouldn't have been worth shit without the big hats. They were both in their twenties, shirts open, straggly hair coming out of their hats. Not powerfully built young men—thank God—but that dirty mean type Bryan had been sending to Jackson for the past sixteen years. He would bet they had put in some hard time at Raiford or maybe a federal lockup. They wore pass-the-time tattoos on their arms, the coarse designs of prison artists.

One of them said, "Hey, lady . . . "

And Bryan thought, Here we go.

Angela was saying, "You have to be excited about what you're doing. If you don't have enthusiasm then your words are gonna just sit there. That's the problem I was getting into with Robbie. My angle was flat."

"Hey, lady, what're you doing with that old fart?"

Bryan looked at them now straight on. He might as well.

Angela said, "What? Are you talking to me?"

"You aren't married to him, are you?"

"Shit, he's too old for'r," the other one said. "Come on over here, talk to us."

Angela said, "Are you serious?"

Bryan liked her tone: quiet, matter-of-fact, but with a put-down edge to it.

The one cowboy raised and recrossed his run-down boots on the chair in front of him. He said, "What you want an old fart like him for? Can't even get it up."

"I like old farts," Angela said, a little more tense. "Leave us alone."

"My, my, my, my," the first cowboy said. "you got a tongue, haven't you? Stick it out, let's see it."

The other cowboy said, "I got something she can tongue."

The first cowboy said, "What's the matter with your old man? He don't say nothing . . . Mister, you mind we take your girl out the van? You stay here, drink your beer."

Bryan edged out of the booth to stand up. He felt Angela's hand touch his arm.

"Bryan . . ."

"It's all right."

"*Bry*-an? That your name?" They thought it was pretty funny.

The second cowboy said, "Oh, Bry-an, Bry-an . . . Where you going, Bryan? You nervous, gonna go take a piss?"

"He's gonna complain to the management," the first cowboy said. "We ain't doing nothing."

Angela watched the Hawaiian shirt cross to the hallway where a sign read *Rest Rooms * Telephone*. The two cowboys stared at her now. She looked past them. Bryan was gone. The waitress came over with napkins; she said, "Will there be anything else?" Angela told her no, just the check, please. The two cowboys stared at her.

One of them said, "Who's the guy you're with?"

"I don't believe this," Angela said.

"Where you staying?" the same one said now. "We'll come visit . . . You like weed? What do you like? How 'bout ludes?" His tone was different: intimate, coaxing. "Get rid of the old man we'll see you later, have some fun."

Angela picked up a napkin and concentrated on wiping her hands.

"You tight with that fella? He don't look like he knows where it's at." A confiding tone. "Some guy you picked up? Girl, you can do way better'n that tourist. Where's he from—up north?"

The other one said, "He come down here in his motor home?"

Angela saw Bryan coming back now, taking his time. She watched him walk over to the waitress at the service section of the bar and stand there while she totaled their check. She watched him take money out and pay her, the waitress laughing at something he said as he waited for his change.

"Tell him you're going with us. What do you say?"

Bryan was coming from the bar. Angela couldn't believe it: he was carrying a pitcher of beer.

"You don't want to tell him don't say nothing, we just walk out. The fuck can he do about it?"

She watched him come past their table to the booth. One of them said, "Well, here's Bry-an back, Hey, Bry-an, you thirsty? He must be thirsty."

Bryan said to her, "I'll see you outside." When she hesitated he said, "It's okay, I'll be right out."

He turned and placed the pitcher of beer on the table between the two cowboys. She was out of the booth now. She heard one of them say, "What's this?" And the other one say, "Trying to suck up, so he don't get hurt." She walked away from the booth. She saw the waitress watching. The waitress and a couple at the bar with serious expressions. The juke box was playing a Willie Nelson piece, "On the Road Again." She looked back and saw Bryan standing above the two cowboys. He was watching and nodded to her. She continued on to the double-door entrance but that was as far as she was going. She saw Bryan turn to the two cowboys.

They were looking up at him with keen expressions at this point, curious, the fresh pitcher of beer between them.

Bryan said, "Can I sit down?" He took hold of the chair where crossed boots rested and pulled the chair out from under the boots, carefully, the cowboy having no choice but to lower his feet to the floor. Bryan said, "Thank you," and sat down.

In a pleasant, normal tone he said, "Fellas, I'm down here on my vacation . . . "

He looked at their showdown stares waiting, those big, sweaty hard-rider hats pointing straight at him and he started over.

He said, "Fellas, let me put it another way," still with the nice tone. "I don't want to see either of you cocksuckers in my sight ever again. I'm telling you the truth. If I do, I'm gonna kick the shit out of you, sign a complaint you tried to assault me or sell me a controlled substance. Then I'm gonna see you get sent back to wherever you got those ugly fucking tattoos." He paused before getting up. "Are we of one mind on this?"

Angela watched him leave the table and cross toward her. She saw the two cowboys looking at each other, starting to move. Bryan didn't look back. He reached her, put a hand on her arm. Willie was still singing. She would remember that and remember going out the door into soft evening light and seeing the gumball on top of the squad car turning without sound, Gary Hammond coming out of the car.

Bryan said to him, "You got a stick?"

Gary said, "I got a flashlight."

Bryan said, "Let me have it."

Gary reached into the squad car. He tossed the flashlight underhand, arching it flat, the chrome catching light. Bryan swiped it out of the air the way you catch a baton and turned to stand squarely before the entrance to Chuck's Bar-B-Que Pit.

Angela was next to the car in the first parking place, looking at the back of Bryan's Hawaiian shirt. She saw one of the double doors bang open and saw Bryan step in and sidearm the flashlight at the first one out, slamming it into him to send his big hat flying and the cowboy stumbling back, grabbing hold of his head. She saw Bryan swipe the other one across the face and saw the flashlight come apart, batteries spilling out. She saw the two cowboys as though they were dancing, the one trying to hold up the one with blood on his face. Gary Hammond came past her, looking at Bryan cop-to-cop, asking no questions, a hand behind him working the cuffs from the back of his belt.

Bryan said, "It's okay. It was a misunderstanding." He said to the cowboys, "That's right, isn't it? You thought we were somebody else?"

They sat in the rented Buick and watched the yellow van pull out onto Federal Highway followed by the squad car. Angela let her breath out in a sigh. Bryan lighted a cigarette and handed it to her.

She said, "You called Gary?"

"I had him radioed—talking fast." He said, "Did you learn anything?"

"I'm shaking."

"But did you learn anything?"

She said, "For a quiet evening, go out with cops."

He said, "I didn't bring them. When you ask questions about people in that business they want to know who you are, look you over."

That brought her eyes open wide. "Those two work for Chichi?"

"Or somebody close to him," Bryan said. He started the car. "If it was me I'd fire them, get somebody can do the job."

In the night she said, "Does everybody have another person inside them?"

They had both been awake for some time, though not speaking. He said, "What if you saw me shoot someone?" And turned to see her staring at a shape on the ceiling, a reflection of the window.

"I've pictured that. I can understand that. Having to shoot somebody," Angela said. She was silent then.

He said, "But hitting the Miami cowboys seemed what? Vicious, unnecessary."

She remained silent.

He said, "Maybe it wasn't necessary. But I thought it was. I had to give them a reason to stay away from you while I'm gone." He felt her turn to him. "I want them to think about it and take their time and by then I'll be back. Unless you want to go with me."

Her head turned on the pillow, looking at him. "You have to go home?"

"Annie called today. They've got a witness in the Curtis Moore shooting, but the guy's holding back, won't tell everything he knows."

"When're you going?"

"Tomorrow sometime. I want to talk to Walter first, if I

can. Walter could be the key to the whole thing." There was a silence again. He felt alone: the same feeling he'd had when she told him she was going to Tucson, the feeling of losing her. He wished she would say something without having to ask her a question first.

He said, "With the two cowboys—maybe I was showing off a little, too."

After a few moments she said, "Maybe I can help you with Walter." Giving him something, but not as much as he wanted.

FOURTEEN

WHEN BRYAN CALLED Walter's wife in West Palm, Irene Kouza said, "Walter? Walter who? I don't know anybody by that name."

Bryan said, "Mrs. Kouza, we met at Lieutenant Daugherty's retirement dinner at Carl's about three years ago."

She asked him if he was down here on vacation. He said yes. Was he having a good time? Yes, a very nice time. She said, then what did he want to talk to Walter for and spoil it? She was way ahead of him and it took Bryan the first couple of minutes to realize it.

Bryan said, while he was down here he was hoping he could stop in and see Walter, say hello. Irene Kouza said both their daughters were down with their husbands on vacation and Mr. Big Shot hadn't even bothered to call yet, her dry tone becoming abrasively cute. Anybody who wanted to talk to Mr. Big Shot had to call over there to the beach and leave their name. She began telling Bryan the cost of lawn service for the tiny yard they had, seventy-five dollars to trim a hedge because Mr.

Big Shot didn't have time no more, he was too busy—and Bryan got off the line as quickly as he could without sounding rude, feeling like he'd made an escape.

The idea had been to catch Walter at home or arrange to meet him there: try to pry open the old Walter in a familiar setting. But Walter was staying clear of West Palm. Bryan had seen it before. A man able to kill other men, but scared to death of his wife.

Angela said, "Let me try something."

She called Walter at the Daniels place and invited him to lunch. She needed a little help with the piece she was doing on Robbie Daniels, an insider's view of how rich people lived. Walter said, certainly.

She said to Bryan, "Charley's Crab at noon. See? You need me."

That was all it took. He felt inspired again.

A light blue suit coat straining, stretched across heavy shoulders—there he was, hunched over the bar with his shot and a beer and a pack of Camels.

Bryan said, "Like getting ready for the second shift, Dodge Main."

Walter turned to him, pompadour rising. "The fuck *you* want?"

"Angela's gonna be a little late. I told her I'd buy you a drink." It was ten to twelve. Bryan watched the bartender, good-looking young guy, serving customers on the other side of the bar pen, giving them draft beers to go with buckets of clams. The hostess was seating others in the near room among planters and plain-wood decor where young girls in black vests took over with smiles. Everything nice on a sunny day in season.

"Walter, what's he want to shoot somebody for?"

"You talking about?"

"He gave me the same routine he gave you. He shows me the guns, he says Walter took one look—he goes, 'What're you gonna do, invade Cuba?' "

"Guy's a collector, he likes guns," Walter finished the bottom of his shot and picked up the glass of beer. He said to the bartender, "Hey, buddy, Do it again."

Bryan ordered a draft. He waited for it to be placed in front of him, gave Walter time to pick up the new shot and sip off half of it.

"He's got some beauties. His gun collection."

Walter salted his beer and pushed the shaker toward Bryan.

"He showed me the Python he used on the guy that broke in." Walter didn't comment. "What I can't figure out," Bryan said, "is how you can have all that money, can do anything you want and still be bored. Christ, we'd think of something to do with it. You imagine?"

"Who says he's bored?"

"He did. He told me. What's he, a little fucked up?"

"He's a very educated man," Walter said. "Guy reads all the time."

"Yeah, but what does he read? All his books're about the same thing. People getting taken out. He says to me, 'Who would you pick? Some universal asshole who deserves to die.' "

Walter said, "What's hard about that? Christ, the way the world is today? Take your fucking pick. There's Castro. You got any number of dictators, shit. You got your PLO assholes, fucking Arabs. Your Cubans, your Haitians coming in, taking over. Go out to Belle Glade and warm up. 'Cause pretty soon everybody's gonna be packing. You won't have no choice, you want to stay alive you better fucking know how to shoot."

There were more sounds in the restaurant now, Palm Beachers coming in for lunch, though most of the places on this side of the bar remained empty.

"I talked to Irene this morning."

"Jesus Christ." Walter came around on his stool. "The hell you trying to do?"

"I was looking for you, I thought you might be home. Then Angela said she was gonna see you . . ."

Walter stared at him before turning back to his beer. He shook more salt into the glass and watched the dissolving crystals rise like foam.

"She says you don't cut the grass anymore."

"Three bills a week I give her, she can have it done."

"She says you've changed."

"Cut the shit, okay?"

Bryan sipped his beer. "She says if I see you, remind you your daughters're down for a visit."

Walter said, "Look, I don't ask you if you're fucking that girl writer. Mind your own fucking business, okay?"

"Okay," Bryan said, "I was just telling you what Irene said." He took another sip of beer, nursing it along. "So, I gather you like your job. Seeing how the other half lives . . . I wondered how much dough he's got in that gun collection."

"Don't worry about it," Walter said. "Guy can pay fifteen bills for a Mickey Mouse piece, he's not worrying about it, so don't you."

Fifteen hundred.

"What, a shotgun?"

Walter looked at him again. "I thought he showed you his collection."

"We didn't get into prices." Bryan waited. "I didn't see the High Standard. The one he had in his office."

Walter remained hunched over the bar on his arms. He pulled out a cigarette without picking up the pack and lighted it.

"I wonder where he keeps it," Bryan said.

Walter exhaled smoke, staring across the bar. He said, "You know who that is over there? The gray-haired gentleman, combed back?"

"Who is it?"

"That's Tony Marvin," Walter said. "He's down the beach at the Hilton. Has a show there."

"Tony Martin, the singer?"

"Tony Marvin. *Mar*vin. Used to be with Arthur Godfrey. He was the good-looking dark-haired guy."

"Oh," Bryan said, "the announcer. With the voice."

"Yeah, Tony Marvin," Walter said. "I see him quite a bit, different places."

Bryan said, "Walter, get me that High Standard. For one day."

Walter said, "You're outta your fucking mind."

"One day," Bryan said.

"I should've known," Walter said. "All the chitchat, bunch of bullshit."

"Walter, you were a cop for twenty-one years."

He came off the stool brushing past Bryan, pushed his way between an elderly couple coming in the door and was gone.

The bartender said, "Your friend left his cigarettes."

Bryan paid for the rounds. Waiting for his change he put the half-pack of Camels in his pocket.

The routine was established. Robbie would sit back with his drink and his peanuts. Sometimes he'd say, "It's showtime." Sometimes he'd say, "Roll it." And Walter would drop the cassette into the recorder and turn on the TV console.

"Okay, boat coming along the Intracoastal. Okay, the patio. I'm waiting for somebody to come out." Slow minutes of stationary shots followed by abrupt jumps to something else, sky, trees, lots of trees, then back to the waiting shot of nothing. Like an Andy Warhol film.

Robbie said, "It reminds me—you've seen those security guards looking at their monitors, a whole row of TV screens. Looking at the lobby. Looking at any empty hallway. Looking at the parking lot . . . And nothing ever happens." He was bored.

"Here she comes now," Walter said.

"Little T and A for our viewing pleasure . . . You're good whenever Dorie shows up, Walter. Old steady-hands . . . What's this?"

"I hear a car," Walter said, "so I go back the road to check. It was the guy. You'll see him in a minute."

"Jesus, I almost forgot," Robbie said. "Guess what washed in out of the ocean? I found it this morning on the beach. A whole bale of grass. Goddamn thing must weight two hundred pounds."

"Waterlogged," Walter said. "Yeah, there's a lot of that. When I was with the cops here we'd find it up and down the beach. The stuff they throw over the side when the Coast Guard's bearing down on 'em. So, you want to use it?"

"Why not? Then we won't have to wait for somebody to make a delivery. I'd rather catch him with coke, but pot's okay."

"What'd you do with it?"

"I had the gardener put it in the garage."

"The *gard*ener?"

"I told him I'd talk to the police about it . . . Well, look at old Cheech."

"Looks like the fucking Shah of Iran," Walter said, "with the robe."

"Gold lamé," Robbie said. "They going swimming?"

"Skinny-dipping," Walter said. "You leave that stuff in

the garage, somebody's gonna say something. The help could cop on you, that fucking cook you got."

"After we're finished here, put it in the Mercedes," Robbie said. "If you can lift it."

"What, two hundred pounds? I can lift more'n that."

"Even if it's half water," Robbie said, "dry it out you'd have, say, a hundred pounds of good Colombian worth on the street about . . . four sixes're twenty-four, four ones're four, carry the two, sixty-four, that's six hundred and forty times a hundred . . . say it's worth sixty grand at least. That should be plenty. You find that in a guy's house, he's a dealer . . . Where are they?"

"See their heads? They're out'n the ocean."

"Frolicking," Robbie said. "I never thought of Cheech as a frolicker."

"I'd frolick her," Walter said.

"Like a shot at that, huh?"

"They're coming out now. Fucking Adam and Eve."

"You zoom in?"

"Zoom in for what? They're coming out. Little grab-ass on the way. The guy knows how to live, I'll say that for him. Plays golf, goes swimming. Never has to work . . ."

Robbie leaned forward in his chair, toward the television set. "He's not hung at all." Sounding surprised. "I thought he was supposed to be hung."

"The guy just come out of the fucking ocean," Walter said. "What do you expect?"

Robbie was squinting at the set. "He's got one of those brown ones. But there's nothing unusual about it. Would you call that a big shlong?"

"I never measured any," Walter said. "That what you guys do, compare 'em? Maybe when I was about eight years old we did that, but not since then . . . Okay, grab their robes, go in the house."

"What's this?"

"I'm moving up on the house around the side. See if I can get a shot through a window."

"Nothing's happening."

"I left the camera, went up to check it out, but it was too dark. I'd have to use some lights."

"You need a gaffer," Robbie said.

"The fuck's a gaffer?"

Robbie was staring at the house on the screen. "Did you see anything?"

"You mean when I looked in? Yeah, Jesus, they were going at it. On the floor. They got this thick white carpeting."

"What were they doing?"

"They were doing it," Walter said.

"I mean *how* were they doing it?"

"Like you do it," Walter said. "You mean *how* were they doing it? Don't you know how to do it?"

"I mean were they just . . . doing it?"

"I'll tell you something," Walter said. "All the things you hear these days—I been wondering whatever happened to just plain fucking. Well, that's what they were doing."

"Amazing," Robbie said.

As far as Bryan was concerned it rained and turned dark at the wrong time. If it had rained and turned dark right after they came up from the beach and were alone in the room, then they could have used the mood of the rain and the dark and they would have gone to bed. By the time they got out of bed they'd be back together and doubts would have vanished. But when they came up from the beach it was still bright hot and he could hear kids playing in the swimming pool and a couple of the maids arguing in Spanish outside Number 15. When Angela was silent, Bryan was silent. He said, what's the matter? And she said, nothing. They could do that forever.

In the car going to the airport he began with, "You're different." She said, "No, I'm not." And he felt dumb, awkward. He said, "Why're you so quiet?"

She said, "I'm trying to figure out what to do with Robbie. I can't make it just another dopey interview. Not if he's got all those guns and he seriously intends to use them . . ."

A Mickey Mouse piece—it went through Bryan's mind, words without anything to picture—*a weapon worth fifteen hundred dollars*.

"Can I? I don't want to throw away what I have," Angela said, "so maybe I begin like it's another dopey interview, then throw Chichi at him and see what happens. But I know I have to talk to Chichi if I want any kind of emotional angle, a point of view, because Robbie's such a cold fish. He thinks he's Mr. Personality, but he's basically a very dull person. Do you see my problem?"

"Is that what you've been thinking about?"

"It's what I do, Bryan."

It got dark and began to rain as they drove through West Palm.

She said, "I'm not moody. When I'm in my head I'm working. I don't stew. If something bothers me I tell you." Her tone softened. "And then you straighten me out. Right?"

He said, "I never worried before this. I'm thinking too much because I don't want anything to happen to us."

She said, "Bryan, I think you're the niftiest guy I've ever known. I love you and all I see are good things happening."

She said it so easily.

He said, "I love you, too."

It hung there inside the car with the sound of the windshield wipers going and the windows steaming over. He felt her hand touch his face, the tips of her fingers gently stroking. He heard her say, "Bryan, don't worry about us, we can't lose."

When they were inside the garage Daniels said, there it is. The bale of marijuana was wrapped in a big gunnysack and stood chest-high on Walter. Daniels told him to put it in the "boot" of the Mercedes.

The boot. T and A. Gaffer. Another one he used, "dailies," referring to the videotapes. The guy loved to use words nobody knew what they meant. The guy had a lot of show-off in him and maybe he should have been an actor, as someone had suggested one time. The guy didn't even help him.

Walter struggled with the load himself and got the front of his shirt and pants messed up. He patted his pocket for a cigarette and remembered leaving them on the bar at Charley's Crab.

"I saw Hurd today," Walter said. "He told me you showed him your guns."

"Some of them," Robbie said. He brought the trunk lid down firmly, pushed on it again to be sure it locked and remained bent over, looking down. "What's that?"

"Where?" Walter said.

"It's a bumper sticker."

Walter looked at it now. The bumper sticker said, *Real Americans Buy American Cars.*

"That's been on there. Probably somebody in Detroit put it on."

"Christ," Robbie said. "Well, get it off."

"When I'm on surveillance or when I'm showing you movies?" Walter said. "Or when you're showing your guns to a police lieutenant investigating a homicide you happened to have committed?"

"I thought they'd gone," Robbie said. "I called the Holiday Inn the other day, they'd checked out."

"Well, he was still here today. He said you give him the same routine you used on me. Like he knew all about it."

"Sounds like he was fishing," Robbie said. "No, I was very careful, gave him only hypothetical situations. I was playing with him, Walter, that's all."

"I think he makes you nervous," Walter said. "I think you don't know whether to try and buy him off or take a crack at him, which'd make you feel better."

"That's your expert analysis?"

"I know him," Walter said. "He comes on like he's so straight he wouldn't even fucking jaywalk. But the son of a bitch—you give him any indication of probable cause, he'll throw the book away and come at you. I've seen it."

"I know him better than you think," Robbie said, "I played golf with him. And you're right, he cheats. But then, who doesn't? Would you feel better if we waited till he went home?"

"I get excited about it, I get all ready," Walter said, "then we sit around. We gonna do it or not?"

"Well," Robbie said, "I've got a late golf match tomorrow. How about the day after?"

FIFTEEN

THERE WERE PICKETS in front of the General Motors Building with signs that read GM HAS NO HEART . . . GM'S TAKING OUR HOMES . . . WAR! GM INVADES POLETOWN! . . . The little guy taking on the big corporation over a land dispute: a neighborhood the city had bought, condemned and already partly razed to make room for a new Cadillac assembly plant.

Bryan said, "Dodge Main's gone, what do they want, a house or a job?"

Annie Maguire said, "If you lived there you might feel differently about it."

Bryan said, "I might and I might not."

They got out of the blue Plymouth parked in the no standing zone and walked past the pickets, Bryan carrying a thick manila envelope, saying, "Maybe they don't have anything else to do," and into the GM Building, Annie saying, "I'm never sure what side you're gonna be on." Bryan saying, "Why do I have to be on either side?" Annie saying, "Ralph Nader thinks they're getting dumped on." And Bryan saying, "Who asked him?"

"You're in a terrible mood today."

"I'm not even supposed to be here."

"The guy we're seeing's name is Bill Fay. He's a nice guy. Try not to bite his head off."

Bryan said nothing, making no promises.

He followed Annie out of the elevator on the second floor to the end of the corridor and into a wing of glass-partitioned offices intersected with hallways. Bryan saw executives, some in shirt sleeves, each sitting between a worktable and a desk; he saw wallcharts and graphs, photos of wives and kids, draperies in some offices, venetian blinds in most. They entered an office where a pair of middle-aged secretaries presided, bore left, and Annie told the lady studying them, "Hi, Mr. Fay's expecting us." Bryan could see him through the glass in a gray pin-striped suit with a maroon handkerchief in the pocket, talking on the phone, gently swiveling from side to side in his executive chair. He looked up and waved them in with an alert eager expression and was off the phone, on his feet, by the time they entered.

"Miss Maguire, gee, it's good to see you again. How're you doing?" Then to Bryan, "Hi, Bill Fay . . . It's a pleasure. Lieutenant, this is some gal you got here. She knows her stuff, I'll tell you. Sit down . . . "

There were Chevrolet magazine ads, mounted and matted, covering most of one wall. A display line in bold, cursive lettering, off by itself, read:

*SEE THE EIGHTY-ONE-DERFUL CHEVROLET
TODAY!*

The line held Bryan's attention. He thought of 1982, new models coming out in the fall . . .

He heard Bill Fay saying, "I'm afraid I'm gonna have to make this one short," and turned to see him shoot his cuff to look at his watch. "I've got an ad meeting in exactly . . . four-and-a-half minutes. *But*, I know your work is as important to you as mine is to me. I know you have to keep going back over the same territory, make sure you don't miss anything . . . But, hey, I had an idea. I wondered, what if you displayed your phone number in the paper? You know, anyone who was around there and just might have seen something strange going on, please contact us at this number. What do you say? I could have the agency speedball you a nice layout. Maybe put a gun in it? Hey, I love it."

"Newspaper stories usually include our number," Annie said. "What we were wondering"—she rose, taking the manila envelope from Bryan—"if you'd mind looking at these photographs again. Just on the chance one of them, you know, might ring a bell."

As Annie pulled the photos from the envelope Fay was studying Bryan, the beginning of a smile in place. He said, "Boy, all the legwork you have to do, huh? Sure, I'd be glad to look at them again," helping Annie now spread the black and white shots of Robbie Daniels over the glass-top surface of his desk. "This is your suspect, huh? He looks familiar."

Annie said, "He's not a suspect exactly, but we're curious about him. We know he *was* in the vicinity of the Plaza that morning."

"Oh?" Bill Fay seemed a little surprised. "Is this a new development? As I recall, you weren't that sure before."

"He was there," Bryan said.

Fay waited for him to say more. Finally his gaze dropped to the photos and Bryan watched his demonstration of interest, row by row, studying all the Robbies, the on-camera shots, smiling, winking, the laid-back, heavy-lidded Hi-I'm-Robbie-Daniels shots and the true candid shots that caught him unprepared, or caught angles that emphasized his posture, his hip-cocked stance, the hand beneath the cashmere sweater.

Bryan said, "Mr. Fay, you checked into the Plaza about nine forty-five Saturday morning?"

"Yeah, about that."

"You told Sergeant Maguire you noticed a black Mercedes sedan."

"It's funny, driving down," Bill Fay said, "my wife and I were talking about foreign cars, particularly the Japanese imports taking close to twenty percent of the market. She was saying they shouldn't be allowed in the country, especially with the economic situation the way it is, and I said, wait a minute, just a darn minute, we got a free-enterprise system here. You don't make it, you pack your bags. It's rough out there, I kid you not. Though I believe there's room for some kind of quota system, yeah, for the time being—"

Bryan said, "You did see a black Mercedes?"

"I'm coming to that. I said, you don't see, really, that many foreign cars in Detroit anyway. I mean it's not anything like L.A. . . . we're pulling into the Plaza, you know, underneath by the entrance, and she goes, 'Oh, then what's that?' " Bill Fay grinned. "Here's a four-fifty SEL Mercedes right in front of us. But wait, here's the kicker. On this big piece of German iron there's a bumper sticker that says, *Real Americans Buy American Cars.*" Fay sat back for reactions, grinning.

Bryan said, "Did you notice the license number, or any part of it?"

"No, I didn't. And I didn't *see* anyone because the car was empty. I remember the door was open. We had to wait before we could pull up. Then we had to stand around there a while waiting for a parking ticket."

Bryan leaned over the desk, pulled out a shot of Robbie wearing a suit and dropped it in front of Fay.

"Nope." He shook his head.

Bryan looked over the selection, found one that showed Robbie in a raincoat, an angle on him going into what was probably his home in Grosse Pointe.

"No," the GM executive said, but kept looking at it.

"Maybe," Bryan said, "if we showed the pictures to your wife . . ."

And Bill Fay said, "No, no, no—she didn't see anything. I know, I discussed it with her. As a matter of fact she went inside right away. She wasn't even there."

Bryan said, "What do you mean, *there?*"

"When I was waiting for my ticket."

"There's still a chance," Bryan said, "she might've seen him before she went in."

"There was nobody there before. I know—she didn't see a thing. We've gone over it and over it."

Bryan said, "Mr. Fay, was your wife with you that morning or was it someone else?"

The executive said, "Now wait just a darn minute. I hope I didn't hear an insinuation of some kind."

"You didn't," Bryan said. "I asked you in plain English if you were with your wife or someone else. You checked in at nine forty-five and checked out at four P.M. It's none of my business what you were doing there or who you were doing it with, but if you saw this man at the hotel, I want you tell me about it."

Bill Fay looked at his watch again. "Listen, we're gonna have to continue this some other time."

Bryan said, "Can I use your phone?"

Fay was putting some papers together, starting to get up. "Sure. Help yourself."

"What's your home phone number?"

Fay held onto the papers and eased down into his chair

again. He straightened the papers now against the glass top of the desk and placed them squarely in front of him, preparing himself, getting ready. He said, "Lieutenant, I can tell you in all honesty she did not see a thing. I'll swear to it."

Bryan said, "Tell me in all honesty if your wife was with you."

"Does it matter?" Fay said. "I mean if she didn't see him it doesn't matter *who* didn't see him, does it?"

"But you saw him," Bryan said. He waited. "The whole thing is, you don't want to be a witness and have to appear in court . . . Where did you tell your wife you were?" He waited again.

"If I told you anything at all"—saying this carefully— "I *would* have to appear, wouldn't I?"

"I don't know," Bryan said. "Your testimony would place him at the scene, but that's all. We'd need a lot more to get a conviction. The murder weapon, for example, and a positive ballistics test. If the suspect's lawyer sees we've got a case then he might enter a plea and there'd be no trial. You're off the hook. I can't promise you anything; but if you tell me he was there, then we can narrow it down, concentrate the investigation, get something that'll stick."

Fay raised a hand to his forehead, spreading his fingers to massage his temples. He wore a diamond on his little finger, his nails were manicured and glistened with colorless polish.

"You saw him there," Bryan said. "The reason you remember him, you know who he is. You saw him walk down the ramp or you saw him enter that area . . . he went down to the garage and shot a parking attendant five times, probably killing him instantly. We don't think, no matter who he is, he should be able to take another's man's life and get away with it. Do you?" Bryan waited.

"He was wearing a raincoat," Bill Fay said. "He walked

into the entrance to the ramp. A gray Lincoln Continental turned in and stopped. I could see the rear end sticking out. Then the car continued on, but he didn't come out. So I assume he got in the car and went down."

"Thank you," Bryan said.

"But I won't appear in court," Fay said. "In fact, if you ever again ask me if I was even there, I'll deny it." He paused. "I told my wife I was going to Cleveland."

Bryan looked at Annie. She got up and began gathering the photos and he looked at Fay again.

"Do you know who that is?"

"If it isn't Robinson Daniels, it's somebody who looks just like him."

"Do you know Daniels?"

"No. I see him at the DAC every once in a while. And I've seen his picture. But why would he want to shoot a colored parking attendant?"

"Why would he want to shoot anyone?" Bryan said.

He got up and waited for Annie before moving to the door. Then looked back at the display of magazine ads and the theme line, *See the Eighty-one-derful Chevrolet today!*

He said to Fay, "What you might say next year—how about, See the Eighty-two-rific Chevrolet today?"

Bill Fay began to nod. He said, "That's not bad," and was making a note as Bryan and Annie left.

Outside, walking past the pickets, Bryan said, "How come they're marching around here instead of looking for a place to live?"

"You're all heart," Annie said. "I'll bet you don't even feel sorry for Mr. Fay."

"He should've gone to Cleveland," Bryan said.

They drove downtown and had to park two blocks from 1300 with the construction of the new county jail wings clogging the side streets with trucks and heavy equipment. Bryan could hardly wait to get upstairs. The first things he did, waving off Malik and Doug Parrish, he placed a call to the Atlantis Villas, Number 16. The phone rang nine times. He was ready to hang up, frustrated, when Angela's voice turned his mood around.

"You just come in from the beach?"

"No, I was washing my hair. How's it going?"

"I'm through. We're gonna have a meeting and that's it, I'm coming back tonight. In fact, if I get the five-thirty Delta flight I'll be there around nine."

"I'll meet you."

"You don't have to do that."

"Are you kidding? I can hardly wait."

"I'm not sure what time it gets in."

"I'll find out. If you miss it and have to take a later flight I'll wait for you. Just come."

"What're you doing?"

"I'm washing my hair."

"I mean outside of that."

"Oh—I called Chichi. Finally got hold of him."

"Yeah? . . ."

"I told him I need some color for a magazine piece I'm doing on Robbie and he said, 'You want some good stories?' He said, 'I've got some you'd never be able to print.' "

"Angela? Why don't you wait till I get back?"

"It's all arranged, I'm meeting him at six."

"Where?"

"The place in Hillsboro. I told him I knew where it was. He said, 'So you're the one.' I told him, don't worry, I'm a user not a snitch."

"Angela—"

"If I don't get him now I may never. But I'll be at the airport, don't worry about that."

"That's not it—"

"Bryan, what about the little girl?"

"What little girl?"

"The one—you found her body inside the car, with her panties pushed down?"

"Rolled down. Nothing. We don't know any more than we did," Bryan said. "Angela," he said then, "why don't you wait?"

"Bryan, who took care of me before I met you? I gotta go. I love you and I'll see you tonight."

She was gone.

SIXTEEN

THE PALM BEACH realtor that Robbie was to play golf with phoned at two-thirty to say he was terribly sorry but there was no way he could make it this afternoon; he was showing a Saudi's place to a West German, Christ, middleman in an Arab-Kraut deal and hoped to God he came out of it in one piece.

Robbie said, "You'll come out of it with about a hundred grand, Tony. But don't ever ask me to play golf with you again. Is that understood?"

The realtor said, "Hey, Robbie—"

And Robbie said, "Get fucked, Tony," and hung up.

He found Walter in his room and brought him up to the study along with two cold bottles of Heineken.

"Change of plans. We move today."

"How come?"

Jesus, everybody was giving him a hard time.

"Because I want to do it today," Robbie said. "I'm

ready. I want to walk in there and do it. Is that hard to understand?"

Walter had to see it clearly in his mind. He took a big swallow of beer and wiped his mouth with his hand.

"How we know the guy's gonna be there?"

"He comes every day between five and seven, doesn't he?"

"Almost every day."

"Okay, if he's not there, we don't do it. We do it tomorrow. There's not that much to plan, Walter. I'm gonna use the MAC-ten with the suppressor. We walk in—"

"What do I use?"

"We walk in," Robbie said, "I open up with the MAC and you open up with the Hitachi."

"The *camera*? You're kidding me."

"I told you that, didn't I? I want to see it, I want to study it—same way a football team studies game films. I want to get it down right, Walter, so when we go for the big ones"—he snapped his fingers three times—"it works like that, like the pros do it. You have a team operation you better have split-second timing or else you're gonna blow it. And when you blow the big one, Walter . . . that's it. No more."

Walter said, "I'm gonna be standing there with the fucking camera on my shoulder—"

"This time you are. I want to *see* it, Walter."

"You're the star—that what you're saying?"

"I'm not gonna be in it—"

"Big movie, Assassination of an Asshole, starring Mr. Robinson Daniels. You want George Hamilton to be in it, too?"

"Walter, you don't shoot *me*. I'm not in it. I want the camera to follow only the guy. I want to see how he reacts, I want to see everything he does."

Walter was silent a moment. "What about the broad?"

228

"Who, Dorie? . . . We get her out of the way. Lock her in a closet."

"Jesus Christ," Walter said, "I thought you knew what you're doing. Lock her in a closet—the cops let her out, they take hold of her finger, this one. They say okay, you know who did it? Point 'em out."

"We cover up," Robbie said. Goddamn dumb Polack. "Wear masks or something. Ski masks—no, we'll tie bandanas around, you know, just our eyes showing and wear sunglasses."

"Jesus Christ," Walter said, "Butch and fucking Sundance. Broad looks at you, hears your voice, or she happens to look out the window, sees a Mercedes and a fucking silver Rolls Royce . . . I think, Mr. Daniels, I'm gonna pass on this one. What I ought to do, get my ass outta here right now."

"Finish your beer," Robbie said quietly. He walked away from the bar, stood with his hands in the pockets of his chinos, then drifted back, taking his time.

"Walter? . . ."

"You're not ready," Walter said. "You haven't thought it out. We went out on a STRESS operation—before we hit that street we knew every fucking move we're gonna make and what we do if different various situations come up."

Robbie said, "Okay, we don't want a witness, there won't be a witness. If Dorie happens to be there, well, that's too bad."

Walter said, "Oh no, uh-unh. The broad's got nothing to do with it."

"She works for him—what's the difference? She's part of an illegal operation."

"She puts out for him," Walter said. "That's all she does I know of or seen her do. I don't want no parts of shooting broads. I told you that a long time ago, I never shot a broad in my life and I hope to God I never get in a position I have to.

You're telling me about all these assholes—were there any broads on your list? No. Broads might *be* there, yeah, but that's all. They're like on the side, what broads do, they hang out. No sir . . ."

Robbie said, "Okay, we call her up. Give her a message to meet Cheech at the polo club. Five o'clock. Which means we got to move."

"Wait a minute," Walter said. "Wait a minute. You got the phone number?"

"Not yet."

"You think it's in the book? Narcotics drop, they got it under *N*?"

"You can get the number, can't you? Call the Broward County Sheriff's Office. Like you did before."

"What if Drug Enforcement's got a tap on the line?"

"You're somebody from the polo club," Robbie said. "Chichi asked you to call her for him. You're not gonna leave your name, Walter."

"They might not have the number."

"They can get it, can't they? Or you call the telephone company. Tell them you're with the Palm Beach office of the DEA. You know people there, you know the routine. Walter, this is your end of it. You know how to do all that kind of stuff. But we've got to *move*."

"Yeah, but what if they want to talk to my superior, something like that?"

"You're the superior, Walter," Robbie paused. "You're the star. For two grand a week, including your combat pay, it doesn't seem like much to ask. A couple of phone calls? Come on . . ."

Walter walked over to the narrow casement window that looked down on the swimming pool and the patio with its umbrella tables. He stared at the immaculate blue, green and yellow orderliness of the scene, the arrangement of color reaching to the ocean. If the guy wanted to he could have the grass painted red and dye the water in the swimming pool purple or cover the whole setup with a golden dome. The guy could do anything he wanted. Easy. It came down to a simple question. Would you rather be inside pissing out, or outside getting it all over you?

Walter came away from the window. "Okay, I'll try the phone company, give 'em some bullshit. But when I call her, I don't think it should be a message from the guy. It's gotta be somebody else, 'cause what if he happens to call her? It's gotta be somebody offering her a deal, like something she can't pass up."

Robbie was sitting at the bar now. It seemed to come to him almost immediately, the way his expression brightened.

"Dorie thinks she's an actress. She does get a few small parts at dinner theaters, the maid, maybe a couple of lines. But how about—tell her they need somebody right away up at Burt Reynolds's place."

"Where, Jupiter?"

"Yeah, it's perfect. By the time she gets there and gets back, it's done."

Walter drank his beer. It sounded pretty good. He looked at Robbie sitting like *The Thinker* now, fist supporting his chin, weighing something heavy.

"What's the matter?"

"Nothing," Robbie said. "I'm trying to decide what to wear."

Angela wore the new white-linen sunback, feeling and looking good; but more for Bryan, later, than any effect it might have on Chichi. Cheech would probably try something just to test her availability—out of habit, part of his nature—come on with some kind of slippery Latin routine and she'd tell him to knock it off and he would. That's what she told herself. The alive feeling of expectation was something else. She didn't want him to make the moves, but at the same time she wanted to see him at least try. After all, how many internationally famous great lovers did you come across when you knew you were looking good and certain you could handle the situation? She hoped.

Then an anxious feeling of impending disappointment: following the gravel, coasting the Buick through the clumps of sea grape to find the circular drive empty; the cement apron in front of the three-car garage empty. The house with a closed, empty look. The son of a bitch.

Dorie, barefoot in bra and panties, a hairbrush in her hand, opened the door and said, "Hi," and disappeared.

Angela entered cautiously, through a hallway past kitchen and den to the spacious front room. A little white dog sniffed her but ran off as she reached to pet him.

"Sit down if you want."

Angela turned to see the red-haired girl halfway up the staircase. The little dog was with her, looking out through the balusters.

"I love your dress. I wear white, I look like some Appalachian kid in a CARE package dress. You know what I mean? I look dumb in plain white things, like they're wearing me. I have to wear something busier so it all like blends together. You know what I mean?"

Angela said, "Is Chichi here?" She held up her slim reporter's notebook, a credential. "I've got an appointment to interview him."

"Good luck," Dorie said. "Listen, I gotta get ready. Unless you want to come up."

"Do you expect him?"

"Cheech shows up or he doesn't. If he told you he'd be here—"

"At six."

"Well, he still shows up or he doesn't. God, is it six already?" She disappeared, the little dog hopping up the stairs after her.

Angela moved to the French doors, looked out at the patio and pool, the stretch of beach beyond. This had to be the most secluded place on the coast; almost as though the great real estate rush had passed it by. There was enough property here for a good-size condominium.

Dorie's voice said from the top of the stairs, "I don't think I know your name. Do I?"

"Angela."

"I'm Dorie and I've got a problem." Still in her bra and panties, pulling the brush through her hair. "You wouldn't do me a huge favor, would you?"

"Sure. If I can."

"I've got a chance to do a walk-on tonight at the—are you ready?—the Burt Reynolds Dinner Theatre. I don't even know the name of the play, I'm supposed to be there practically right now and my fucking car's at a gas station in Deerfield, getting fixed. Actually it's done. I thought Cheech would be here to drive me, but the son of a bitch, you can't rely on him."

"You need a ride just to Deerfield?"

"God, if you would."

"I'd be glad to," Angela said. "But hurry, okay? I'll leave him a note in case he comes—" and looked up as she heard the door open.

Chichi, in person.

In golf clothes and a linen sports jacket over his shoulders, the sleeves hanging empty. Angela watched his entrance, coming in to see two women waiting for him—one in a white sundress, one in a bra and panties—the inspector of embassies showing mild surprise one moment, a gesture of inevitability the next, no more than his due.

Then coming alive. "Angela!" Coming toward her,

both hands extended, limp—the sports jacket somehow clinging to his narrow shoulders—to touch her gently, to kiss both of her cheeks . . .

Dorie said, "Cheech! I'm in a play tonight!"

He turned to look at her with genuine concern. "Ohhhh, Dorie, you're leaving us? . . . And Mr. Piper . . . How are you today, Mr. Piper?"

Dorie left in the rented brown Buick, not trusting herself in Chichi's Rolls. The Buick would be at the Mobil station in Deerfield. Then, later on, Chichi would drop Angela there on his way back to Palm Beach. No problem.

"Alone at last," Angela said, playing the game, smiling to show him she was playing.

"I'm going to bathe," Chichi said, holding his dog, trying to hold Angela's hand, drawing out his exit, "and change into something comfortable."

"After a hard day at the club," Angela said.

Chichi's eyes smiled. "You've had your bath."

"Yes, I have."

His eyes smiled and smiled.

She would make a note that they "flashed and danced" and see if she could work up an analogy to Caribbean moonlight, reflections on tropical waters—if she could do it unpretentiously and if Bryan didn't think it was dumb.

Walter had said, "First, we want the cars turned around so they're facing out, you never know. But that road's too narrow, all the trees and shit, to turn around once you're in there. So you have to back in from Ocean Drive. Wait'll you don't see anybody coming. You go in, I give it a couple minutes, then I go in."

This is where they were, on the access road to the beach, about a hundred yards from Chichi's house.

Over his jeans, a dark cashmere and the Colt Python in a shoulder rig, Robbie wore a light canvas shooting coat with deep pockets. He was hot, but needed a good deep pocket for his extra ammo clip. He wore a blue bandana rolled and tied around his forehead like a sweatband. (Walter had said, "You gonna blacken your face, too?") Walter wore his wing tips, his light blue suit pants and a dark blue poplin jacket that covered the Browning nine-millimeter holstered on his right hip.

He hung the VCR, the tape recorder, over one shoulder and crossed the strap holding the battery pack over the other, each one as heavy as a dictionary, and hefted the video camera to his shoulder—like a goddamn native ready to follow the white boss—the white boss in his commando outfit and tennis shoes half inside the "boot" of the Rolls now putting his submachine gun together. The "fag gun" Walter called it, all cammied up in shades of blue and rose. Robbie was screwing the suppressor onto the barrel stub, the silencer bigger and longer than the gun itself. Then fitting the thirty-two-round clip into the slot on the underside, just behind the trigger. If you couldn't hit one guy with thirty-two rounds you weren't going to hit him and you might as well take off the coat and leave the extra clip in the car. But Daniels was going in like it was a fucking assault on enemy headquarters—the guy probably sitting in there in his underwear, scratching his ass.

Robbie came out of the trunk. "Ready?"

"Okay," Walter said "Just his car's there when we drove by. But we got to check, be sure nobody else's come in the meantime. We don't want no surprises. We stay in the trees and shit till we get to the house. Only the one car's still there we go in through the back, I'm right behind you. Do it, then we come back, get the grass out of the trunk."

"I don't think there'll be enough light inside," Robbie said, looking up at the sky that was pale gray-blue, without glare.

"Let's wait and see," Walter said. "We stand here we're not gonna have any light anywhere."

"I think I'd like to get him out by the pool."

"You might not have any choice," Walter said. "The guy makes a run, you have to drop him. I mean that's why we're here, right? You see him, you hit him, no fucking around, give him a chance to get away."

"Yeah, but I want to see him fall in the pool," Robbie said. "He's running—give him a burst, he falls in the swimming pool and you see him floating there, face down, the water turning red . . . "

"Jesus Christ," Walter said, "let's get it done."

Chichi called down from upstairs, "I won't be a minute. I hurried, so, I didn't have a chance to shower at the club . . . Why don't you make yourself a drink?"

"I'm fine."

"Well, sit down. Watch the telly if you like."

Angela looked about the sitting room that resembled a Cape Cod summer home more than it did a place in Florida. The sofa and chairs, slipcovered in a beige fabric, reminded her a little of Bryan's apartment. Comfortable, but indifferent to fashion. She was gathering impressions. The side-table bar offered a skimpy selection of several brands of whiskey, one gin and a blue siphon bottle. Now the room looked English. A cottage in Brighton. Apparently there was no ice. But she didn't want a drink anyway.

Angela looked up toward the top of the stairway as she said, "I'll be outside . . . "

Bryan was put on standby for the five-thirty Delta flight to West Palm. He told the ticket lady behind the counter he had to make it. "I'm getting married." The ticket lady glanced up at him and said, "Congratulations." He told her he was also a police officer—"See? My shield"—working on a very important case that was taking him to Florida and that's why they were getting married down there. The ticket lady looked at him again, into his solemn unwavering blue eyes. He would tell her anything.

All that, his stomach in a knot, then hearing his name called and grabbing his canvas bag.

He sat in the back of the plane and smoked cigarettes, drinking down the first bourbon over ice then sipping the second one, trying to make it last.

He would tell her about his former wife about to get married. It had nothing to do with them, yet somehow it did, because it relieved him and gave him no more reason to look back or think of reasons to feel guilty. He could concentrate on Angela. Tonight they'd have dinner in a dark place and go back to the Villas, sit by the seawall alone and look at the ocean and touch her and feel the familiar feel of her hand that was like no other hand and feel her arm, the soft hint of down, and feel her face—later, lying down, feel her face and trace the delicate line down her nose to her mouth and feel her breath. Jesus. He said, I love you. He said it again and then again, trying the emphasis on a different word each time. He said, I'm in love with you. He said, God, I love you. He said, I love you so much that . . .

She would know.

She had said, "You don't have to say a word if I feel it."

And he had said, "Start feeling."

But he would tell her so she would be absolutely sure.

They crossed a strip of lawn from the trees to the back of the house, Robbie running with his head down, shoulders hunched, the flowery submachine gun at port arms—the way it was done.

Walter carried the video camera in front of him, using his arms beneath it for support. He didn't hoist the curved, saddlelike support to his shoulder until they were in the entranceway.

Robbie said, over his shoulder, "The door's locked."

Walter said to himself, Get out; right now. He said, "I 'magine it is. Kick it open."

"It's too heavy."

"Okay, you got a credit card?"

"Christ," Robbie said.

"Come on, gimme a credit card, I'll see what I can do."

Robbie gave him his gold American Express card from his wallet and held the camera while Walter tried to work the card into the crack between the door and the molding and slip the lock. It wouldn't budge.

"We'll have to go around the front," Walter said.

Robbie gave him the camera back and they moved along the north side of the house, pausing to look in a window at the empty living room. At the front corner of the house, Robbie raised his left hand to hold up his troops. He crouched, his gaze scanning the patio and pool area, then out to the empty stretch of beach. Rising now, Robbie moved around the corner. Walter lifted the camera to his shoulder again and followed his leader across the brick patio and in through the French doors.

Robbie stood in the middle of the room, the machine gun held close to him, the silencer pointing up past his head. He glanced at Walter and swept his left hand toward the back of the house.

Whatever the fuck that was supposed to mean. Walter said, "He's upstairs. You hear the shower?"

Listening, Robbie shook his head.

"It stopped," Walter said. "Get back in the hall there, wait for him."

They crossed quickly. Robbie poked his machine gun

into the kitchen first, then looked in the den to be sure and shook his head at Walter.

Walter said, "I just told you, he's upstairs."

They waited in the hallway.

When Chichi appeared, coming from the right into his frame of vision, Robbie was looking at the man's back, at a gold lamé robe, the skirts hanging nearly to the floor, a little dog running to keep up with him. He could hear Chichi's slippers slapping his heels as he crossed the room, approaching the bar now, rubbing his hands together. Chichi selected a bottle, stooped to bring out a leather-covered ice bucket from underneath. It was when he straightened, coming around, that he saw Robbie holding the gaily colored submachine gun and the heavyset man with the camera mounted on his shoulder, the man moving carefully to the side now, his face pressed to the eyepiece.

Chichi said, "Robbie—what are you doing, making a film? Can I be in it?"

"You're in it all right," Robbie said. "You're the star."

"You know, I did appear in a film once when I was married to Valaria," Chichi said. "I seduced her in the first reel and I was shot in the second reel by that weight lifter, very popular with the Italians. Muscular young man—I can't think of his name. Steve something . . . What's this picture about, Robbie?"

Walter kept the gold robe in the center of the viewfinder that was like a tiny television screen in front of his eye. The camera whirred in his right ear. He heard Robbie say something.

"Death."

Then Chichi. "The film is about death?"

The gold robe on the little screen was turning to the bar again. "Should I ask whose?"

"Yours," Robbie's voice said.

"You wouldn't prefer a drink, would you?" Chichi's voice said.

Son of a bitch—the gold robe was moving again. Walter heard the popping sounds like a heavy automatic B-B gun firing and saw the bottle on the side-table bar shatter. He saw the stunned expression on the guy's face for only a split moment—beautiful, got it—but now the guy was moving and he heard the hard popping sounds again and the little dog barking and saw the guy stumble like he was tripping over his robe and several panes in the French door exploded.

Angela heard glass breaking.

She was coming back from an anxious walk that had taken her a little way down the beach—carrying her sandals—restless now, feeling she was running out of time and wanting to postpone the meeting, put Chichi aside for another day—Bryan was right, he was always right—and get out to the airport. Be there waiting. Her mind wasn't on this at all. The ocean was even different, oily, uninviting. She didn't want to be here.

She heard the sound of breaking glass in a lull, coming clearly and by itself as the heavy sound of the surf receded and was still for a moment.

She came away from the ocean, crossing the littered sand, looking down to avoid patches of tar and seaweed, then looking toward the house again . . . at a figure in gold coming out. The Great Lover. God, in a gold bathrobe. He seemed drunk. She was halfway there, between the ocean and the grounds. She saw him coming out toward the swimming pool, staggering, the little dog coming with him. How could he have had that much to drink? He was fine when he came in. She saw two more figures, one of them carrying something on his shoulder. She moved toward them but not hurrying now, not understanding what was going on, but beginning to think now, to realize there were people associated with this man, like the two in the restaurant . . . She saw the other figure raise something in front of him that began to jump up and down as he held it and tried to control it and she saw Chichi in the gold robe running, stumbling, the thing still jumping in the other man's hands and she could hear it now, hard little muted pops, as Chichi staggered and went into the pool. She stood still. She saw the figure looking this way. She saw his arm extend, pointing directly at her. Angela dropped her sandals and began to run.

Walter said, "Who was that?"

Robbie was sweating. "Christ, I don't know." Concentrating, squinting at the section of beach in front of them, empty now, as though if he looked hard enough the figure in white would reappear. "Come on." He started off.

"Was that a broad?" Walter said.

Robbie reached the edge of the sand and looked back. "Whoever it was—we were *seen*. You understand? That's a witness."

"Was it the broad?" Walter said, his eyes open as wide as they would open. "It looked like it might be the broad."

"It was a *witness*," Robbie said. "Will you get it in your goddamn head? Come on—I want you to shoot it, whoever it is"—slipping as he started off in the sand—"shoot it, goddamn it!"

Walter started after him, then stopped. He'd better change tapes, shove a new cassette into the recorder. He saw Robbie look back and yell at him again as he pulled out the first cassette and slipped it into his jacket.

Walter used to believe in always carrying a knife. You shoot fast in a street situation, okay, and you find out the guy wasn't armed or he was only reaching for his I.D., you put the knife in the guy's hand and you swear to God at the hearing the son of a bitch was coming at you and you had no choice but to shoot. You had to protect your ass. You had to protect it from people claiming to be witnesses, too, who were just as bad as the people you had to shoot. What was the difference? You gonna go up because somebody that works for him, just as fucking bad as he is, saw you do it and copped? He wants you to shoot it, Walter said, getting the goddamn camera on his shoulder and moving now, heading for the trees, then shoot it. Get it done.

He went into the scrub—almost used to it now, with the knack of moving without getting his straps and cases tangled up. He told himself not to think about whoever it was. Anybody goes to work for a guy like that guy in the pool, tough shit, that's how it comes out. It's your ass or the other person's. You going up for some fucking hooker? You bet he wasn't going up. It was no different here than on the street.

He saw her then. He saw something white. Moving along the beach at the edge of the trees. Crouched down now, trying to hide. Robbie would be coming up on her. She heard him, it looked like. She was coming into the scrub now, looking back but coming this way.

Walter snugged the camera to his shoulder, pressed his eye to the viewfinder and turned it on. He heard Robbie yell something. Robbie had spotted her. The white figure was in the sea grape, moving across Walter's tiny rectangular field of vision from left to right, looking back as she angled toward him head turned the other way. He panned the camera on the white figure. He heard the hard little pops of sound, Robbie opening up. He saw leaves flying apart. He saw the figure in white closer, looking back, no idea where she was going, then looking

242

this way and he saw the awful expression of terror on Angela Nolan's face—not the other one, *Angela*.

It was like he was looking through the slit window of a tank and she was out there and wanted to get in, coming toward him to get inside with him where it was safe. He saw her face and heard those hard grunting pops and saw leaves flying, snipped off, and that was the end of it for him. Walter raised the camera in both hands above his head and threw it as far away from him as he could. Threw it and turned to get out of there and felt the cables still attached to the camera pull tight and now he was dragging the camera, unable to detach himself from it until he untangled the equipment straps, lifted them over his head. Robbie was calling something now, but he couldn't see him. Walter dropped the battery pack and the VCR. Then stopped and went back to hunch down over the recorder and yanked the cassette out, wanting it and not wanting it and not having time to think. Reacting then, rather than making a decision, he threw the cassette away from him hard overhand, and began running again—past the swimming pool. Where the little dog sat at the edge and the gold robe floated in the water, stretched open like wings, ran into the scrub on the north side of the house, all the way through the trees to the access road. Walter got in the Mercedes and took off.

He was on Sample Road moving west toward the Interstate before he realized he had a cassette in his jacket. The first one, the one that would show Chichi Fuentes in his robe. Walter pushed a button. The window next to him slid down into the door. He drove perhaps another mile staring straight ahead at the road. He pushed the button again and the window slid closed.

Give it a little more thought. Soon as it was dark enough he'd stop somewhere and dump the bale of wet grass. But the tape of the rich guy doing the playboy—that was something else.

SEVENTEEN

SHE WASN'T AT the airport to meet him.

He hung around the front of the Delta terminal, walked over to Eastern and looked around there just in case, head raised moving through the crowd, all the last-minute vacationers down for Easter, then walked back to Delta. He had to keep moving. Goddamn it. He wasn't mad at her. He was mad at standing here watching people throwing their arms around each other, pretty soon standing alone with his canvas bag but without a sense of the policeman's patience. He wasn't aware of being a policeman. He wasn't too aware of himself, for that matter. He wanted the sight of her. He was on the edge of feeling what he would feel when he saw her, ready to turn it loose, and she wasn't here.

The taxi took Southern Boulevard over, followed the right-hand curve coming to the beach and passed along the wall of the Daniels estate. It was dark. The place felt dark. Bryan sat in front with the driver but they didn't talk much. Big cars poked along in front of them. There was nothing you could do.

Finally Bryan said, "There it is. On the left."

The driver said, "Villas Atlantis," like he was making an announcement.

They had to wait for a stream of oncoming cars. As the last of them crept past and the taxi turned in Bryan saw the police car. He paid the driver and got out. He didn't see the brown Buick Century anywhere in the parking rows.

The Palm Beach City police car was parked in front of the first unit, the office, where a neon sign said *No Vacancy*.

He went up the walk with his canvas bag, past the swimming pool where the underwater lights were on and kids were splashing around, their parents sitting with drinks, watching. They said good evening leisurely, with all the time in the world, waiting to see if he would stop and talk. He had never seen them before. He nodded once and said good evening. He kept walking, the line of cement villas leading to the ocean. Anywhere along here he could cut through to Number 16, over in the third row of villas. Or he could go all the way up the walk to the seawall . . .

He saw the uniformed officer, hatless, coming across the front walk from the left, out of darkness. He knew the uniform would be brown and beige when they were closer, when they met at the point where the walks intersected . . . But the uniformed officer was shortcutting, not hurrying, almost taking his time, but still he was shortcutting across the grass now, past the aluminum lawn chairs in a row, coming toward him at a slow walk.

He knew who it was.

"Lieutenant? . . ."

Bryan said, Oh, Jesus . . .

He knew who it was and knew what his expression would be like. From the tone of that one word he could look at the ocean or up at the sky and he would still see that solemn-neutral cop expression and know what it meant.

"Lieutenant?. . ."

See? Nothing else. Nothing more to expect or hope for in just that one word.

He said, "Gary, get away from me. I mean it. Get the hell away from me."

Bryan refused to look at him. He kept his eyes on the impersonal ocean and continued to the end of the walk until Gary was no longer in his vision.

Gary Hammond followed as far as the pipe railing. He put his hand on it and watched Bryan go down the seawall steps to the beach, becoming a small dark figure out there alone. He watched the figure walk into the surf to stand where the ocean reached land and came exploding around him. He heard him scream something. He heard the homicide cop standing out there in his good suit scream something that was maybe a word, two words. But he wasn't going to outscream the ocean. Nobody was going to do that.

EIGHTEEN

GARY HAMMOND PICKED him up the next day. They drove down to the Broward County Sheriff's Office in Fort Lauderdale. They wanted to ask him a few questions and show him something. He had already identified her body.

There were people here from the Florida State Police and the Drug Enforcement Agency as well as Broward deputies, most of them in plainclothes. The meeting was in a cement-wall conference room with fluorescent lights above a long table. A television set had been placed at the end of the table away from the door; a videotape recorder was hooked to the set.

A girl by the name of Dorie Vaughn was here when he arrived but left shortly after. She was the one who had discovered the body of Mr. Rafael Fuentes in the swimming pool and called the operator who contacted the Broward County sheriff. The Palm Beach Police were alerted because Mr. Fuentes lived in their city. In the meantime the Broward crime-scene people had discovered a second body, a camera bag full of blank video cassettes and, partly hidden in the scrub among the matted, dead leaves, one video cassette with something on it. No weapon or videotape equipment was discovered at the scene, but it became obvious both had been used. The crime scene people collected seventeen nine-millimeter shell casings which they believed had been fired from an automatic weapon. Very possibly a submachine gun.

And once again Bryan thought of the Mickey Mouse gun that might cost fifteen hundred dollars. He said nothing about it to the law-enforcement officers.

He was asked to describe Miss Nolan's activities in Florida; they wanted to know specifically what she had been up to. He told them she was writing an article on rich people and had gone to see Mr. Fuentes to interview him.

A DEA agent lounged half-sitting against the conference table, wearing a straw cattleman's hat over his eyes, a creased, outdoor look about the man, asked Bryan if Miss Nolan knew Chichi Fuentes was a drug dealer. Bryan said yes, she did.

Roy Spears was the DEA agent's name. He said, when you run with that crowd anything can happen to you.

Bryan told him she wasn't running with anybody, she was on an assignment.

Well, how come they didn't meet at one of his clubs or some Palm Beach cocktail lounge? Roy Spears asked. How did she know about the place in Hillsboro? That was supposed to be a regular love nest, he'd heard, where Chichi kept his broads and they had all kinds of orgies there and apparently, it seemed, shot some pretty weird films. Was that a possibility? If she was that close to Chichi, Roy Spears wondered if she might not've been working for him, or at least fucking him.

Bryan hit Roy Spears across the table. He went after him but the Florida cops came alive, swarmed all over Bryan and finally sat him down. They helped Roy Spears out of the room to have a paramedic look at his mouth. They remained cordial to

Bryan and seemed more relaxed after Spears was gone. One of them leaned close to Bryan and said don't worry, enough guys here would swear Roy Spears provoked him, if it ever came to that.

They asked him if Miss Nolan had contacted or interviewed anyone else in Palm Beach. Bryan said none that he knew of. He gave Gary Hammond a look.

They said they would inspect her personal effects later on. Bryan nodded. He had already gathered her notes, her typewritten sheets and her cassette interviews with Daniels and put them in his suitcase.

They said they were sorry they had to show him the one videotape they'd found; it wasn't pretty. But since he knew her, and especially since he was a police officer, maybe it would tell him something that would be of help to them. They turned on the machine.

The picture on the TV screen was of trees, dense growth, brief glimpses of the beach and the ocean, the picture jumping erratically as it moved, a camera looking for something but without a plan, never holding still.

Until Bryan saw the white linen sundress, not seeing it at first as a woman in a dress but knowing it was and who it was.

He saw her twisting through the trees like someone in pain and realized she was barefoot. He saw her clearly now. He saw her eyes pleading. He saw her eyes close and open, her expression change, her mouth stretch open in a silent scream and saw the red splotch appear on the front of the white dress. He saw another red splotch and another red splotch and another red splotch and another red splotch and red strings coming out of those red splotches pulling her, yanking her off her feet, and then leaves flashing across the screen round green sea-grape leaves filling the screen and then a pattern of mechanical lines jumping until the screen went gray and then went black.

They waited.

They said, Lieutenant Hurd?

He shook his head.

They asked him if he would look at it again.

He shook his head. He got up and walked out without saying a word, without ever mentioning the name Robbie Daniels.

He accompanied Angela's body to Tucson, remained for the funeral and flew home to Detroit that evening.

Annie Maguire called him the next day. It was in both papers, a two-column story with a smiling shot of Chichi, "the playboy of the western world," and a brief reference to the other victim of the apparent drug-related double homicide. Annie said everyone was worried about him and stumbled over her words until Bryan said he wasn't going to talk about it right now if she didn't mind. He would, pretty soon, but not right now.

NINETEEN

WALTER STAYED AT his sister's house on Belmont in Hamtramck. For three days he didn't leave the house. He drank. Finally he got in his sister's Monte Carlo and drove over to a bar on Jacob just off Joseph Campau. Lili's.

He wanted it to be like a homecoming. Walk in and the guys at the bar see him. "Hey, look who's here!" . . . "Walter, where you been? How the fuck are you?" And he would see if he could slip back into another time, back around '57, '58 when they'd come in after a softball game, CYO League or Catholic War Vets—fast pitch, none of this blooper-ball shit—and drink Stroh's and play the juke box and argue about American League batting averages and ERAs. Now there was a kid named Art he had never seen before working the bar and Lili wasn't around. Four o'clock in the afternoon Art said she'd gone to have her dinner. Her dinner? What was going on here? The place had a strange feel to it. It was different. The only thing that hadn't changed, Kessler's was still fifty cents a shot. Walter said they used to call it Polish Canadian Club. Art said they still did.

"Don't anybody come in here no more?"

Art looked at him like, what kind of a question is that? Though right now there were only two others in here, an older couple at the other end of the bar. Art said, "We do more business'n this place ever did since it opened."

"Everybody must be out taking a leak," Walter said, " 'cause I don't see 'em."

"Stick around," Art said.

Walter wasn't going anyplace. He ordered up-and-downs, Kessler and Stroh's, looking at all the strange fruit-flavored brandy on the back bar, the—Christ—egg-nog punch. He sat sideways to the bar, comfortable, looking around and not remembering much. The place seemed darker: a long narrow storefront-type bar with windows painted over and a small neon *Lili's* the only identification. He had been drinking all day for three days. He might be shit-faced, but he was vaguely confident he had his head on straight.

On his way north in the Mercedes Walter had stopped off in Deltona, Florida, to visit the sister he hadn't seen in about five years. He sat down as long as he could, talking about Irene and how much she liked West Palm, before asking his sister if he could stay at her house a few days, while he wound up some business in Detroit. His sister kept asking him questions. Wasn't he working for this Mr. Daniels? Living—I mean to tell you—in Grosse Pointe? No, he was quitting, getting into something else—Christ, having to explain everything until he thought he was going to have to take the goddamn house key off her. His sister would call Irene, there was nothing he could do about that; but he'd be out of her house in about a week. Once he contacted Robbie and made the deal. He had dropped off the Mercedes the first day. Robbie wasn't back yet. Or his wife. The maid didn't seem to know anything about them.

Walter would wake up hungover, the top of his spine like a spike sticking up through his head, still half-drunk, jumpy and in pain, with urges to look in the empty rooms. He'd have a couple of cold ones to settle him, fry some eggs and sausage, then spend about an hour in the can with the door locked, even though he was alone in the house. Mornings he had to keep moving, walk through the dark rooms with the shades drawn, figuring out where he stood and what he was going to do with the video cassette that showed the death of Chichi Fuentes—and a little more. So far he had hidden it in three different places. It was in a good place now, protected.

Coming here, staying here, was to settle him down. Look out a window and see a street that could have been back in '57, '58, or before that. The row of straight-up-and-down two-family houses with their imitation brick facings, grillwork guarding the porches and postage-stamp front lawns. They belonged to people who were proud to live in Hamtramck with a church around the corner, football games at Keyworth Stadium, "Home of the Cosmos," and doing a job at Dodge Main along with about eighteen thousand hourly working three shifts when you couldn't buy a better car for your money and the fucking Japs were still making birthday-party novelties and toys that fell apart. No more. People were moving to Warren and out to Sterling Heights. Well, you could still drink Kessler's for four bits and could listen to Johnny Shadrack's Polish-American Matinee, WMZK, and still hear in this hot-shit new age "The Beer Barrel Polka" once in a while. But that was about it.

At least he felt safer in the bar than at his sister's house, in there in the dark waiting for the phone or the doorbell to ring. Darker than in here even. He felt pleasantly numb after the painful morning.

He felt like everything was going to work out.

He felt like talking.

He felt he knew the guy coming in now. And when he found out he was right he didn't know what to feel.

It was Bryan Hurd.

Bryan took the stool next to him and placed a flattened pack of Camels on the bar. He said, "You left these, Walter, in Florida."

"How'd you find me?"

"I'm a policeman," Bryan said. "You used to be a policeman. You remember that?"

Walter had too many words in his mind at once and it was hard to pick the right ones. He tried, "I read about it, I want to tell you I was shocked, I couldn't fucking believe it." He tried, "Jesus, you never know, do you? You get mixed up with—you get like involved with these people you're writing an article about, I guess it can happen, being at the wrong place, you know, at the wrong time. It's a shame, an innocent person. But you got a job, what can you do? You can't sit home. Right?"

Walter stopped. The way Bryan was looking at him all he could see were Bryan's eyes, the eyes not saying anything, except every time he looked away and looked back there were the fucking eyes, the eyes fixed on him. He wanted to get it over with. If Bryan was going to say something he should say it.

Walter thought of something else. "You want a drink? Art, fix us up here. Kessler and whatever the lieutenant wants." He said to Bryan, "Fucking Kessler's still four bits. You believe it?" It gave him an opening. "The only thing in this town hasn't changed. I used to live over by Geimer, when I was growing up? The house's gone. Hamtramck High School, where I went? Gone. Not a trace of it. Dodge Main? Fucking gone. There's a couple brick walls standing there I think was the boiler room, it's got so much steel in it they can't fucking knock it down. Kowalski's still there. St. Florian's still there. St. Florian's, you'd have to shoot the priests and blow it up. But Immaculate Conception? It's not in Hamtramck but it's close enough, right there. GM's tearing it down. Sure, taking all that land there and

256

where Dodge Main was for a new assembly plant. Cadillacs in Hamtramck, for Christ sake. Everything's changed. I mean everything. Go over look at the juke box. They got on there The Mutants, the Walkie-Talkies, Adam and the fucking Ants. What else? The Fishsticks. The Plastics. The Infections, for Christ sake. What's going on? Look—picture of the broad over there on the wall?" He pointed to a poster shot of David Bowie. "You know who she is? They got Iggy Pop, all this shit, they got *one* Frank Sinatra on there, on the juke box."

Walter thought as fast as he could to come up with something else, to fill the silence beginning to settle.

Bryan said, "Walter, I want the gun Robbie used. I don't want a stroll down memory lane. I want the High Standard twenty-two and I want the suppressor that goes with it."

Walter looked away and back again, knowing he had time and knowing what he wanted to say, the one word, the key word, *gun*, giving it to him.

He said, "Bryan, I don't know if you're a Catholic, but how about the pope, uh? You believe it, somebody would shoot the fucking pope? John Paul the Second, best pope we ever had. Yeah, hey, his cousin use to live right over here on Mt. Elliott. You know that? You knew he was Polish, right? Educated—shit, he can speak seven languages, goes all over the world, seen by millions of the faithful and where is he? He's home, he's in St. Peter's Square, this Turk pulls out a Browning starts popping away. Fucking Turk." Walter stopped, a dramatic pause.

"Bryan, it was a Browning nine-millimeter, the exact same fucking gun I've been packing the last, what, three, four years. And you know what I'm gonna do with the gun, Bryan? I mean my gun. I'm gonna drive over on the Belle Isle Bridge, I'm gonna get out of the car and I'm gonna throw the fucking gun in the fucking Detroit River. I'm gonna tell you something I haven't told nobody at all. You think I'm in the fucking bag and I'm drunk, but I promise you that's what I'm gonna do. Throw the gun away and never pack again as long I fucking live and that's a promise."

Bryan said, "I want that High Standard, Walter, and whatever barrels go with it. I want you tell me where it is."

It didn't sound right to Walter. He said, "The twenty-two? He didn't use the twenty-two."

He saw Bryan's eyes fixed on him again and tried to remember—shit—what he had just said. He said, "Wait a minute . . . "

But it was too late. Bryan said, "You want to talk about Florida, Walter? You want to get into that?" Bryan unbuttoned his sport coat and held it open with both hands. "You notice anything different, out of the ordinary?"

Walter shook his head. "What?"

"I don't have a gun on me," Bryan said. "You know why? I was afraid I saw you the first thing I'd do, I'd stick it against your head, Walter, and pull the trigger. I thought about it a long time and then I put it out of my mind and stopped thinking about it. You understand? I'm not talking about Florida, I'm talking about Detroit. Curtis Moore. I'm not gonna give him to anybody in Florida. I want him here . . . You listening to me?"

"Yeah," Walter said, "Curtis Moore. Was shot with a High Standard twenty-two. Got a big fucking suppressor on it."

"That's the one," Bryan said. "Listen to me."

"I'm listening."

"Robbie's due back sometime tonight."

"How do you know?"

"Just listen. Sober up. Go in there and find the gun before he gets back. Don't touch it, leave it. Then call me and tell me where it is. When I go in I'll have a warrant, but I want to know where to look."

"You getting me into this?"

"If you're in it, you're in it."

"I didn't know he was gonna do Curtis. Honest to God, he never said a fucking word. He just pulls this cool shit and does it."

"He told you about it after?"

"Like that night."

"But you didn't tell anybody."

"Somebody was gonna do Curtis sooner or later," Walter said. "What's the difference? Go down the morgue, see all the fucking Curtises they got there."

"Walter? Call me at 1300 soon as you know where the gun is. I'll talk to you later about a statement."

"What statement?"

"Whatever he told you. Write it down and sign it."

"Not without immunity."

"I'll see what the prosecutor says."

"What about the other deal?"

"Walter," Bryan said, "if you're talking about Florida I'm gonna give you one more chance to keep your mouth shut. Don't mention it again, okay? Don't say one fucking word."

Walter got as far as saying, "I think you're imagining things that happened—"

Bryan hit him, spinning him off the stool. Bryan stood over Walter and said, "I saw it. I don't have to imagine anything, I saw it."

Art had to come around to help Walter, straining to get him on his knees and his arms over the side of the pool table—like a sack of cement—so he could pull himself up. Then had to help him away from there so he wouldn't be sick on the table. Walter looked awful, staring out bleary-eyed.

"Where'd he go?"

"Your friend?" Art said. "He left. What'd he hit you for?"

"It's okay," Walter said. "He's pissed off about something."

Malik and Doug Parrish were waiting in front of the General Motors Building, watching the pickets who were trying to convince everyone that GM had no heart and that GM was taking their homes. New signs today read:

DON'T TAKE OUR CHURCH!
SAVE IMMACULATE CONCEPTION—PLEASE!

Parrish said, "Wait a minute. If the archdiocese thinks it's a good idea, they sell the land the church's on to the city and the city sells it to GM, what're they bitching at GM for?"

Malik said, "You asking me? Ask the cardinal. These people're parading around trying to save their church hardly any of 'em go to, he's out at Gucci's, some shoe store, blessing the grand opening. They open up a new Thom McAn he sends an altar boy."

Parrish said, "You got that from the *Free Press,* the guy on the back page. I read it."

Malik said, "So? He got it from somebody else. What's the difference?" He nodded toward the blue Plymouth pulling in behind the blue Plymouth already in the no standing zone. Then watched Bryan closely, the way he moved as he came past the pickets to join them.

"What's the matter with your hand?"

"I'm trying to keep from killing people," Bryan said, "and I'm having a hard time."

Malik and Parrish looked at each other. As they walked into the building Parrish said, "How do you want to handle this?"

"I want a statement," Bryan said, "I hope without hanging the guy out the window. Stare at him and crack your knuckles, I don't know . . ."

It was past five and they were moving against a rush of people coming out. On the second floor, down the glass hallways, nearly all the offices were empty, desk tops cleared. Bill Fay's secretary had gone. He looked out from his desk with a weary grin, extending his hand as he got up, shaking his head, and Bryan knew he was rehearsed, ready. Not that it mattered. There would be no handshaking or introductions.

Malik and Parrish came up to the desk one either side of him as he said, "I'm gonna have to have a statement from you, Mr. Fay."

Bill Fay smiled and frowned, made several faces as he thought it over and finally said, "I'm prepared to say, from now on, I don't know what in the hell you're talking about."

Bryan picked up the phone and began dialing a number, paused after three digits, looked up and said, "Eight-five-one, seven-one-three-one?"

Fay said nothing, holding on.

Bryan finished dialing. He held the phone out so Fay could hear the rings.

"All right, put it down."

"You'll give me a statement? Everything you saw?"

The phone continued to ring. A woman's voice came on, a pleasant tone. "Hello?"

"*Yes!*" A half-whispered hiss. "Put it down!"

Bryan said into the phone. "I may call you back in a minute," and hung up. He watched Fay sink into his chair and begin to swivel slowly from side to side.

"You seem to be experienced in ruining marriages," Fay said. "What's the least destructive way to do this?"

"I want a signed statement," Bryan said, "a positive identification of Robinson Daniels, what you saw him doing, the fact you saw him go down to the garage."

"I didn't actually see him go down."

"Tell what you did see."

"This is under duress, you realize."

"If you think I'm forcing you, don't do it."

"What else do you call it? You think I'd freely sign a statement?"

"It's called good-citizen cooperation," Malik said.

"Can I tell my wife that?"

"Tell her you just wanted a strange piece of ass," Malik said. "It might work."

Fay wrote his statement with coaching, editing help from Bryan. When he had finished and signed it, Bryan gave him some hope. He said, "Don't tell her anything yet. You never know what might happen between here and the Frank Murphy Hall of Justice."

It was dark, early evening, when Robbie got home. He left the front door open and walked into the hall yelling, "Hey! Where is everybody? Come out, I won't hurt you—I'm a friend!" He'd had four first-class Delta martinis on his first commercial flight in years.

A maid appeared, hesitant. Robbie couldn't remember her name.

"Where's Walter?"

He wasn't here. He *was* here a little earlier, but he wasn't here now. Greg talked to him.

Robbie went through the dining room and kitchen to the back stairway and called up, "Greg, where are you? I need you, Greg!"

The cook came down the stairs slicking his dark hair back with his hands, wearing his white shirt and his black pants. "Yes sir." They went into the kitchen and Robbie got a bottle of white wine out of the refrigerator while Greg quickly washed his hands at the sink. When Robbie couldn't find a glass Greg got one out of the cupboard, an everyday glass, and Robbie told him to bring one for himself.

"You see Walter?"

"As little as I can," Greg said. Greg was about thirty-five and looked to Robbie like a day laborer, but he could cook.

"I got to find him."

"He was here," Greg said. "He went in your study and I told him hey, you don't work here no more, what are you doing in there? The other day he brings the car back he says he quit."

"He was in my study?"

"About, well a few hours ago he was here."

"Where'd he go, do you know?"

"No sir. I could care less."

"Care," Robbie said, "just for a minute. I thought you two were from the same neighborhood. Hamtramck, right?"

"That doesn't give us anything in common. You know what he does all the time? He bitches . . ."

"It's a trait," Robbie said.

"He comes in here for a beautiful meal cost him twenty dollars outside, he starts bitching. Beef Wellington, he says take the fucking bread off. I fix veal Oscar you like? He want golabki, pirogies, he wants placki for breakfast. All the time telling me I don't know how to cook."

"He's a rustic at heart," Robbie said, not having any idea what Greg was talking about. "But where can I find him? You know any places he goes, where he hangs out?"

"I don't know if he goes, I know what he talks about, over there."

"Over where?"

"He talks like Hamtramck was Grosse Pointe, like Under the Eagle was the London Chop House. He don't know anything."

"Under the Eagle?"

"Yeah, I used to eat there sometime, till I learned how to cook. You go in there and get fat."

"Call the place up, see if anybody's seen him. You know any other spots?"

"Couple of bars maybe."

"Call 'em. See if he's been in lately, the past couple of days." Robbie started out of the kitchen with his wine glass, paused and looked back at Greg. "There's a footlocker out on the front steps the goddamn cab driver wouldn't bring in the house. But make the calls first, okay?"

Goddamn Walter. Robbie walked through the marble front hall to his den, flicked the light switch on and the switch next to it off as he went in.

The room seemed in order, everything in its proper place. No—some books were pulled half out of the shelves and the cabinet doors were open behind the desk. The dumb shit. Looking for the gun. That had to be Walter's purpose. Walter the cop turned driver-aide turning snitch. Scared to death. Or blackmailer, that was a definite possibility.

Robbie sat down in his chair with his glass of wine, picked up the TV remote control gadget and pressed the on button.

"It's showtime . . . "

He watched Walter appear on the television screen, Walter coming into the lighted room, looking around, weaving a little as he moved to the desk, placed his hands on it flat and leaned heavily, resting. He was drunk! Unbelievable. The guy comes in to burglarize the place smashed. Walter was groping around now, edging his way to the cabinets behind the desk while those sneaky cameras that resembled light fixtures followed every move. He'd even explained to Walter how the surveillance cameras worked, these particular ones programmed to look on a subject and follow until the subject left the camera's scan and walked into the field of another, the cameras activated when a light switch was turned on. But Walter was drunk, or wouldn't have remembered anyway. Walter's attention span was about from A to B. He desperately needed someone to wind him up and point him in the right direction. Walter stumbled around, going over to the bar now . . . standing there trying to decide what to drink. That's what he needed. Probably not recognizing one single label. Christ—no, Walter, not the seventy-five-year-old stuff!

Greg appeared in the doorway.

"He was in there today, Mr. Daniels. Under the Eagle? Waitress says he acted drunk. Told her he'd been to Lili's Bar, where he used to hang out. She says she stopped in there for a pop after she was through working and he was in there again. Art told her, the bartender, Walter would go out, come back in, go out, come back. Like he didn't know what he was doing."

Robbie looked over, clicking the picture off. "You know where Lili's is?"

"It's right off Campau on Jacob."

"Give me some directions."

Greg said, "Yes sir, but I don't know you want to go there at night."

On the first sheet in the pile of notes and typewritten pages was a list of working titles written in Angela's straight-up-and-down hand.

"Hi, I'm Robbie Daniels"

"What's It Like To Be Rich?"

"I Was Just Saying To My Very Good Friend George Hamilton The Other Day . . . "

"Who Would I Rather Be Than Anyone? . . . Me!"

"Split Images: How Rich-Kid Robbie Daniels Defies Your Viewfinder"

A note below the list of titles said, "Maybe a short dialog exchange would work." And below that, "What would Tom Wolfe call it?"

Bryan got up from his desk. Crossed the squad room toward the wall of mug shots, stopped and turned around, without purpose. He had nowhere to go. He didn't want coffee. He didn't want to turn on the radio. He wanted the telephone to ring and hear Walter's voice, sober. At this moment it was all he wanted because he would not let himself think of anything else. He was standing when Eljay Ayres came in, the inspector of Homicide dressed in a tailored tan three-piece suit, raincoat over his arm, tired eyes looking at Bryan, wondering things.

"Tell me if you're doing something I should know about."

Bryan shrugged, raised his shoulders a little and let them drop.

"You can think it long as you don't do it. You know what I'm saying to you? Ain't worth it."

"How do you know?" Bryan said.

"I don't know much," Ayres said. "Nobody sits down and tells me stories anymore. I have to ask questions, get bits and pieces." He studied Bryan with his tired gaze and began to shake his head. "You don't even have the gun for the job. Little thirty-eight with the bands 'round it so you don't lose it in your pants. What kind of a gunslinger are you, Bryan?"

Bryan said, "You know how many guns he's got?"

Ayres said, "Has only one I'd be interested in. From what little bit I hear . . . I'm gonna tell you something I would never tell anybody else. Gonna come right out and say you, Mr. Hurd, are the best homicide dick I know or know of. That includes me, giving you maybe a half a step, no more than that. The point being, the best homicide dick I know doesn't fuck up, does he? Doesn't carry the blade to put in the man's hand after, does he? He wins most, he loses a few. But he doesn't ever fuck up. Does he?"

Bryan turned, moved toward his desk. "I've got to write a letter."

"That's cool," Ayres said. "Keep your mind occupied."

Walter parked his sister's Monte Carlo next to a bulldozer that stood in the drive of an abandoned gas station. Every parking place up Jacob and around on Campau was taken. Like somebody was having a party. There were three girls in front of Lili's, standing in the dark smoking, passing around a cigarette. He could smell it now; he was still a cop he could bust them. The hell with them. He had slept about two hours and was still whacked out, half in the bag. The girls moved away, one of them looking at him as he approached the bar, the girl saying, "The Babies bring out the weirdos every time."

What? He put his hand on the door and felt a vibration. The same girl was saying, "Down here, dad."

The fuck was going on?

They went through a board gate and along a passage with walls that squeezed in close, Walter following sounds in darkness, a girl's laughter, smelling the grass, seeing the glow as the girls took last tokes and went in past a sign that said *Pagan Babies*. Pagan *what?* Art was looking at him through a window in a red door. Art said, "Three bucks."

Walter said, "Wait a minute. I got turned around or something."

Art said, "Three bucks, for the band."

Walter dug in his pocket. He said, "For the *band?* That's the band? I though it must be the fucking wreckers tearing down a building, Art. Hey, Art?" But they were moving him into the wall-to-wall racket of rock sound filling the bar, people behind him now crowding him into people standing inside, the people moving but moving in place, moving up and down, skinny people with painted hair, pink hair, Kraut hair, moving like puppets attached to the beat, skinny girls wired to it together, thighs shining, sliding together with sex on their faces, mouths moving, speaking, but no sound coming out of them, no room for voice sounds in a room filled with electronic sound. Five guys up there by the front with tight suits on and no shirts—no, four guys and a girl playing with them as alike as the guys were alike, moving alike, mechanically, one eating the microphone, saying something about the pope. The pope? *"The Turk did it during her afternoon soap—"* It sounded like the guy singing was saying the girl was pissed off, she missed all her children, yeah, *"She missed 'All My Children'—"* And people around him as he tried to get through them, as he used his shoulders to ram his way, were repeating it, their mouths saying, "She missed 'All My Children'—" But the girl was gonna go straight to hell because she was pissed and the guy up there in the suit and no shirt was saying, *"Don't forget your Sea and Ski—"* And now everybody was mouthing, saying, "Don't forget your Sea and Ski—" Walter raised his face to breathe. He saw Lili, a striped tiger drinking a white drink. He saw a pair of barmaids in shirts that glowed pure white and saw the labels of the fruit-flavored brandy glowing white, girls at the bar moving with their eyes closed and a girl licking the sticky inside of her glass, getting it all, girls squirming in pain to the guys in the suits and no shirts who looked diseased. The sound stopped. It was in the room filling the room and then gone like a plug had been pulled, leaving screams that were moans in comparison. A voice close to him said, "Oh, man, who's got some blow?" Another voice said, "You're busting caps now, man. What do you need with blow?"

Lili's voice said, "Walter? Come on—is that Walter Kouza?"

He stared at her, at her tiger dress.

Lili's voice said, "Walter, you sick? Please don't throw up on my customers, Walter. Go outside."

Art's voice said, "He doesn't know where he is."

Another voice said, "I'll take care of him."

Walter turned to the voice.

To Robbie Daniels smiling at him. "Come on, Walter, let's go outside."

Walter heard his own voice say, "I'm messing up . . ."

Bryan wrote in longhand on a legal pad. He wrote lines and scratched out words and tried other words, trying to explain in the letter why he was writing it. He started again and stopped, picked up the phone and dialed a number. He listened to it ring. He hung up and dialed an out-of-state number.

"Irene? . . . Bryan Hurd. I'm sorry to bother you again. Are you sure Walter's at his sister's? I called a few times, there was no answer . . . Yeah. No, I did see him this afternoon . . . He's fine. Sort of unwinding. Give me the number again, make sure I have it right." He wrote numbers on the yellow pad. "And the address? . . ."

The quiet was good, the sensation of gliding in silence, protected, staring at the gleam of the hood as they passed beneath street lights.

"Is this Belmont?"

"Next one. Hang a left. Go down the second block."

"How do you feel?"

"Shitty. I don't know what happened to me. It was like—you really want to know what it was like? It was like dying and going to hell."

"That's interesting," Robbie said.

They went in the front door. Walter switched on a lamp, walked through to the kitchen and turned the water on to let it run and get cold. A phone rang.

"That's Irene," Walter said. "She thinks I'm gonna answer it she's crazy." Still, he walked back out to the living room to watch it ring.

Robbie, wearing a bulky knit sweater that hung to his hips in soft folds, leaning in the kitchen doorway, straightened. His hands went behind him, beneath the sweater, as his eyes moved over the kitchen. He'd better do it now. Not wait. Bringing out the Colt Python he stepped to the refrigerator, laid the gun on top and stepped back again as the ringing stopped and Walter returned from his vigil. Robbie said, "You know things don't always go as planned."

"The first thing I'm gonna do," Walter said, "is quit drinking. The second thing—I don't know, I'm fucking beat. But I was gonna call you."

"To offer me a deal?"

Walter took time to drink a glass of water. He refilled the glass and sat down at the kitchen table. He said, "Okay. Two hundred and fifty thousand for the tape I got."

"You mean tapes," Robbie said. "Two of them."

"I got one, that's all. I threw the other one away."

"You sure?"

"I'm telling you I did."

"Which one do you have?"

"The one you're doing Chichi."

"Why do you think it's worth a quarter of a million?"

"You're in it too. The headband—fucking Cochise."

Robbie pulled out the other kitchen chair and sat down. "I had to pick up after you, Walter. You leave me in a spot and now you're blackmailing me."

"Bet your ass I am."

"If in fact you do have the tape."

"Take my word."

"Forget it," Robbie said. He rose, pulled his sweater down and started out through the hall to the living room.

Walter said, "Hey, you think I'm kidding?"

Robbie stopped and came half around. "About what?"

"Pay or I mail it to the cops. How's that grab you?"

Robbie came back to the kitchen doorway, hands on his hips, slim, hair mussed. Walter thought of a cheerleader, the first time in what seemed like years.

Robbie said, "Walter, you send it in, I get picked up. What's the first question they ask me?"

"Why you shot him."

"No—who shot the film? I'll give you a hundred grand, flat deal. But only if you prove to me you've got the tape. I mean right now. Otherwise, fuck off."

"I'm sober," Walter said, "you think you can pull anything."

"Come on, Walter, Jesus Christ, I want to go home and go to bed."

Walter got up from the table. He approached Robbie carefully and felt the bulk of the sweater around the middle. "You stay right here, you don't move. Right?"

He went out through the kitchen door, down the steps and across the yard to where his sister had set up her shrine to the Blessed Virgin Mary, a four-foot plaster statue on a pedestal: Mary standing on top of the world, a snake held firmly beneath her foot. Walter looked back at the light showing in the kitchen door before he carefully tilted the statue, bringing it toward him to let his shoulder support the weight, reached into the hollow base and drew out his Browning nine-millimeter that he would throw away right after this deal was completed. He stuck the automatic into his belt, reached under again and drew out the cassette, done up in Saran Wrap.

Robbie had moved a little. Enough to see Walter coming up the back porch steps with a gun in one hand and something wrapped in the other. Enough to place himself next to the refrigerator with his hand resting on top.

Walter stuck the Browning into his belt again so he could unwrap the cassette.

Robbie's hand came off the refrigerator with the Python. He shot Walter squarely in the chest, three times, giving him one more than he had given the Haitian, and watched Walter stumble around rearranging the table and chairs before he hit the linoleum floor. He felt for a pulse in Walter's throat, something he had not done with the Haitian. It was how you learned.

Twenty-one seventy-two Belmont.

Bryan had to go up the walk almost to the house to read the number next to the aluminum storm door. He rang the bell and waited. The house was dark; the entire street seemed dark, no one up watching late movies. He went around back, along the narrow walk separating Walter's sister's house from the one next door. It was a clear night. He could see a statue standing in the backyard, a robed figure with hands extended: come to me. The back of the house seemed darker than the front.

When the knob turned in his hand he realized the door wasn't shut tight. He pushed gently. The door swung in and stopped, obstructed; but the opening was wide enough for Bryan to slip through, to step inside and feel the bulk of Walter's body against his foot. He turned the kitchen light on.

A Browning automatic and a glass of water were on the table. Walter lay face down, blood on the back of his poplin jacket. Bryan knelt down, tired. He said, "Walter, you dumb shit," raised the jacket and shirt, pulling them up enough to see a ragged tear in pale flesh, blood oozing. He pulled the jacket down, rolled Walter over and opened his shirt. Three entrance wounds, one through and through. Two bullets were still inside Walter. Bryan stood up. He opened the cabinet door with the gouge in it, sifted through broken china to find the third slug and studied it in the palm of his hand. A chunk of misshapen lead. From something bigger than a twenty-two. Bryan turned the light off and sat down at the kitchen table. If police evidence technicians had been watching him up to now they'd have him thrown off the force. And if the Hamtramck Police knew what he was going to do next they might scream or they might thank him, it was a toss-up. But either way, this one was his.

He'd find a shower curtain in the bathroom. Or a blanket.

He'd bring his car around to the alley.

He'd place a call as soon as possible to West Palm and get Gary Hammond out of bed. In fact, before he left the house.

He needed just a little luck. Or kneel by that little statue for a minute. It wouldn't hurt.

TWENTY

ROBBIE COULDN'T BELIEVE how beautifully the video-tape came out. The assassination of Chichi Fuentes. Like he'd directed and choreographed it. The bottles on the bar and the door panes shattering, Chichi staggering out in his golden robe turning red and then, *aggggggggh*, falling into the swimming pool. Chichi was a good dier. He even liked—liked?—he loved the unplanned flashes of himself, the bandana and the sun-glasses, firing the grease gun, holding it low and letting it rip with that great gutty sound, muted but very heavy. The whole scene was heavy. Inspirational. It reaffirmed his convictions, made him dead certain he wanted to go on to more significant projects, bag some really bad ones. Maybe not Carlos, but there were some giant assholes out there waiting.

He was learning fast. He'd lucked out with Walter. Walter had been a mistake. Scratch Walter, a genuine pain in the ass. His body probably wouldn't even be discovered until the sister came home from Florida; whenever. The type he needed was not a cop but a seasoned mercenary, a former

Green Beret or Recon Marine who'd been to Africa and back and knew the game. A heavyweight. He'd look in the classified section of *Soldier of Fortune* and get in touch with a pro looking for action. Some guy practicing his karate moves, opens the letter, the guy wouldn't believe it.

God, it was fun.

Write the real book about it someday.

Robbie watched the tape three times that night after he got home, about ten times or more yesterday and a couple of times this morning. It kept getting better.

Right now he had the footlocker open, going through a seasonal rite: taking out his handguns, oiling and wiping them clean before mounting them in the wall cabinet behind his desk. He liked to keep the handguns handy, show them off. The heavy stuff, the submachine guns, he kept in a half-ton safe that was bolted to the cement floor of the utility room in the Palm Beach house.

There were guns spread all over the desk when the maid knocked on the door, opened it a few inches and said, "Someone here to see you, Mr. Daniels."

He had been half-expecting this so he was ready. The unannounced visitor who would try to catch him off-guard. What surprised him was that Lieutenant Hurd was not alone.

Annie Maguire came in first and Robbie widened his grin as he saw her glance up and around at the sneaky cameras. His hand found the switch under the front of his desk and he flicked it on to activate a record of this meeting, just in case. Robbie's expression changed, became somber. He said to Bryan, "Lieutenant, I can't tell you how sorry I am. If I'd known what Angie was getting into, believe me—"

Bryan cut him off. "You better not say anything. All right?"

"Well, I want to express how I feel—"

"No. Don't say anything."

Robbie said, "You're not inferring, I hope, that anything I say might be used against me."

"I'm not inferring anything," Bryan said. "Can we sit down?"

"Please." Robbie gestured, watched them sink into the soft leather chairs across the desk from him. He remained standing, deciding to feel his way a little deeper into it. "I thought, since I introduced you to Fuentes—remember, at Seminole? . . . Well, I'm sure you've talked to the police in Florida . . . " He paused a moment, not sure what to say next. Hurd was staring at him. Not with an expression that described an emotion, but simply staring. It gave Robbie a strange feeling, the thought that he might have overlooked something. But if it wasn't about Florida . . .

"How're you doing with the Curtis Moore investigation?" Robbie's gaze moved to Annie Maguire. Much better, a definite sign of life in her eyes.

"Well, since you asked," Annie said. "We know you were at the hotel. I mean at the time of the homicide."

"I told him that." Robbie's eyes flicked at Bryan and returned. "I was at the Renaissance Center about ten o'clock. I picked up some Mexicans. I told him all about it and he checked it out."

"You forgot to say you went down to the parking garage," Annie said.

"Are you serious?"

"We've got a witness."

"Where, down in the garage?"

"Right by the valet parking."

"I might've stopped there. I was looking for the Mexicans. But if you're trying to tell me somebody *saw* me down in the garage, that's pure bullshit."

"Where was the pistol, in your car?"

"What pistol?"

"The one you used on Curtis."

"Jesus Christ—"

"The same one you showed us in your office. The High Standard."

Bryan watched him begin to smile, getting back on safe ground.

Robbie said, "You ran a ballistics check on the shells you picked up, didn't you? Compared them to the ones you got out of Curtis Moore? Isn't that the way it's done?"

Annie said, looking at the desk, "Do you have it here?"

Now Robbie looked over his display of handguns. "I don't see it. Oh shit, that was the one I lost in Florida. I was out in a boat, shooting, and dropped it over the side . . . Gee, I'm sorry."

Annie said, "What were you shooting, fish?"

"Yeah, I like to shoot fish." He gave Annie his interested, serious look. "Is this the way you do it, honest to God?"

Annie said, "Well, you asked about Curtis Moore."

"And that's all you have?"

Annie said, "No. As a matter of fact we have a warrant for your arrest . . . "

"You're kidding." Beginning to smile.

". . . on a charge of first-degree murder."

Robbie was smiling sincerely now. It was a con, he was positive. These rinky-dinks were giving him the grim-cop number, Hurd playing stone-face, and he was supposed to, what, break down? Confess? He couldn't believe it.

"You're not serious, are you?"

Annie said, "You have a constitutional right to remain silent. You don't have to answer any questions . . . "

"Wait a minute."

". . . or make any statements. If you do . . ."

"Wait a minute, goddamn it! Hold it!"

There was a silence.

"Now then," Robbie said. "You've got a witness who wasn't actually there. You don't have a murder weapon . . . How in the hell can you associate me, in any way, with Curtis Moore? It's impossible."

Bryan said, "The warrant doesn't mention Curtis." He waited to make sure he had Robbie's full attention. "It's for doing Walter Kouza."

Bryan waited some more. He liked this part. The chair was comfortable, soft but firm. It was Robbie's turn. He watched Robbie pull up the high-backed desk chair, giving himself a little time as he sat down on the edge and tried to look interested in an objective way, at ease, slouching over to rest his arms on the desk full of handguns.

"Let me get this straight," Robbie said, giving himself more time, "Walter Kouza was murdered?"

"The night before last," Bryan said. He had the hook in now.

"Wait a second," Robbie said, but added nothing to it.

Bryan said, "I understand you were with him at Lili's about eleven." Giving him a little more of the hook. In a moment now he'd watch Robbie jump.

"Where," Robbie began, and then said it quickly. "Where was his body found?"

"In front of the art museum," Bryan said.

Robbie jumped. "The *Art* Museum!"

"Lying under that statue. *The Thinker*," Bryan said.

"You found his body—you're telling me in front of the Art Museum on Woodward Avenue?"

"Why," Bryan said, "did you think it was someplace else?"

"I dropped him off—" Robbie stopped, but knew he had to go on. "It was a house in Hamtramck. That's where I saw him last, in Hamtramck."

"And you're wondering how he got over to Detroit,"

Bryan said, "with three bullets in his chest from a Colt Python, three-fifty-seven Mag, that match a couple bullets taken out of a Haitian burglar and sent to us courtesy of the Palm Beach Police. Is that what's bothering you?"

Hunched over the desk, his blue cashmere hanging loose, Robbie stared with a numb look, his mouth slack.

Bryan said, "You want to hear the rest of your rights, or you want to call your lawyer first? . . . Don't know what to think, huh? We've also got a search warrant that says we can pick up evidence. That Colt Python you think so much of and the tape over in the VCR. You got any movies you want to show us?"

Annie said, "If you do make a statement it can be used against you in a court of law. You have the right to have a lawyer present—"

Robbie said, "Goddamn it, shut up!" He came alive and hung there in a knot, losing his good looks, before easing back into the chair. Now he seemed stunned, amazed. He said, "Walter *Kouza?*"

Bryan said, "There must be some mistake, huh? Who's Walter Kouza?" Poking at the nerve center of Robbie's pain. "He sure wasn't one of your international assholes, was he?" Bryan said, "No, Walter was just a local asshole trying to make it big."

Bryan got up. Annie dug into her bag before she rose and came out with a pair of handcuffs. Bryan took them, jiggled them at Robbie and he got up very slowly.

Robbie said it again, "Walter Kouza. . ." Like he would never get over it.

Bryan said, "Put your hands behind you, we'll ride down to the Wayne County jail. It ain't Seminole, Smiley, but they do serve a lot of macaroni and cheese."

TWENTY-ONE

HE SAID TO himself, Shit, just write it. It's only a letter. Go ahead.

Under *Dear Editor* he wrote:

Here is the material that Angela Nolan was preparing for your magazine according to the assignment you gave her on rich people. You will notice there are 15 finished pages of the interview typed up that are great and seem to describe exactly the kind of dangerous show-off Robinson Daniels is, or at least was. He is going to have to change his ways very quickly where I hope he is going or else get his ass knocked off. (If you need any information about the Southern Michigan Prison at Jackson, which has the largest inmate population in the nation, let me know.) There are also some very interesting notes you can fix up a little and use to finish the article yourself. (Enclosed also are photos of both Daniels and Angela.) If you are in not too big a hurry, wait and I will let you know how the trial comes out. I'm betting the son of a bitch will get mandatory life. If he doesn't, I'll settle for 99 years.

Bryan was going to end it there and sign it, but he thought of something else and added:

If you have trouble deciding whether or not to run this great article by Angela Nolan, let me know. I'll come to N.Y. and hold you out the window by your heels until you decide.

See if they had a sense of humor.